I0451268

DEATH
AT
LARCH
BRIDGE

An absolutely gripping WW2 historical
murder mystery full of twists

GRETTA MULROONEY

Daisy Moore Mysteries Book 2

Joffe Books, London
www.joffebooks.com

First published in Great Britain in 2023

© Gretta Mulrooney 2023

This book is a work of fiction. Names, characters,
businesses, organizations, places and events are either
the product of the author's imagination or are used
fictitiously. Any resemblance to actual persons, living
or dead, events or locales is entirely coincidental.
The spelling used is British English except where fidelity to
the author's rendering of accent or dialect supersedes this.
The right of Gretta Mulrooney to be identified as author
of this work has been asserted in accordance with the
Copyright, Designs and Patents Act 1988.

Cover art by Jarmila Takač

ISBN: 978-1-80405-991-3

AUTHOR'S NOTE

Oxfordshire and Oxford are of course real. The author has invented Fernfield and surrounding villages.

CHAPTER ONE

'That's a pretty bit o' tomfoolery, me old china, I've not seen it before. Did you treat yourself? Am I paying you too much?'

JB is pointing to my neck, where I'm wearing the only jewellery I possess, an amethyst pendant that was my grandmother's.

'My mum gave it to me. It was her mother's.' I'd been wearing it the night the house caught fire and I hadn't taken it off when I went to bed, so it survived with me. This is the first time I've worn it since I woke up in hospital. It's not that my guilt has faded, I just saw it this morning when I opened my sock drawer and had a sudden need to put it on. I should have realised that JB would spot it. He doesn't miss much.

'Ah, I see. Sorry, Daisy. Foot in mouth. Didn't mean to prod painful memories.'

'Don't worry. Where did you pick up "tomfoolery", JB?' He regularly drops into cockney slang with me, but I haven't heard him use that one before.

'One of those gangster films I was in pre-war. I played a fence from Bermondsey who ran into trouble with the big boys in Soho.' JB waves his knife at me and snarls from the side of his mouth. '*If you bleat to the rozzers abaht the chordy gear, it'll be bona nochy.*'

I chuckle and start clearing away the breakfast dishes. We've eaten our routine meal, hard boiled eggs for me, soft boiled for JB so that he can dip his toast soldiers. JB's usual accent is fruity and upper class, befitting a man living in the lodge to a manor house in the Oxfordshire countryside. His wife, Rosalind — who he refers to as 'the *kommandantin*' — lives half a mile up the track in Brize Manor and owns the properties and acres of land, which she strides over shooting pheasants, rabbits and any other wildlife that catches her eye. As well as being my employer and landlord, Jeffrey Berrow — always JB to me — is an actor in films, theatre and on the wireless, and a semi-detached husband to Rosalind, who owns and permits him to run the Dolphin hotel in nearby Fernfield. I work at the hotel, doing any job needed. Vera Crampton, the manager, calls me her 'floating staff'; JB says I'm his 'factotum'. 'General dogsbody' sums it up best.

JB pushes aside his copy of *The Times* and flexes his fingers. 'I might tinkle the ivories, practise 'We'll Gather Lilacs'. I promised the *kommandantin* that I'd play it at one of her soirées for her Oxfordshire Ladies coven.'

'What do the Oxfordshire Ladies actually do?' I'm a working-class Londoner, a recent arrival at the lodge, and the activities of the shires are still a mystery, like an onion that I've hardly started to peel.

'They're a cross between the WI and the Mafia. Genteel and do-gooding, but intricately and invisibly woven together. Cross them at your peril! They sip tea in a refined fashion with little fingers crooked; play bridge, lawn tennis and croquet; bake cakes and make jam and pickles; hunt, shoot and fish; support flogging and the death penalty and vote Tory. Are you staying to hear me play?'

'I can't this morning. Vera has to go to the dentist, so I'm covering for her.'

'Everything tickety-boo at the hotel?'

'It's hard to find new staff, so everyone's mucking in to cover all bases and I'm going to be working more evenings for a while.'

'Jolly good. How's Vera coping with the pregnancy?'

'She's doing well. We all make sure that she puts her feet up when she gets tired.'

'She must be pretty big by now. When's the miracle infant due?'

JB insists on calling the baby this name because Vera struggled to get pregnant and was ecstatic when she learned that she was expecting. 'Mid-July. She plans to be back at work by October. Her mum's going to look after the baby.' It's unusual for a pregnant woman to continue working and return to work after the birth, but Vera is a determined sort who's keen on her job, and JB is an enlightened employer who recognises when he has an excellent manager.

'Knowing Vera, she'll have everything carefully planned.'

'Down to the last detail. This baby had better show up on schedule, or it'll be in trouble. I must get going, I don't want to be late and incur her wrath.'

'I'm free and easy today, but I'm attending an audition in Soho tomorrow, reading for Mr Bung the publican in *Aaron's Field*.'

'Is that a play?'

'Indeed.'

'Never heard of it.'

'It's a short piece in verse, so not too much to learn.'

'See you later, then.'

'Ta-ra, me old fruit. Give my best to the darling Dolphin.'

* * *

I wheel my bike out of the gubbins room, where we keep all the bits and pieces, and set off for Fernfield, which is around five miles away. I've named the bike Lucinda, in honour of Lucinda Laidlaw, the woman who was murdered in the Dolphin last autumn, a crime I helped to solve. I'm grateful to Lucinda, whose death provided me with much-needed mental stimulation and prevented my brain from atrophy-ing in the sedate atmosphere of Fernfield. I'm sure that she would rather be alive, doing good works in the town, but if her spirit is lingering anywhere, perhaps it's of some comfort to her that her terminal cloud held a silver lining for me.

The bike squeaks and pulls to the left, an idiosyncrasy I've grown fond of. For a while, I timed the squeak to the song 'A North Country Maid', but I've recently swapped to 'Molly Malone' for variety.

It's a watery but sunny Friday morning in May, crisp and bright, and the war in Europe has been over for a year. I sing as I get into rhythm with Lucinda.

'In Dublin's fair—' *squeak*
'Where the girls are so—' *squeak*
'I first set my—' *squeak*
'On sweet Molly Ma—' *squeak*
'As she wheeled her wheel—' *squeak*
'Through streets broad and—' *squeak*
'Crying, "Cockles and—' *squeak*
'Alive, alive—"' *squeak*.

I'm much fitter physically than I used to be when I lived in London. Cycling ten miles a day to Fernfield and back has toughened me, although my brain isn't benefiting as much from the country air. Compared to many, I had a 'good' war. I escaped from my job in a biscuit factory, drove buses and then signed the Official Secrets Act and worked for the government in a covert decoding team in Whitehall. It was exhausting, often frustrating, occasionally terrifying, but always mind-blowingly amazing.

Unfortunately, as well as these achievements, I managed a significant entry in my personal liability account when I inadvertently burned down our house, causing my mother's death from complications shortly before VE day. The matricide is my guilty burden. No one else is aware that I hung my socks over the fireplace and forgot the fireguard. My mother and I had a difficult relationship, and especially so after my dad died at Dunkirk and wasn't there to provide our buffer zone. Although my father willingly went to war, he was by nature a peacekeeper, and his refusal to argue or take sides neutralised our bickering. But since my mother died, I've come to understand that it's possible to miss an antagonistic bond as much as a treasured one.

Mum's parish priest, Father Declan Hickey, found me aged twenty-four, living in a hostel in Tottenham, homeless and jobless. (After hostilities ended, the Whitehall mandarins quickly discovered that they no longer needed young women with few educational qualifications, and I was advised to find a husband.) Although I wasn't one of his flock, my father having insisted I was baptised C of E, the priest took it upon himself to watch over me — *'Sure, aren't ye an orphan o' the storm, Daisy darlin', and wouldn't yer poor mother, rest in peace, want me to mind ye in these troubled times?'*

Father Hickey hails from County Offaly in Ireland's midlands, which he describes as a flat vista of soggy bogs and screeds of rain. He was on the stage in Dublin and London before entering a seminary, and he directed me to his old acting chum Jeffrey Berrow, who needed a general factotum. We met, liked each other, and within months I found myself in Oxfordshire, living in a cosy annexe to the lodge, making breakfasts, cosseting Tybalt and Oberon, JB's cats, answering his fan mail and mucking in as needed at the Dolphin hotel.

I slow to wait for half a dozen sheep to cross the road. Inevitably, there's one who stops and stares at me and we engage in a mutually mindless eye-lock. Its vacant, idle gaze seems to sum up the inertia of rural life. Since Christmas, I've been restless, dissatisfied. The festive season itself was good fun. Father Hickey stayed for a couple of days. We drank too much, played cards and JB thumped the piano while we sang rebel songs, with Father Hickey's brogue growing ever richer as he belted out 'Kevin Barry' and 'The Foggy Dew'. The *kommandantin* ordered us to Brize Manor for Christmas dinner — which she called luncheon — when I visited her home and ate duck for the first time. The manor was as roomy and grand as I'd imagined: layers of cheery chintz, richly

5

coloured rugs, gleaming cabinets and sideboards, porcelain ornaments, ranks of oil paintings featuring fruit and animals (sometimes together), a profusion of flowers in vases and plump sofas that swallowed you in a deep embrace. There were also some of Rosalind's own watercolours in the dining room. She specialises in coy, smirking fairies grouped in dells, glens, churchyards and on mountainsides. I have one of her works on my bedroom wall and I suspect the fairies are laughing at me.

Father Hickey flirted madly with his old friend Rosalind, who responded to his chiselled features, thick dark hair and warm voice, which grew deeper with each glass of wine. He's something of a chameleon, moving effortlessly through different echelons of London society. To his East End parishioners, he's the kindly, approachable priest, and among his actor friends, he's witty, flamboyant Declan, who drinks at their favourite bar in Belgravia, attends first-night theatre parties and hobnobs at the Chelsea Arts Club. After lighting the brandy on the Christmas pudding, he kissed the *kommandantin*'s hand, declaring, *'From the east to western Ind, no jewel is like Rosalind'* before singing 'In the Blue of Evening' to her in his strong tenor.

I was still riding on the crest of success with the Laidlaw murder — although my efforts also made some people wary of me, not least Vera. Her good friend Dora, the cleaner at the hotel, was revealed as the murderer, and during my investigation I discovered that Ray, Vera's husband, was a bigamist, still married to a woman in London. He's currently serving a prison sentence in Oxford, which is hard on Vera, especially with a baby on the way. Well, you can't make an omelette and so on.

Come January, the drab winter brought my spirits low. Fernfield is a pretty, sleepy town by the Thames, but its attractions are limited and I especially miss the cinema. I'm a film fan, the one interest I shared with Mum. (Although she favoured syrupy crooners like Bing Crosby and Rudy Vallée, whereas I prefer film noir with Barbara Stanwyck and Robert

Mitchum.) Some of our most peaceful moments had been spent in the Walthamstow Granada with a bag of sherbet lemons. I was used to catching a double bill in Walthamstow or hopping on a bus to Leicester Square. The nearest cinema now is in Oxford, some miles away.

I yearn for the tension and stimulation of my Whitehall work, that sense of belonging to an inspiring team and doing something important. I've stood in a room with Churchill while he urged us on in our crucial tasks. Replacing bath plugs and soaps at the hotel and tramping the muddy lanes around the lodge, tripping over dead foxes or badgers, doesn't quite match up.

I've tried to hide this from JB, because he's become a good friend, and he realises that there are times when I desperately miss the city where I was born and grew up. I'm terribly fond of him, and don't want to hurt his feelings. He fascinates and entertains me, makes me laugh, and I love the quiet snugness of my little annexe. And yet I often hanker for the pace and spark of London life. I tell myself that I should be grateful that I have a job and a place to live when so many people are dispossessed, hungry and suffering.

Even this sparkling morning doesn't quite lift my mood. I envisage reaching the Dolphin and carrying out the usual scintillating tasks of chasing supplies, tracking missing bedding at the laundry and lending a hand peeling carrots in the kitchen.

I ring my bell and the stationary sheep trots off. As I pedal away, a car roars up close behind me and sweeps past, so near that its heat washes me. I wobble madly and almost pitch over. I shake a fist, shouting, '*Road hog!*' It's gone in a flash, speeding around a bend.

The car is about to complicate my days and fire up my brain. I push on, back to singing 'Molly Malone', oblivious to the delightful trouble ahead.

CHAPTER TWO

The Dolphin smells of bacon and beeswax polish. Vera is perched on her stool at reception when I arrive. She's smart in a blue-checked maternity dress with little flaps over the pockets. She has a number of natty maternity numbers that her mother has run up for her. Vera's big on standards, and no matter how out of sorts she's feeling, she's always well turned out.

'Hi, Vera. You said you were going to the dentist.'

'Good morning to you, Daisy. I am, in ten minutes. I just wanted to check that Seahorse is spick and span for the Carpenters, who are arriving at lunchtime.'

The rooms at the Dolphin have marine names, which seems bizarre for an inland hotel. No one has been able to explain the reason to me.

'Your hair's great,' I lie. It's been tortured into a victory roll, which has to be one of the least flattering styles invented, but Vera rates it. These days, I'm careful to say positive things to her, in an effort to make amends for the turmoil I've helped cause in her personal life. She's a temperamental sort, prone to crankiness, and the strains of pregnancy have rendered her even more capricious. We tread carefully around each other, being ultra-polite. Vera can't help a tart comment at my expense occasionally, but I allow her those — after all, she has been left on her own with local gossip, a baby on the way and prison visits. (She is standing by Ray and visits him weekly.) Also, after years of living with my mother's unpredictable moods, I'm used to skirting around changeable people.

She pats her head. 'Thank you. I had it done at Pincurl.' She glances meaningfully at me. 'They've a half-price deal this week.'

I've been chopping my own wiry hair for years, keeping it short and springy. I can see that Vera despairs of it, as well as my penchant for wearing trousers and lace-up shoes.

'Anyway,' she says briskly, 'I'll get going and leave everything in your capable hands. Call that chap to find out when he's coming to fix the guttering, the curtains in the bar need some hooks replaced and check the butcher's delivery this afternoon. I've left a list here.' As she reaches for her coat I hear her mutter, *'That shouldn't get you into any trouble.'*

When she's gone, leaving behind a mist of Yardley lavender, I head to the kitchen, where Leslie, the chef, is rolling pastry.

'What's for dinner tonight?'

'Sausage and onion pasties and carrot mash.' Leslie casts his eyes upwards at the thump of the hoover. 'Our new cleaner has a heavy hand. She's very dolled up for a char, if you ask me. More like Jean Harlow than Mrs Mop.'

Sharon Billing is our glamorous newish cleaner-cum-chambermaid-cum-waitress. She's replaced Dora and Susan, who used to be with us. Susan was evacuated from London during the blitz, but decided she missed it too much and moved back to a job in a guest house near Victoria. There are days when I envy her.

I tease him, 'Is Sharon a bottle blonde?'

'Definitely, and with curves in all the right places.' Leslie grins, showing his gappy teeth, and makes a wave shape with both hands.

'Don't let your fiancée hear you going on like that.'

9

'I can keep my trap shut, especially as her dad's helping me with my inheritance.'

Leslie's discovered that he's the illegitimate son of deceased gentry at Granville Grange, a local estate.

'Have you struck a deal?'

'Too right. I'm getting some land, going to build a house for when we get married.'

'You'll be too grand for the likes of us.'

'Get away with you.' He beckons me closer. 'Between you, me and the gatepost, Vera told me Ray's getting a divorce. They'll marry as soon as it's finalised.'

'That's good news. Will we be invited?'

'Doubt it. I reckon Vera will want it low key — a quick turn around the register office. They had a big party for the first wedding. She won't want to tempt fate.'

'You could make her a cake, if you can get the ingredients.'

'I might be able to beg, borrow or steal enough. My neighbour got married in forty-three and she had to make do with a cardboard cake for show and slices of bread pudding for the guests. I'd best get this pastry made. You can chop onions if you've nothing better to do than annoy me, Lazy Daisy.'

'Sorry, I have important business regarding guttering.'

I sidle away and pursue my tasks. Sorting out the man who's mending the gutter takes an hour or so, by which time Mr and Mrs Carpenter have arrived for two nights. There's a huge kerfuffle when I show them up to Seahorse, which overlooks the front, because he insists that he asked for a room at the rear of the building.

'My wife is a very light sleeper, the least noise disturbs her. I was explicit about that when I made the booking.'

He's a big man with a narrow head, trim moustache, a booming voice and general air of being in command. His diminutive, pallid wife says nothing, clinging limply to his arm. She has dun-coloured hair, parted at the side and curled under at the shoulders.

'I'm sorry about that, let me see if I can offer you an alternative.'

Vera manages bookings and such a mistake is unlike her, but then she is juggling a lot in life at present. Luckily, Porpoise, which has a view of the back garden, is empty, so I invite them in there. Mr Carpenter gazes at the discoloured wallpaper with sprays of cherries and the small double bed, and snaps that it's a little *cosy* and the ceiling is rather low, but it will have to do.

'Are you having a country break?' Making small talk is quite an effort for me, but Vera has explained that the guests expect it.

Mr Carpenter doesn't care for my conversational sally. 'We're here for a friend's engagement party,' he says brusquely.

'It's tonight,' his wife ventures in a whispery voice, 'at a place called the Marquis. D'you know it?'

They both have posh accents, and it strikes me that they're slumming it at the Dolphin, which is middle-of-the-road at best. I'm surprised that they're not booked in to an Oxford hotel, but maybe they prefer to be more local.

'I've heard of it, but I haven't been there. It's about three miles east of town on the Banbury road.' The menu is beyond my earnings, but JB sometimes dines there, partial to the roast beef when they can source it.

Mr Carpenter is glancing at his watch and shifting from foot to foot. 'We should unpack, dear, and you need a rest after the journey if you're going to be on form for tonight.'

'I am a bit bushed,' she agrees.

'We'll let you know if we need anything,' Carpenter says in my direction, turning his back and hefting a suitcase onto the bed.

I can take a hint and I've no wish to linger in his overbearing company, or wait around for him to find fault with something else. 'I'll leave you to settle in. Enjoy your stay.'

I get sidetracked by the butcher's assistant, who's lost our order, and then several phone enquiries from potential guests, so it's nearly half three when I climb on a chair in the bar to sort out the curtains. I struggle and try my best, but they defy me. I might be skilled at codes and cryptic puzzles, but eyes, hooks and unwieldy fabric get me in a sweat. I'm swearing quietly when I hear Sharon's rich laugh.

'What on earth are you doing, Daisy?'

'Trying to fix these.'

'Break your neck, more like. Want me to have a go? I'm taller than you and I'm pretty good with curtains.'

I step down from the chair. 'Please. I'm just getting in a tangle.'

Sharon's a touchy-feely woman and a heavy smoker. A fug of nicotine hangs around her, as if she moves within her own haze of cloud. She puts a warm hand on my shoulder and squeezes. Her brown-and-yellow striped dress is tightly cinched at the waist, and her impressive cleavage is peeping from the low, square neck. Vera appointed Sharon reluctantly, commenting to me that, 'She is a bit common and she could do with putting less in the shop window, but she's the only applicant for the job, so it's a case of Hobson's choice.' Sharon kicks off her navy pumps with decorative bows and hops up on the chair. Her legs are bare and smooth, with well-muscled calves.

'You've made a right pig's ear of this — you've got the hooks too close together. Easily sorted, if you've any notion what you're doing. Hold the chair steady while I fiddle about.'

I'm watching Sharon deftly manipulate the gathered fabric when there's a little cough and a breathy murmur at my side.

'Excuse me, but have you seen my husband?'

It's Mrs Carpenter, a bit creased and dazed, still wearing her grey skirt and blue blouse from earlier.

'No, not since I left you in your room.'

'Oh. It's just . . . I dozed off, you see. He said he had to pop out, wouldn't be long. I woke and I can't find him.'

I glance at the clock. It's almost four. 'What time did he go out?'

'Well, I suppose just before one. I didn't mean to sleep for so long. I must have been more tired than I realised.

I never sleep well at night and we made an early start this morning . . . Where can Ronald be?'

Sharon calls down, 'Did he say where he was going?'

'No, at least I don't recall — just to get some air, I imagine, and so that I could rest.'

'Where have you looked?'

'In the parlour. Our car is outside. I don't understand.' She's biting the edge of a nail and there are little puckers of worry between her pale, wide, slightly fishy eyes.

'I bet he's in the pub,' Sharon says. 'You know what men are like.'

'Oh, no.' Mrs Carpenter shakes her head. 'Ronald is teetotal. We're Rechabites.'

'Wreck a what?' Sharon jumps down with a thud, her bosom bouncing.

'The Independent Order of Rechabites. We're part of the temperance movement.'

'Crumbs. Can't imagine life without a gin to kick-start the evening,' Sharon tells her.

Mrs Carpenter smiles nervously, her eyelids quivering, and crosses her arms tightly.

'Would your husband have met up with someone from the party you're attending tonight?' I ask.

'I shouldn't think so. We don't know people locally — just Charles, who's getting engaged. He's Ronald's old school friend from London. Charles lives in Oxford now, he's an accountant and his fiancée is from around here. I'm so sorry about this . . . taking up your time. I expect I'm being silly.'

I can't help wondering if her domineering husband often tells her that she is. 'Why don't you sit down in the parlour, Mrs Carpenter, and I'll get Sharon to bring you some tea. I'll search around the hotel and the centre of town. I'm sure your husband will be back soon.'

'Oh, thank you so much. I'm sorry to be such a bother. I would like a hot drink.'

Mrs Carpenter drifts away to the parlour and I ask Sharon to organise a pot of tea.

13

'She looks right anaemic, as if she could do with something stronger inside her — like a bottle of milk stout,' Sharon remarks. 'I've never heard of Rechabites, have you?'

'New to me.'

'She's a bit drippy. What's the husband like?'

'Big and bossy. I'd better see if I can find him.'

I do a sweep of the hotel, but can spot no sign of Mr Carpenter. I stand outside scanning the street and then trawl up and down the nearest High Street shops, asking if anyone has seen a man of about six feet two with a moustache, wearing a brown gabardine overcoat. 'Bit careless of you, losing a guest,' Jock calls in the Napolina café.

I draw a blank everywhere. Back in the Dolphin, I run up to Porpoise in case Mr Carpenter has returned, but he's not there. I find Sharon sitting on the parlour sofa with Mrs Carpenter, who's sipping treacle-coloured tea and toying with a piece of shortbread. Sharon's puffing smoke over her, waving a cigarette as she holds forth.

'. . . So I said to him, I said, you needn't try to give me a fatty cut like the one you slipped me last week, you must think I've got eye problems . . .' She turns to me as I come in. 'I was just telling Mrs C here about how our butcher takes the mickey.'

Mrs Carpenter starts up anxiously. 'Have you found him?'

'No. No one seems to have seen him. Maybe you should ring your husband's friend, in case he's heard anything.'

Her tea trembles in her hand. 'I'm afraid I don't have his number. Ronald made all the arrangements.'

Sharon raises an eyebrow at me and pulls deeply on her cigarette.

'What's his surname?' I ask.

'Harrington. Charles Harrington.'

'Let me see if I can find his number.'

I'm flicking through the phone book at reception when Vera arrives back, as pale as Mrs Carpenter.

'I had to have a filling,' she says, with stiff lips. 'Did you fix those curtains?'

'Yes, with Sharon's help, but we have another problem at present. Mr Carpenter's gone AWOL.' I explain about his absence and my search along the High Street.

'But that's almost four hours now!'

'It is a long time, for a man who supposedly popped out. I've found a Charles Harrington. I'll try this number.'

'Where's Mrs Carpenter?'

'In the parlour, with Sharon.'

Vera bustles away holding her jaw and I try the Oxford number. A man answers with an easy bonhomie that suggests he has a glass in his hand — not a Rechabite, then.

'Harrington here.'

'Good afternoon. I'm calling from the Dolphin hotel in Fernfield. Are you Mr Ronald Carpenter's friend?'

'I am. Is Ronnie there yet?'

'Yes and no.'

'Eh?'

I recount what's happened. 'I wondered if maybe you and Mr Carpenter had met, or if you'd heard from him.'

'Damned strange. I haven't chatted to him since early last week, when he confirmed he and Tommie would be there tonight. What's the silly chump playing at?'

'Is there anyone else he could be visiting locally?'

'He didn't say he was planning to. And his car's there, you say?'

'Yes, Mrs Carpenter checked. She's very worried.'

'I can imagine. She's a nervous sort at the best of times. I've no idea about this. I'm getting ready for the bash right now.'

'What time does it start?'

'Seven. Twelve of us for dinner and a cabaret. I'm sure Ronnie will turn up any time now. Probably gone for a walk and lost his bearings. He'll wander back.'

'I hope so. Let me give you the hotel number, in case you hear from him.'

I give him the number and return to the parlour. Sharon has vanished and a window has been opened. Vera is perching on the arm of the sofa.

'Well?' she asks.

'Mr Harrington hasn't spoken to Mr Carpenter since last week. He's getting ready for the evening, but he'll ring if he hears anything.'

'Oh!' Mrs Carpenter is wringing her hands. 'It's half past five. Where can he be? He must have had an accident or been taken ill! He could be lying in a ditch somewhere!'

Vera moves her jaw tentatively, draws herself up. 'What time is the engagement party?'

'Seven o'clock, at the Marquis,' I tell her.

'Very well. Listen, Mrs Carpenter, it's best if you go and get ready for your evening. I'm sure that your husband will be back any minute now, and you don't want to be in a terrible rush to get to your party.'

Mrs Carpenter looks from Vera to me, then back again. 'You think that's what I should do?'

'Absolutely,' Vera says. 'He's been delayed for some reason, so you need to get the show on the road. Have you a special dress?'

'Pardon? Oh, yes . . . it's pre-war, but a Madame Isobel.'

'How lovely. You go on up and we'll keep our eyes peeled for your husband.'

Mrs Carpenter doesn't seem convinced, but she gets up and leaves the room, head lowered.

Vera shuts the door. 'Where *is* the dratted man? He can hardly get lost in Fernfield! It's all most peculiar.'

I'm about to suggest that he might have run away, but stop myself in time, Vera's husband having done a runner from his other wife. 'Heart attack? Fell in the river?'

'Very helpful,' Vera says. 'I'm going to get some aspirin, my mouth's killing me. The least that a guest could do is not go missing as soon as he's arrived!'

CHAPTER THREE

At seven fifteen, Mrs Carpenter is sitting on her bed, decked out in a beautiful apple-green silk dress with matching clutch and wearing silver peep-toe shoes. She's grasping a damp hanky embroidered with 'T', her eyes are reddened and the green of the dress does nothing for her drained, waxy complexion. There's been no word from her husband and Charles Harrington has phoned to report that he hasn't turned up at the Marquis.

'Something dreadful has happened, I just know it,' Mrs Carpenter gasps. 'Ronald's a strict timekeeper, he'd never be tardy, especially for an event like this. There's something wrong.'

I have to agree with her. It's Vera's evening off, so I'm in charge. I check the time. 'Your husband's been gone for more than six hours. I'd better ring the police.'

'The police! Oh, gosh, that's so . . . I suppose . . .'

I'm sad for her, all dressed up with nowhere to go and her husband vanished into the ether. 'You should eat something,' I tell her. Two cups of tea sit untouched on the bedside table.

'I couldn't, really. Oh, why can't he just walk through the door?' She brims up.

'Come downstairs with me while I call the police. They might want to speak to you.' And it will be better to have something to occupy her.

She goes down in front of me, shimmering in her finery, which makes the faded wallpaper and scuffed paintwork appear even drabber. The army requisitioned the hotel for training for a couple of years during the war, and it still shows the wear and tear of energetic soldiers. I park her back in the parlour, which is empty and rarely used in the evenings, while the other guests enjoy their sausage pasties or sit in the bar.

There's no answer from the local police station, so I ring Oxford, crossing my fingers and ask for Inspector Thaxted, the detective who led on the Lucinda Laidlaw murder last autumn. I haven't seen him since just after Christmas, when he was driving through town and tipped his hat to me. He might be at home eating a vegetarian supper with his mother, but after a few clicks, I hear his scratchy, world-weary voice.

'Miss Moore, we haven't crossed paths for a while. How are you?'

'I'm very well, thanks. And you?'

'Yes, all is well.'

There's a little pause. 'The thing is, I'm at the Dolphin and there's a problem.'

'Oh. Not a body, I trust.'

'The lack of one, actually.' I picture him pinching the bridge of his narrow nose.

'Explain.'

'A guest, Mr Ronald Carpenter, told his wife he was popping out around one o'clock and he hasn't returned. The car's outside, so he didn't drive anywhere. They're supposed to be at an engagement party at the Marquis right now. She's very distressed.'

'Have you looked for him?'

'In the High Street and around. No one's seen him. His friend who's throwing the party is a Charles Harrington. He hasn't heard from him and Mr Carpenter hasn't turned up at the Marquis.'

'When did this couple arrive at the Dolphin?'

'Around half twelve. They're from London — Chiswick.'

Thaxted gives a little dry cough. 'Is Mrs Carpenter there? I'd like to speak to her.'

'I'll fetch her for you.'

She's pacing up and down, blinking at me with her glassy eyes.

'I've got hold of Inspector Peter Thaxted at Oxford Police,' I explain. 'I've met him before and I've given him brief details. He'd like to have a word with you.'

She says nothing but accompanies me to the phone in the tiny office behind reception. I move away to sit at the reception desk while she speaks to Thaxted in trembling tones. I hear her giving their home address and phone number, and a description of her husband.

'No . . . he didn't say where he was going exactly. He mentioned stretching his legs . . . I was resting, you see . . . I fell asleep. No, he has no real friends in the area apart from Charles. We've never been to Fernfield before. Oh, please find him!'

She starts sobbing. For such a slight woman, she produces deep, gusty wails, so I hurry to take the phone from her. Sharon, who's serving dinner, sticks her head through the dining room door to see what's happening, and I motion for her to take Mrs Carpenter back to the parlour.

'Hello, it's me again, Inspector. Mrs Carpenter is very upset. She's gone to sit down.'

'Sounds sensible. I'll start the ball rolling here and then I'll be on my way to Fernfield. Please call in immediately if this man turns up.'

'I will. Thanks, I appreciate—'

But he's gone, the line dead. Typical of him. I tidy the desk, which is already neat. Thaxted and I didn't get off to a good start when I became involved in the Laidlaw enquiry, provoking his anger at times. When I discovered information that helped to solve the crime, his attitude gradually mellowed. We ended with a kind of stand-off involving mutual respect. Thaxted is related to the *kommandantin*, but he lives with his mother in Oxford and rarely visits our neck of the woods. He's told me little about himself, but I've gleaned information from JB, just as Thaxted has found out from Rosalind about my war work and the circumstances that brought me to Fernfield.

Sharon skims through the door in a tight apron that sculpts her chest and hips. I can imagine why she's so popular with the gentlemen guests.

'I've persuaded Mrs C to have some toast, otherwise she'll keel over. Are the police coming?' Her eyes are lit up.

'Yes, they should be here soon. I'd better ring Vera. She said to keep her updated with what's happening.'

'The trouble with Vee is that she can't relax and let go,' Sharon says sagely. 'She'd be better off staying at home and looking after her bun in the oven, instead of running herself ragged.'

'Vera enjoys her job and I expect she needs the income.'

'True enough, with her old man banged up. What a rotter, pretending he was free to marry her! They should have locked him up for years.'

'I don't agree with you. He was sentenced to six months, and I think that's harsh. I was hoping he'd get fined, but he was unlucky, the judge at his trial was a moralist.'

'You're having me on!' Sharon folds her arms and cants a hip against the wall. 'What he did was bloody awful. If I was Vera, I'd have dumped the two-timing cheat, baby or no baby.'

'I don't approve of what he did, but there are much worse crimes. Vera's mad about him and it doesn't benefit her or the baby for Ray to be in prison, with his business just about surviving.'

I can see that Sharon is struggling with my viewpoint. She fluffs her hair. 'You're a strange one. Tell you what, glad I'm single and fancy free. D'you want a pasty? They're not bad.'

'I'll have something later. Can you tell Mrs Carpenter the police are on their way?'

I phone Vera to update her. She lives next door, in a flat above the bakery that her husband ran before he was imprisoned. Leslie is keeping the bakery ticking over for him with an assistant, opening it mornings only. He's up at dawn to prepare the dough and claims that he can't work out if he's coming or going, but he seems to thrive on the activity.

'I'll stay over tonight,' I tell Vera. 'I'd say it's going to be a long evening and I don't want to cycle home very late. Shark is empty, I'll sleep in there, which means I'll be here first thing in the morning, so you can have a later start if you like.'

'Yes, thanks for that, it would be handy. I reckon I could do with a lie-in for once.'

* * *

At just gone nine that evening, I'm sitting with Mrs Carpenter in the parlour while she nibbles toast and crumbles the crusts between her tiny fingers. We're on first-name terms now. She's Thomasina, 'but people always call me Tommie'.

'Have you phoned your family?' I ask. 'Is someone coming to be with you?'

'Oh, no. I don't want to bother them just now and cause a lot of worry. Ronnie would be cross with me. He hates fuss. Gosh, the mess I'm making!' she mumbles. 'Ronnie aways tells me off for picking at my food. I've a small appetite. It's one of the things that annoys him about me.'

'And what about you?'

'Pardon?'

'What annoys you about him? Doesn't it always work both ways in a marriage?'

'Oh . . . well . . . men have their little ways,' she says mysteriously.

'How long have you been married?'

'Eight years now. We met at the theatre, a production of *Invitation to the Waltz*. Such a lovely musical. I was with a friend who introduced me to Ronald in the interval.'

21

'My friend's an actor. Jeffrey Berrow.'

'Oh? I'm afraid I haven't heard of him.'

'He's not been in anything big. He's a support player, calls himself a jobbing thespian.'

The door opens and Peter Thaxted limps in. He removes his hat, nods to me and addresses Tommie. 'Good evening. Mrs Carpenter? I'm Inspector Thaxted, Oxford Police.'

'Oh, Inspector, I'm so glad you've come. There's still no sign of my husband and I'm beside myself with worry. I rarely go anywhere — I mainly stay at home, but Ronnie persuaded me that this little trip would do me good, so I agreed to come. But now . . . I wish we'd both stayed put!'

He sits, resting his stick beside his chair, and runs a hand over his wavy white hair. His eyebrows are striking, a contrasting black. JB told me that the inspector's hair turned white overnight after he was injured at El Alamein and sustained a terrible leg wound.

'Try to stay calm, Mrs Carpenter. We've contacted local hospitals and your husband hasn't been admitted, nor have any accidents been reported. We have commenced a search.' He casts me a look that asks, *Why are you still here?*

'Would you like some tea?' I offer.

'That would be good,' he says.

But as I start to rise, Tommie grips my arm surprisingly firmly, pulling me back down.

'Oh, can Daisy please stay, Inspector? She's been so kind and helpful and I'd find it a great comfort.'

I keep a neutral expression and avoid his gaze.

'Very well,' he replies.

'I'll ask Sharon to fetch the tea. I won't be a moment.'

When I return, Thaxted is making notes and listening to Tommie with his placid, inscrutable expression.

'Ronald is in insurance, a loss adjuster. The company kept his job for him during the war. He was in the navy, a lieutenant in the Mediterranean fleet. He was at school with Charles and they've been friends since. Charles brought Linda Merchant, his fiancée, to visit us a couple of months ago. Her parents own the Marquis, that's why the party is being held there. Linda works there as well.'

'You and your husband were anticipating this engagement celebration?'

Tommie has perked up a little. No doubt a response to officialdom and the welcome feeling that someone has taken charge. Thaxted isn't exactly a reassuring presence, but his sombre, spindly appearance strikes a note of seriousness.

'I can't say that I was, Inspector. I find socialising such a strain and a worry. But Ronald has been terribly busy at work and Charles is his oldest friend, so he persuaded me to come along.'

'Did Mr Carpenter take anything with him when he went out?'

'No . . . just his coat. He must have his wallet, it's not in the room.'

'Did he have much money on him?'

'Oh . . . I can't really say. Some cash, yes . . . he usually carries some. His chequebook is in his suitcase.'

Thaxted stretches out his injured leg. 'Did your husband seem worried at all recently?'

'No. He didn't mention anything to me.'

'Has he ever vanished like this before?'

'Goodness, no! What an odd question!'

Thaxted doesn't respond. Tommie glances at me and I smile reassuringly.

'And your husband didn't refer to anyone else he needed to meet while he was in Fernfield?'

Tommie slumps. 'It was just a little break, a chance to attend the party, and Ronnie was keen to spend a couple of nights away from London. He was looking forward to it so much. He only came home last summer, and then his work has been frantic with so many claims, we've not had much time together . . .' She's caught by a sob and buries her head in her hands.

Thaxted snaps his notebook shut. 'I'm sorry, Mrs Carpenter, I realise how distressing this must be for you.

Please let me assure you that we'll do all we can to find your husband.'

He manoeuvres himself up from the chair. His well-worn serge suit hangs loosely on his skeletal frame. It's easy to see that a broader man filled it before he was diminished by bullets ripping through his leg. I follow him out to the hall, closing the door gently.

He leans against the wall by reception, under a painting of three leaping dolphins. 'You said you met Carpenter briefly. What was your impression of him?'

'Opinionated, confident. I'd wager he rules the roost at home.'

Thaxted's lips twitch. 'You didn't take to him.'

'Not much.'

'And he didn't say anything to you about his plans, or where he might be going?'

'No. He wasn't a conversationalist.' I pause. 'He was keen for his wife to have a rest. Maybe he needed to go out without explaining why. Although I'm not sure she would question him about where he was going, and she did say she's a poor sleeper, so she was very tired.'

Thaxted dons his hat. 'Goodnight, Miss Moore. I'll be in touch as soon as there's any news.'

'They're Rechabites,' I tell his back.

He turns. 'Pardon?'

'Mrs Carpenter said they're Rechabites. Teetotallers.'

'The things you find out!'

I don't take to being patronised. 'Just as well you're not a Rechabite as well as a vegetarian. The combination might make life a bit bland.'

He stares at me. 'Quite so. Night.'

I watch him lean heavily on his stick as he leaves. My little gibe has left me with a grubby conscience; the man can't have much fun in life with that permanent injury. I phone JB to tell him I won't be back tonight and why. I can hear that he's sipping a late-night whisky.

'The missing guest!'

'Fascinating, isn't it? He didn't much like the room and said the ceiling was too low, but that's no reason to disappear.'

JB chortles. 'Keep me posted. Peter's in charge, then?'

'That's right.'

'Don't tread on his toes, Daisy. Keep your fascination under wraps. You've plenty to occupy you at the Dolphin these days, so don't go interfering.'

'Why would I do that?' JB has put my back up. I don't suppose he'd find gutters and curtains especially riveting.

There's a snort at the end of the line. 'Well, let's hope this guest turns up soon. I don't want the Dolphin getting a reputation.'

CHAPTER FOUR

The following morning, Ronald Carpenter does turn up, but not in the way his wife or any of us would wish. I've just come downstairs at seven o'clock when the phone rings.

'Bad news, I'm afraid,' Peter Thaxted tells me. 'We've found Carpenter's body a couple of miles from town, in a car down a farm track near Bidwell.'

'How did he die?'

'I can't comment at present and Mrs Carpenter must be informed first.'

'Whose car?'

'We don't know as yet. It's a navy-blue Ford Anglia.'

'Should I tell Mrs Carpenter?'

'Absolutely not! I'm at the local police station and I'm about to come round.'

A flash of memory from yesterday morning nudges me. 'Just a minute. When I was cycling in yesterday, a Ford Anglia almost ran me off the road. It was dark blue.'

'You're sure about the make of car?'

'Yes, I can identify cars easily from when I drove London buses early in the war.' I picture it speeding away. 'It had an AA badge by the boot handle.'

'Excellent recall, Miss Moore. I'll speak to you about this later. I have to go. Don't tell anyone else this news and stay away from Mrs Carpenter until I get there.'

'But what if she—'

He's gone. One day, I'll put the phone down on him. A childish aspiration, but a satisfying one.

Tommie Carpenter took a sleeping tablet late last night, so I hope that she won't appear just yet asking about her husband. I help Leslie and Sharon with breakfast service, which isn't onerous. We have only six guests at present. One is dead, his wife is unlikely to want bacon and eggs, and Mrs Ward, our permanent guest, eats in her bedroom, so the remaining three are easily catered for.

When the inspector arrives, I see that he's wearing one of the unlovely V-neck tops his mother knits for him under his flannel jacket. He asks Sharon, who's observing him with interest, to take Mrs Carpenter a cup of tea and tell her that he's here to speak to her.

He parks himself at reception. 'A coffee wouldn't go amiss when you have time,' he tells me. 'I also need to use your phone.'

I show him into the office, fetch him a coffee and leave it by his elbow. 'Stolen? From where?' I hear him say into the receiver.

Twenty minutes later, Thaxted has seen Mrs Carpenter and is back downstairs, asking to speak to me in the parlour. The sun is razoring through the window beside him, emphasising the transparency of his skin and the fine web of lines around his eyes.

'Mrs Carpenter is in a bad way. I asked if she wants to return to London, but she insisted on staying here for the time being. She's going to phone family when she's more composed. She wanted to be left alone for a while, then she'll come down.'

'I'll keep an eye on her, make sure she can call people in private. Did I hear that the Ford was stolen?'

'Yes, early yesterday morning, from just outside Fernfield. It has an AA badge on the boot, so it sounds as if it was the car that passed you. What time was that?'

'About a quarter to nine. It was a mile or so out of town. It was going fast, came up behind me suddenly and flashed by, very close.'

'Any impression of the driver?'

I close my eyes for a moment. 'No — it was so quick, and I was trying to keep the bike stable. Where was Mr Carpenter found? I expect you can tell me now.'

'Can I, indeed?' He writes in his notebook, then relents. 'The car was on land belonging to a farm called Broadmeadow.'

'Was it a robbery?'

'No. We identified him from his wallet, which had bank notes inside.'

'How did he die?'

He weighs up the question. 'I've told Mrs Carpenter that her husband was shot.'

'Shot! I suppose that there might be quite a few guns floating around post-war.'

'You'd suppose correctly. Some not handed back after active service or stolen, others bought.' Thaxted points his pen at me. 'You can tell the other hotel staff that we've found Mr Carpenter's body, but no other details for now and nothing about the shooting. Understand? I'll release details as I see fit.'

'So, he must have met the car driver somewhere. Seems as if he knew them. Why not tell his wife? Unless he was kidnapped, maybe attacked and knocked unconscious, then—'

'Miss Moore!' Thaxted stands and grasps his stick. 'Please don't start theorising about this murder or becoming involved. This is a violent crime. Just remember that last year, you could easily have become another of Dora Sullivan's victims because of your interference.'

He's gone, the door banging. I sit for a few minutes, irritated and marshalling my thoughts. I have to admit that he's right, albeit begrudgingly — I did narrowly avoid being murdered by Dora and her syringe full of morphine, and I was rescued due to Thaxted's quick actions. In my defence, I had discovered crucial information, which had forced Dora's hand and in doing so, helped solve the case. And I am already involved here, through no effort of my own, because I saw the killer's car. I could even have been injured (or worse) by it if I hadn't swerved.

As far as I'm concerned, I'm perfectly entitled to ask questions.

I'm still musing when Sharon elbows the door open and comes in with a cup of tea and a bacon sandwich for me.

'Here. I reckoned you might need these. I got Leslie to do the rasher extra crispy, how you like it.'

'Thanks, I am running on empty.' I take a bite of the salty bacon.

'So, what's happened?' She sits, pops a cigarette between her glossy red lips and flicks her brass lighter.

'The police have found Mr Carpenter's body.'

'Oh, crumbs!' Her mouth drops, the cigarette glued to her bottom lip. 'What happened to him?'

'I haven't heard any details yet,' I lie. 'I expect his wife's been told.'

'That poor lady!' Sharon's pencilled eyebrows arch up towards her hairline. 'She must be in bits! She's a delicate little thing, isn't she? This will knock her for six. I wouldn't be surprised if she has a breakdown.'

'I'll go up and see her in a minute, when I've finished this.'

'That Inspector Thaxted's a strange one, with the limp and walking stick. He's ever so scrawny, all skin and bone, but he's sort of attractive in a funny way. Interesting eyes. Was he fighting in the Far East?'

'I'm not sure. Why?'

'My cousin was, and he lost most of his stomach because of the starvation and dysentery in the prison camp. He can only eat soft food and he still looks like a skeleton. I'm surprised that the inspector can work in the police with such a gammy leg.'

'How d'you mean?' I croak through a mouthful of sandwich.

'Well, he could hardly chase down a criminal, could he?'

'He's got constables to do that. He has a good brain, that's the most important asset for a detective.'

'Leslie said you and he are friends. He gave me the low-down on what happened last year with Dora. I mean, I'd heard a fair bit, but I'd no idea you almost died!' She's sitting forward, one hand cupping her chin.

'I'd say Inspector Thaxted and I are acquaintances rather than friends.'

'Oh, right. How old is he, then?'

'Mid-thirties, I suppose.'

'He looks much older, but then a lot of blokes have lived-in faces these days, after what they've seen and done.' Sharon reaches for an ashtray. 'So what will happen now, with Mrs C?'

I finish my tea. 'I'll go and speak to her, see what we can do to help.'

* * *

Tommie Carpenter is sitting on the bed, still in her dressing gown, her eyes unfocused.

'Oh, hello,' she whispers, drawing a hand listlessly over her hair. 'Have you heard the news?'

'Yes. I'm terribly sorry.' I perch on the window ledge, next to a stone porpoise. 'Can I call anyone for you, or do anything?'

She seems half asleep and I wonder how many pills she swallowed. She twines the cord of her dressing gown around her finger.

'No, that's kind, but . . . I'll have a wash and get dressed and then I'll come down and phone family. And Charles — I must ring Charles. I can't . . . I can't believe this. Why would anyone do that to Ronald?'

'I'm sure the police will find out.'

'Yes. It's so peaceful here, such lovely countryside. Ronald will simply have wanted a quiet walk . . .'

She goes back into her trance state. I take a cold cup of tea from the table, where there are four brown bottles of tablets, two with the lids off.

'Mrs Carpenter — Tommie, would you like me to contact Mr Harrington for you?'

'Please, that would be kind. He must be worrying.'

Vera's arrived. She's on the phone in the office, giving short shrift to someone who was supposed to provide an estimate for redecoration of the hotel. 'I'd have expected you'd need the work,' she snaps. 'You've cancelled twice now! And don't give me any of that old nonsense about problems with supplies, I'm only asking you to give me a price, not reproduce the Sistine Chapel! Right . . . good. Next Friday.'

She slams the phone down, rests her hands across her stomach and grimaces at me. She looks as if she's slept badly, but her make-up gives her a false bloom. 'That put a flea in *his* ear, giving me a load of codswallop about shortages. Sharon told me about Thaxted turning up and what's happened to Mr Carpenter. What a to-do! Where's his wife?'

'Still in her room. She's going to come down and call family soon. I said I'd ring Mr Harrington, their local friend, for her.'

'Yes, you'd better.' Vera shoves the chair back, knocking it against the waste-paper bin. 'Is it too much to ask to run a quiet country hotel, rather than an annexe to the police station?'

I assume it's a rhetorical question and a dig at me — since I arrived, so has trouble. She turns on her heel and taps away. I call Mr Harrington, who sounds hungover and stunned. He says he'll be straight over.

* * *

Charles Harrington is lithe and earnest, with floppy fair hair. He's wearing a blue sweater with red trim at the neck and wrists and a motif of a hare on the upper left chest. Tommie is hovering on the stairs. When she sees him she runs down, bursts into tears and sinks onto his chest. He pats her back and bites his lip, then they vanish upstairs.

When he reappears, I offer him coffee, hoping to detain him for a chat. He accepts and I bring it to him in the parlour. He's ashen, pressing his temples.

'I had rather a lot to drink last night. Celebrating until late.'

'Did your evening go well?'

'It was terrific except for worrying about Ronnie. His absence did make it all seem a bit odd, cast something of a cloud. Tommie's told me he was shot in the head. For God's sake . . . unbelievable.'

'It must have been hard for your fiancée too.'

'Yes, poor Linda, it wasn't quite the evening she'd been hoping for. Ronnie was going to be our best man, so this has a huge impact.'

'Have the police spoken to you?'

'Not yet. An Inspector Thaxted has asked me to pop into the police station at noon. Tommie said you've been very helpful, she appreciates it.'

'It's the least I can do. She seems quite an anxious person.'

'Yes, she does suffer awfully with her nerves. Sees a doctor and so on.'

'Are any family coming to be with her?'

'No, she doesn't want that. She's phoned Ronnie's widowed mother. She lives in Bournemouth and is quite frail. Tommie's dad is in Exeter — he remarried after her mum died and she doesn't get on with the new wife. She said she'd rather just see to whatever the police need from her and then get back to London. I'll drive her and catch the train home.'

'It's so strange. I showed them to their room yesterday and then Mr Carpenter just vanished.'

'I can only imagine that he needed to stretch his legs after the drive and decided to take a walk around Fernfield.'

'This was his first visit here?'

'That's right. He'd been to Oxford, we'd meet there now and then, and I'd catch up with him in London.'

'Tommie told me you'd been friends since school.'

'We were good chums. Hadn't seen quite so much of each other since I moved to Oxford, and then of course there was the war, but we've always kept in touch.'

'Was he a popular man?'

'A regular sort. Straightforward.'

'No enemies, then.'

'Enemies! Gosh, no.' He tilts his cup, finishes his coffee. 'Thanks, that's cleared the head a bit. I must push on, lots to do.'

* * *

I'm bushed as I cycle home late that evening, pedalling wearily against the gusting wind that's buffeting me head on. There are no lights on when I reach the lodge and park my bike.

Tybalt and Oberon are in the gubbins room, where they have comfy beds and food bowls. They're both midnight black, the only distinguishing mark being the little white dot like a splash of paint on Oberon's tail. Their personalities are quite different. Saucy, daring Tybalt makes a beeline for me, twisting around my legs and miaowing. Oberon, who is a slyer, more watchful character, stays on the window ledge and fixes me with a sphinx-like stare. I feed them with mashed-up rabbit shot by the *kommandantin* and top up their water.

It's chilly in the sitting room, so I light the fire before I have a wash and don pyjamas and the lovely damask dressing gown JB gave me. It belonged to his previous factotum, Joe, who was killed in the war. It's far too big and long, but if I tighten the cord around my waist, I can hitch the fabric off the floor. I like snuggling into the shawl collar, putting my hands in the deep pockets and imagining I'm in a Noel Coward drawing-room comedy.

I make tea and sit by the fire with the wireless broadcasting the Billy Ternent Orchestra. It's a comfy room, with deep-red velvet armchairs and dark green rugs on the oak floorboards. Bookshelves flank the fireplace and the walls are covered with sketches of famous writers. After a while, Tybalt and Oberon join me, both carrying out a thorough cleaning routine before settling on either side of the fireplace.

While I'm drinking my tea, I recall the way Tommie Carpenter crumbled her toast and clutched my arm. I'm sorry for her loss, but I find her an irritating woman, with her nerves, her timidity, her poor appetite and insomnia. Although I have noted that some men like that type, a woman who can be relied on to flutter and needs a manly chest to rest against.

When the phone rings, it's Rosalind.

'Good evening, Daisy,' she says coolly, in her accent that's a notch posher than JB's. 'May I speak to Jeffrey?'

'He had a rehearsal in London today. He's not home yet.'

'Would you be so good as to leave a message for him? Samuel Baines, the sculptor, and his wife are coming for supper next week and I'd like Jeffrey to attend. Ask him to confirm with me, please. Tomorrow morning will be convenient.'

'Will do.' I wonder whether or not to tell her about the incident at the hotel, as she's the owner, but I decide to leave that to JB.

'Please read the message back to me,' she demands.

I repeat it to her satisfaction and she bids me goodnight.

I leave the note by the phone and return to the fire, which is now glowing with rich ambers. The cats are deep in sleep. I'm intrigued by Rosalind's and JB's arrangement, with her in the huge country house and him down the lane in what used to be the groundsman's lodge. He moved to the lodge some time ago, but they've never divorced. Rosalind owns his home as well as the hotel, so in many ways, he's a kept man. The deal seems to be that in return for her largesse, she has a key to the lodge and is allowed to call in whenever she wishes — which is rarely — and he visits her every week, obeying orders to attend luncheons and suppers. When they're together, he treats her in a gallant, courteous manner, which she accepts graciously.

My thoughts return to Tommie Carpenter. She and Rosalind are chalk and cheese. I can't imagine the *kommandantin* suffering with her nerves or allowing a man to make all the arrangements. When JB fell into a doze after Christmas dinner, she prodded him awake with a snappy, '*Night-time is for sleeping, daytime for activity!*'

I reach for a notepad and pen, review the last twenty-four hours and make notes.

CARPENTER

Where did RC meet the car driver & why did he go with them? Must be someone he knew, but he hadn't visited around here before.

Motive. Could it be a random killing?

Stolen car. Someone from outside the area? Any other crimes like this committed recently around Oxfordshire? Check newspapers.

Did anyone at Broadmeadow Farm see anything?

The wind rattles a windowpane and Oberon twitches. I'm more used to the countryside now, but I'm still not keen on being alone in the lodge at night, listening to creaks, stirrings and animal cries. I get up to draw the curtains tighter and I'm pleased to see the beam of JB's headlights turning into the drive.

'Ah, hearth and home!' He beams when he comes in and heads to the whisky decanter. 'A wee noggin, Daisy?'

'I'll join you.'

He's dapper, in a plum shirt, yellow cravat and black braces. His auburn hair is a little longer these days and it curls around the nape of his neck.

'There, the medicine that cures all ills. My rehearsal went well and I got the part. Just a little wireless thing, but work, so not to be sneered at.'

I clink glasses with him. 'Cheers and congratulations.'

'Ta, me old fruit. Have we found the missing resident?'

'I'm afraid we have.' I fill him in on the day's events and my experience with the Ford.

'Oh, Lord! What's Peter saying?'

'True to form, not much. I'm not supposed to have told you Carpenter was shot.'

He puts a finger to his lips. 'I won't grass you up, honest. Well . . . what to say? People around here worry about entering the fleshpots of London and coming to harm. It doesn't usually work the other way round.'

'That had occurred to me. Tommie Carpenter's made several comments about how they were looking forward to their quiet rural weekend. I'm so annoyed that if I hadn't been trying to keep the bike upright, I might have caught a glimpse of the murderer. I've been making notes.' I hand him the notepad and sip my whisky while he finds his reading glasses.

'Good start with this, Daisy chain, very pertinent questions. You'll find the local papers in the library. It's open on Mondays.'

I hold a hand to my ear. 'Hang on, am I hearing correctly? Didn't you tell me not to get involved and concentrate on the hotel?'

JB peers at me over his glasses, his bright blue eyes gleaming. 'I didn't mean that. As your employer, I had to say the correct thing. Now that's out of the way, I expect you to focus your underused brain on the serious matter in hand. I realise that you will anyway.' He wags a finger, says with a sigh of mock regret, 'You take no notice of what I say.'

'My mum always complained that I was headstrong and went my own way.' She'd also said that I'd be the death of her, which had been prophetic.

'Parents are supposed to be baffled by their children. And just as well you did go your own way, otherwise you'd have stayed working in the biscuit factory, and custard creams' gain would have been my loss!'

We sit in companionable silence for a while, listening to the music. The orchestra starts to play 'She's My Lovely'. JB rises and holds out his hand. I yank up my dressing gown, holding it out with one hand, and we dance around the floor, as we do on many nights. 'Whisky and waltzing', as JB calls it. Tybalt opens an eye and observes us. When I first met JB, I'd worried that he might be seeking a factotum-cum-mistress, but he'd quickly put my fears to rest and I've always been at ease with him. I've heard comments in Fernfield indicating that his affairs might have caused Rosalind to expel him from the manor. I've not seen him with any women, but he stays over in London sometimes, so perhaps he confines his romantic liaisons to the city.

'Oh, I almost forgot. Rosalind left a message for you, it's by the phone. You're summoned to supper with a sculptor.'

'Marvellous. There'll be lots of highfalutin nonsense about form and medium, all of which will fly over my head. But the wine will be good. The *kommandantin*'s papa laid some of it down years ago. Did you tell her about the dead guest?'

'I decided to leave that to you.'

'Yes, that'd be for the best. I'll walk up to see her in the morning. It's not that she'll be particularly shocked. But she finds it terribly bad form when people end up as corpses.'

CHAPTER FIVE

I have the day off on Sunday. I cycle into Fernfield in the morning, watching the good people of the town making their way to St Clement's for a service. The church bells are pealing and the sun is out, striking warmly on the stone and brick of houses. I head to Market Avenue, to visit my friend Felix Koller. Felix is an Austrian Jew, a refugee whose architectural studies in Vienna were ended by the Nazis. He managed to flee, but his family died in a concentration camp. After several years in a British internment camp, Felix became Lucinda Laidlaw's lodger and, for a brief time, was suspected of her murder. Lucinda left him her house and money, which is some consolation for his being beaten up and hospitalised by a local bigot after her death. He's bought a car, a small Hillman, with some of his inheritance, which I borrow sometimes. I'm pleased that, for now, he's decided to stay, despite the fact that some inhabitants of Fernfield — Fernies, as they call themselves — dislike people they refer to as 'wals', from an Old English word for foreigners.

A large box for charity donations stands in the porch of the house. I peek and see that it's half-full, a battered tin of whale casserole balancing on top of a knitted blanket. Felix is continuing Lucinda's work of collecting for people left destitute by the war.

He's expecting me and has coffee and a plate of biscuits ready. He understands my sweet tooth — it was the only way in which the biscuit factory satisfied my needs — and has made my favourite, an Austrian speciality called *Vanillekipferl*, which is a crescent-shaped mouthful of vanilla delight.

We sit at the table in the shady kitchen. Felix's curly black hair frames a long, fine-boned face. He has new glasses, round and tortoiseshell. His eyes are large and intelligent behind the lenses. When I first met him, he was terrified and wary. Now he's more at ease, although I'm sure that Felix will always be alert for the unexpected knock at the door or the shadow at his back.

'I have news,' he tells me with his hesitant smile.

'Go on. These vanilla things are amazing.'

'I've been accepted at Oxford University to study architecture in October. They've agreed that I don't have to start my degree again, but can join the second year.'

'That's wonderful. When did you hear?'

'On Friday. I was going to phone, but I wanted to tell you in person.'

'So that means you'll stay here?'

'Yes, that's my plan. With the car, I can travel in and out easily.'

I'm delighted. He's the only friend I have in Fernfield, someone around my own age who I can talk to. He's different, courageous and resourceful. Also, as well as mouth-watering biscuits, he makes amazing potato dumplings and stews with garlic and herbs, the kind of food that Leslie would describe as 'foreign muck'. When I took a bulb of garlic from Felix's garden to Leslie, he reacted as if I'd offered him poison and asked if I wanted to give everyone bad breath and screaming habdabs.

'I just wish Lucinda was here to celebrate the news,' Felix says. 'She was so supportive of my applying to Oxford, encouraged me when I lost confidence.'

'It's her success as well, then, in a way.'

'That's true.'

Lucinda's knitting bag is still on the counter, a grey balaclava she was making peeping out. Felix has been teaching himself to knit and hopes to finish it one day.

'I've got strange news for you, Felix, and a request.'

'I'm all ears. More coffee?'

'Please. How do you make it taste so good?'

'A pinch of cinnamon added to the warmed milk.'

'One of our guests was murdered.' I tell him the whole story. 'Peter Thaxted is investigating.'

He brings me my refilled cup and says drily, 'You mean you're allowing him to assist you with the inquiry?'

'What a strange observation, I can't imagine why you assume I'll be involving myself.' I crunch my fourth biscuit. 'I am interested in following up a few things.'

Felix laughs, takes a biscuit in his long fingers and dips it in his coffee. 'Such as?'

'I want to visit Broadmeadow Farm, see if anyone there has heard of Ronnie Carpenter. The killer might have chosen the place for a particular reason.'

'It could be coincidental, a handy, isolated location.'

'Worth poking about, though.'

'You'll annoy Inspector Thaxted, trespassing on his territory again,' Felix warns.

'Not necessarily, and anyway, what's he going to do? He can't arrest me for being public spirited. I'll tread lightly. I wondered if I could borrow your car to drive there. Unless you want to come with me?'

'When do you want to go?'

'Now, this morning, if possible.'

'I can't come along. Someone from the Red Cross is visiting me shortly. I've offered accommodation for a refugee, so they have to check me out. It seems shameful, to be living alone here when there are people who are desperate for a home. I should share my good fortune.'

I lick my sugary fingers. 'You might annoy some of the Fernies, bringing in another wal.'

40

'How awkward for them. What will they do, beat me up, put me in hospital?'

'Fair point. Let them get used to post-war reality.'

'Actually, I'm finding most people in town are friendlier these days. Now they've learned that I'm not a murderer and that this house is mine, they're civil to me. I might even become an honorary Fernie one day.'

'JB would say, "Steady on, you'll frighten the horses!"'

Felix smiles. 'How is he?'

'A busy man. Up and down to London for work, the urbane actor in town and the country gent at home. He keeps the *kommandantin* sweet. I still puzzle as to why they stay married.'

Felix puts his head to one side. 'People have their reasons. It's undoubtedly convenient, a trade-off.'

'I suppose. So, can I borrow the car? I'll top up the petrol.'

'You're welcome to it. Just don't get into any trouble. I'd like you and the car back in one piece.'

* * *

I love being in the Hillman, back at the wheel. I'd enjoyed my time on London buses, driving empty vehicles through the fissured roads for maintenance and repair. The responsibility and autonomy had suited me. The easy camaraderie had been good too, and I'd got to know dozens of drivers by name. We'd meet at canteens for cups of tea from enamel mugs and swap tales of obliterated streets, broken gas and water mains and fire hazards, and exchange tips on which roads to avoid.

I crank open the window and let the fresh breeze ruffle my hair. This beats mundane tasks in the Dolphin. I have a love–hate relationship with the hotel. In many ways, I've grown fond of it and the foibles of its staff, but I do get fidgety in its confines.

I turn onto a track with a wooden sign to the farm, and drive past herds of chocolate-speckled cows flicking their tails as they graze. There's an overpowering smell of manure, strong enough to make my eyes water, so I close the window again. The track is stony and straight, with grass growing down the middle. A figure is cycling fast towards me, a man in blue jacket, peaked cap and trousers. I pull in against the hedge to let him pass and he gives a little salute. Another hundred or so yards, and I see a higgledy-piggledy whitewashed farmhouse that appears to have been built in random stages. The windows are odd shapes and sizes with wonky lintels, and the building slants to the right like an uncoordinated drunk. Some roof tiles are missing and there's moss in the gutters. A column of grey smoke drifts from a tall chimney with a diagonal crack through its centre.

I park in the muddy yard, which is scattered with bits of machinery, and wave to a woman hosing down her wellingtons by the side of the house.

I pick my way over to her, my feet squelching as she turns off a tap. 'Hello, my name's Daisy Moore. I was driving by and decided to call in to see if you sell eggs.'

She's early twenties, bleary-eyed and wearing dungarees the same murky shade as cowpats under a hairy black cardigan. Her hair is tucked into a felt hat. She looks like a woman who could do with a week in bed.

'We do beef and dairy, no hens. Want to buy an Ayrshire?'

'Ah, no.' I don't have a plan B. 'There is something else I'd like to discuss, if you don't mind.'

'Should I mind?' She yawns widely, showing neat teeth.

'I work at the Dolphin hotel. One of our guests was found dead near here.'

She stares past me. 'You don't need to tell me. I found him.'

This is more than I'd expected. 'I'm sorry, that must have been an awful shock.'

'Can't say it did a lot for my day. I was glad I hadn't had my breakfast, or I might have lost it.' She leans a hand against the wall and lifts each foot to shake water off her wellingtons. 'Didn't your guest like the room you gave him?'

'Actually, he didn't. It was too small.'

She gives a grunt like a laugh. 'What do you want with me?'

'I'm not sure. His wife's very upset and it's all a bit strange.'

She rubs her hands together. 'You might as well come in, no point in standing around here decorating the yard. I'm due a cuppa and a bite to eat. Take those shoes off, I washed the floor this morning.'

She slips her wellies off in the porch and I unlace my mucky shoes and pad after her in my socks. The kitchen is warm, clean and neat, as if it belongs to a different house, and I guess that it's her corner of order amid the chaos. The chairs have striped cushions, the table is scrubbed and the brass pans lined up on hooks are sparkling.

'Park yourself,' she says wearily. 'Want a sarnie?'

'Just a cuppa, thanks. What's your name?'

'Pearl Armitage.'

She bangs about with a teapot and cuts two thick wedges of bread from a loaf, which she crams with dark yellow cheese and a dollop of chutney. She demolishes half of the sandwich while she fills the teapot and brings it over with two chipped mugs and a bottle of milk.

'We're out of sugar, but I expect you're sweet enough,' she says. 'I'll let you pour your own when you're ready.'

'Thanks. I am sorry to disturb you. I'm sure you're busy with a farm to run.'

'I am indeed. It's non-stop fun around here and the police have been taking up a lot of our time.' Pearl removes her cardigan, hitches a chair with her foot and rests both legs across it. Her socks are red wool with darning at the toes and heels. 'What is it you want?'

'Well, if you could tell me about how you found the deceased — Mr Carpenter.'

'I was out getting the cows to the milking parlour early morning, about six o'clock. I saw a car parked in the hedge by the lower field, on our land. I walked over and saw your man in the passenger seat with his brains blown out and blood all over the window. I came back here, told my dad and he phoned the police while I went back to the herd.'

She's matter-of-fact about her discovery — detached, almost. I presume that farming's made her resilient. Even so, she's calmer than I would be if I'd seen a man with his head blown apart. I pour tea and offer to do the same for her. She nods and picks grime from her thumbnail.

'Has the car gone now?'

'The police fetched it away late yesterday.'

'Any idea why someone would have left his body on your land?'

'No. Bloody nuisance, though. What was the chap doing in Fernfield?'

'He and his wife had come from London for an engagement party.'

'Shame, and a nasty shock for her.' She takes the last bite from her sandwich.

'You didn't hear or see anything suspicious around the farm?'

'Suspicious? No. Me and Dad work our socks off on this place and it's a bloody struggle. Just about making ends meet these days. We're discussing going over to some arable, as we've heard there are going to be fixed prices for crops. That way, we'd have guaranteed income.' She shrugs. 'That's if the bloody place doesn't fall down around us first. There's so much needs doing, it's a case of working out where to start. I've got buckets in my bedroom to catch the rain. Mind you, I wouldn't mind if it did all fall down, then at least I'd be free of it.'

She gazes at the floor, in a moody reverie. I sip my tea, which is eye-wateringly strong.

'Do you like your job?' she asks suddenly.

'It's OK. Bit boring at times and there's not a lot to do in Fernfield.'

'You can say that again. Not that I have much chance of a social life, stuck here.'

'Can't you get out at night?'

'It doesn't matter, ignore me. And I've run out of bloody wool now. I crochet in the evenings to stop myself going nuts.' She goes to the range, opens the lid and chucks a log in.

'You haven't seen any strangers around here recently?'

She snaps back at me, stretching her arms up and flexing her joined fingers. 'Neither of us see anything except cows, grass, the inside of the milking parlour and dairy churns.' She gestures at a photo of two young men in uniform on the dresser. 'Both my brothers died in the war, so me and Dad just have to get on with it all now. Speak of the devil . . .'

A figure strides past the window, the porch door bangs, there's the clump of wellingtons dropping and a tall, rangy man with a beaky nose and a cross expression comes in.

'There's a car. A visitor, I see.'

Pearl leans against the wall by the range. 'This is Daisy, Dad. She works at the Dolphin, came to ask about their dead guest.'

'Oh, yes?'

'Pleased to meet you,' I say. 'The man's name was Ronald Carpenter.'

'So the police constable said.'

Mr Armitage fetches a mug, stands at the table and pours a cup of tea. He's wearing spattered oilskin trousers and a waterproof jacket, which give off a ripe pong.

'What's Mr Carpenter to do with you?' he asks in a gruff voice.

'I was just interested in finding out a bit more about what happened to him. I met him briefly at the hotel, then he went out and disappeared.'

Armitage takes a filthy hanky from his pocket and blows his nose. 'Ask the police if you want more details about him, my dear. What happened to him is nothing to do with us.'

'Not quite true, Dad,' Pearl points out. 'I did find him in the car.'

'And that's all we can tell you,' her father says. 'Someone did us the huge favour of leaving him on our land, and Pearl here saw him. Now that the police have stopped traipsing everywhere and getting in our hair, we've plenty to catch up on. There's been a reporter sniffing around too this morning. I told him to clear off. We still need to clean out the cowshed and sterilise equipment today. If you've finished your tea, I'll walk you out. What's for dinner, Pearl? I'm famished.'

'Sausage and mash.'

'Get it on the table soon, girl.'

Perhaps hunger is making him grumpy, but he seems in a hurry to get rid of me. I say goodbye and lace up my shoes with Mr Armitage watching. He stands in the doorway while I find a patch of grass under a hedge to clean my claggy soles on. He's still there when I start the car, a poker-faced figure holding his mug.

I drive back to Fernfield, frustrated by the scant information I've gleaned, and hoping that Felix won't find the car too redolent of cowpats and other muck.

CHAPTER SIX

On Monday morning, I wake from a jumbled avalanche of dreams featuring my mother, the biscuit factory and a fire that destroyed all the stock. My mother was furious, accusing me of starting the fire and damaging everyone's livelihood. I should be ashamed of myself, she lectured.

My head is cloudy, my mouth parched. I stagger to the bathroom and see an arsonist in the mirror. I'm convinced that I'll be found out one day and instead of sympathy, people's faces will be etched with horror. The police will come calling, saying that they've reviewed the blaze and examined the ruins of our house again. There's reason to believe that the fire wasn't caused by a Doodlebug after all, and they need to ask me some questions.

JB asks me if I'm unwell over breakfast, noting that I'm only having one egg. I reply that Tybalt kept me awake, paddling on my pillow. On the way out, I mouth an apology to the cat, who's sniffing grass, apparently riveted by clinging dewdrops. He ignores me.

The cycle to Fernfield in relentless drizzle does nothing to improve my mood, which is matched by Vera's grouchiness when I arrive at work.

'Here at last, Daisy.'

'I'm not late.'

'Oh, is that so? There was a reporter here just now, wanting information about the Carpenters. I showed him the door. Dead pushy he was. I told him in no uncertain terms that I'm a busy woman with no time for his claptrap.' As she's in the mood for censure, she brings Sharon and Leslie into her sights. 'Sharon hasn't hoovered the stair carpet thoroughly. If she spent less time on making herself glam and more attending to her job, this place might shine a bit more. And I've had to have words with Leslie. He isn't making enough effort with the menu. Now the war's over, guests are going to expect something a bit more imaginative than pasties and casseroles.'

'He could try using garlic,' I suggest.

'*Do* be sensible, Daisy. Can you take a cup of tea to Mrs Ward?'

Amelia Ward is in her seventies, a widow who's lived in the hotel for several years since her husband died. She's hugely fat and hardly ever leaves her room. She reminds me of a cottage loaf, with a small head balanced on a wide body. I always find her sitting in her armchair with her ulcerated leg raised on a stool, gaping at the park across the road and listening to the wireless. That appears to be all she does. I anticipate that one day, she'll become welded to her armchair and the fire brigade will need to extricate her.

When I take a tray of tea and biscuits up to her room, I'm surprised to find Tommie Carpenter there, perched on the end of her bed. Mrs Ward rarely takes an interest in anyone else, unless to complain about them. Her sole occupations are eating, her health and medications, and lamenting her dead husband: *'I wish I could be with my Harold.'*

'Hello, how are you both? I'd have brought an extra cup if I'd known you were here, Tommie.'

'Oh, I'm not staying long,' Tommie says, relief crossing her face at my arrival.

I'm glad to see she's washed her hair and is wearing a fresh skirt and blouse.

'We met on the landing,' Amelia says in her flat, droning voice. 'I went for a little walk. I'm trying to be good and get some exercise, like the doctors tell me. I came over a bit queer and Tommie was good enough to help me back.'

I'm not sure that half a dozen steps up and down the landing is quite what the doctors mean, but any movement must be better than none.

'We've been discussing our sleeping tablets and the awful torture of insomnia,' Amelia continues. 'I was telling Tommie that I haven't had a decent night's sleep since my Harold died.'

'It is a terrible affliction.' Tommie twines her fingers restlessly.

I can see a trapped look in her eyes. Amelia is an expert at playing the helpless old lady and drawing people into her web.

'I can't comment,' I say. 'I nearly always sleep like a log.'
Apart from when I have remorse-fuelled nightmares about my mother.

'Tommie told me about her husband. Sharon did mention it, how he was found and everything. So terrible.' Amelia is relishing the drama. Anything to inject some interest into her monotonous days. She adds tactlessly, oblivious to Tommie's flinch, 'Sharon brought me a couple of newspapers so I could read about it.'

Sharon and Amelia have got very thick. Sharon does home perms for her, causing a terrible ammonia stink that lingers around the landing for days, and runs lots of errands for Amelia in her own time. I suspect that she's paid handsomely.

'Take it from me, dear,' Amelia says, 'you'll never get over this. There's not a day I don't long for my Harold and wish I could be with him.'

Tommie winces. 'It's been lovely to meet you. I really do have to go, there's so much to see to.' She almost runs from the room, tripping at the door.

Amelia takes a digestive biscuit from the plate. 'Funny little thing, isn't she? Awful knock she's had, but I predict she'll marry again before too long.'

'What makes you say that?'

'She's still young and pretty enough in a dull way, no kiddies and she'll no doubt get the house. Men like young widows and I expect she'll have a decent pension from the husband. He worked for Strallen Insurance. That's a big company, my Harold did business with them. Can you pull the stool a bit further away from me?'

I do as she asks, taking care not to nudge against her huge, bandaged leg.

'Thanks, dear. I don't know what I'd do without you all to help me. When you see Sharon, ask her to pop up. I need a few bits of shopping.'

Sharon's on reception when I go downstairs, rubbing cream carefully into her hands and nails. When she sees me she beckons me over, her eyes glinting.

'There you are! I've just read today's paper. It was a shooting! I've seen him!'

'Who?'

'There's a photo of that Mr Carpenter!'

She has the local paper folded at the page. There's a head-and-shoulders photo of Ronald Carpenter in naval uniform, slimmer and clean-shaven, beside a brief article.

MAN FOUND DEAD NEAR BIDWELL

The body of Mr Ronald Carpenter, aged thirty-one years, has been found in a stolen Ford Anglia car at Broadmeadow Farm near Bidwell. The car was taken from the Fernfield area after 10 p.m. last Thursday evening. Police have confirmed that Mr Carpenter was shot. He died between early afternoon on Friday, when he went missing, and just after 6 a.m. on Saturday, when he was found.

Mr Carpenter was a guest at the Dolphin hotel in Fernfield. He was visiting the area from London with his wife to attend the engagement celebrations of their friend, Mr Charles Harrington. When contacted, Mr Harrington informed us that he and Mrs Carpenter are distressed and have asked for privacy at this difficult time.

A coroner's inquest has been opened and adjourned pending a post-mortem and further investigations.

Inspector Thaxted of Oxford Police issued the following appeal: 'This is a violent, horrible crime. If anyone saw Ronald Carpenter after lunchtime on Friday, spoke to him or saw him in a Ford Anglia, or has any other information regarding the victim, please contact Fernfield or Oxford Police immediately.'

'Has Vera seen this?' I ask. She'll be furious that the hotel has been named.

'I'm not sure. I haven't heard her blow a gasket, so I expect not. She's a cross patch this morning, isn't she? She criticised my hoovering and I told her that I haven't got eyes in the back of my head. I'm not responsible for guests making a mess after I've cleaned.'

'Where is she?'

'Getting stomach powder or something. Baby's giving her indigestion.' Sharon taps the photo with a manicured nail. 'But listen, what I'm trying to tell you is that *I* saw him!'

'Mr Carpenter? When?'

'Friday, around half one. I'd gone to the chemist for Amelia's sinus pills. He was standing outside when I came out, looking at his watch, a bit lost. He asked me where Larch Bridge is, so I pointed the way to him.'

The chemist is at the far end of the High Street and Larch Bridge is ten minutes' walk out of town, on the road that eventually leads to Bidwell and Broadmeadow Farm.

'Have you told the police?'

'Haven't had a chance yet, I'd just seen the paper before you appeared. Could you ring them? I'm not much good with officials, I get my words all twisted.'

'Let's go in the office. I'll call, but you'll have to stay around because they'll want to speak to you.'

'Let me just pop to the loo. I'm nervous already!'

I phone Fernfield station while she's in the toilet and ask for Inspector Thaxted. He's there and I'm put through with little delay.

'Yes, Miss Moore. We speak again, and so soon!'

Am I being too sensitive, or is there a definite hint of sarcasm? 'Sorry if I'm bothering you, Inspector.'

'As if you could! How can I help?'

I frown down the receiver. 'I've called to help *you*. Sharon Billing, who works here, saw Ronald Carpenter on Friday. He asked her for directions to Larch Bridge, which is just—'

'Yes, I know where the bridge is. Is Miss Billing there?'

'She's just coming now.'

'Yes, good. Put her on.'

I hand the phone to Sharon. Judging by the waft of fresh rose from her, she's applied scent to give herself a morale boost. She's starting to describe the scene outside the chemist when Vera marches into reception and hisses at me.

'What's Sharon doing in there on the phone? It had better not be a personal call!'

I explain about the newspaper and Sharon's sighting of Mr Carpenter. Vera puts her head in one hand, cradles her bump with the other and leans against the counter.

'That's all we needed, involving the hotel more in this. If the press get wind of it, that reporter will be back. Seems to me, the way this is going, we might as well just move the police station and the coroner's office in here! Where's this newspaper?'

'Here, on the desk. I'll get you a cup of tea.'

She doesn't reply, flicking through the paper while Sharon continues to talk on the phone. I head to the kitchen, where Leslie has his head in a cookbook, the *Woman's Home Companion*.

'Trying out new recipes, Chef?'

'Huh! Her ladyship reckons my dinners need to be more interesting. I told her, we do still have rationing! I'd like to see her manage with the stuff I get hold of. There's only so many ways with Spam. Right, we're going to have cheese and ham parsley pancakes with buttered caraway cabbage for dinner. That sounds poncy.'

'And pudding?'

'Coconut tart and custard.'

'Why don't you call the custard *crème anglaise*, that'll make it sound upmarket. I had it in a café in London and I'm sure it was out of a tin.'

Leslie sniggers. 'I'll do that. You're not just for decoration, are you, Daisy?'

'Thanks, I'm overwhelmed.'

'Can you keep an eye on this stock? I need to pop to the bakery for a mo, make sure everything's shipshape and the takings have been secured. Mind, I worry what will happen with the business come July, when bread's going on the ration. I dunno, we won the bloody war, but now things are getting even tighter. Ray will be lucky to come back home and find the shop still open.'

'At least we're not starving. People are all over Europe.'

'Remind Vera. It might shut her up. But don't do it today, she's cranky enough as it is.'

I make tea, mulling over Ronald Carpenter's movements on Friday. He must have agreed to meet someone at Larch Bridge, and that person picked him up in a car, drove him to Broadmeadow Farm and shot him. What was the meeting for and why didn't he tell his wife about it? Why the secrecy? I'm so wrapped up in my thoughts, I manage to splash steaming water on my finger and I catch the stock just before it boils over.

CHAPTER SEVEN

By the afternoon, Vera's mood has improved, no doubt helped by pink indigestion medicine and the news that Tommie Carpenter will be leaving in the morning.

'Seeing her teary face around the place isn't much fun for the other guests,' Vera comments. 'I'm sorry for her, but her own home is the best place after what's happened.' She tells me to have a break if I want one. I accept, as it will give me a chance to go to the library.

She presses her fingers to her eyelids. 'I wish I could get a good night's sleep,' she says. 'The baby kicks and keeps me awake, then I get awful heartburn and I've been worrying about Ray. When I visit, he tells me he's fine, but I worry so. The food in prison's awful and he's lost weight. It's such a noisy, dingy place. He's sharing a cell with three other men and I can tell that it's getting him down. Ray does like his peace and quiet.'

'You've got a lot to handle.'

Vera smiles wearily. 'Tell me about it. Mind, Ray being Ray, he's trying to educate other prisoners about the evils of capitalism and convert them to the Communist Party. He was going on about prison being a capitalist reservoir for the lumpenproletariat, where they make the inmates slaves of the state.'

Ray is, as far as I'm aware, Fernfield's only member of the Communist Party and a fervent supporter of Stalin. He's an odd companion for staid, middle-of-the-road Vera, but she indulges his political beliefs as if they're a quaint hobby.

'What *is* the lumpenproletariat?' she adds. 'Ray's told me before, but I can't remember most of the stuff he goes on about.'

'I'm not sure. The disadvantaged workers, possibly.'

'Oh, I see. Well, I suppose it gives him something to do while he's in there, crossing the days off until he comes home.'

'How long until he's served his sentence?'

'He'll be home end of July. Then we can settle down and be a proper little family.'

I ask a question I've been skirting around for some time. 'Would you mind if I visit him?'

'You? Well . . . it's no skin off my nose and I'm sure he'd welcome it. Leslie's been in, and a couple of his friends, but not everyone wants to go to a prison.' She colours up. 'Are you sure you'd want to do that? It's a depressing place.'

'That won't bother me — after all, I'll be able to walk out again. I'd be happy to. Ask him next time you see him.' It might assuage my guilt at the part I played in putting him there.

I wander down the High Street to the library, which is just past the post office. The newspapers are in a tiny room off the non-fiction section, lined up in wall racks. The librarian explains that they keep papers for six months and back copies are in the drawers below the racks, in descending date order. There's one table with four chairs, so I sit and work my way through a selection of Oxfordshire newspapers, searching for violent or gun-related crime. I find a number of cases of serious assault, all of which have been committed by family members against each other. There are various robberies, frauds, vehicle thefts, sheep rustling, public disorder, petrol theft and black-market prosecutions. No random shootings involving cars or unsolved murders. Some headlines catch my eye: the Bank of England has been nationalised; Churchill has made a speech about an iron curtain in Europe; the jitterbug craze is sweeping the country; pine needles are being used as a tea substitute in Germany.

As I flick through pages, I note Charles Harrington's name and stop to inspect the sport section, where I read that he led his polo team, Oxford Hares, to victory against the Warwick Greens. There's a tiny, grainy photo of the victorious team, with Charles holding up and kissing a large shield.

I replace the newspapers and head to the Napolina café, where Jock, the owner, is playing his usual samba music. Carmen Miranda sings 'The Lady in the Tutti-Frutti Hat' while I order coffee and a slice of sponge cake. Jock's pet monkey Rindi is sitting on his shoulder wearing his green fez and a cloth satchel full of nuts, which he likes to throw at the customers. He provides a sort of floor show that I find trying. The little grey monkey eyes me, recognising an adversary.

'Don't think about it,' I warn him.

'Aye, leave Daisy alone, Rindi. She doesn't care for your old nonsense.' Jock cuts a slice of sponge. 'I read about the murder, that chap Carpenter being found in the car. Bloody awful. Was he the man you were looking for last Friday?'

'Yes, after his wife got worried about his absence. It's very distressing for her.'

'I can well imagine.' Jock puts my coffee and cake on a round metal tray. 'He was in here a while back. I don't suppose the police would be interested because it was some months ago.'

I pause with the tray and put it back on the counter. 'Are you sure?'

'Aye. It was late in the day, almost closing time and pouring down. The place was empty. He needed a bite to eat before he started back to London, so I stayed open for an extra half an hour. He played with Rindi, they hit it off.'

This doesn't fit with information from Tommie and Charles Harrington that Ronnie was visiting Fernfield for the first time. 'When was that?'

'Oh, now you're asking.' Jock scratches his stubbly chin. 'It was dark, November time.'

'Were you chatting? Did he say why he was here?'

Jock takes a cloth from his apron pocket and wipes the work surface. 'He'd been doing some insurance-type business in the area. He mentioned a museum in Goswick, something about a burglary.'

'That's not too far from Bidwell, is it?'

'Four miles or so.' The monkey jumps to his head, chattering loudly. 'Now, Rindi, quieten down, you wee devil, or you'll have to go upstairs!'

Several women arrive with full shopping bags. I can tell from the acrid smell of setting lotion that at least one of them has come from the hairdresser. I move away to a table and tuck into my cake. I can taste powdered egg, but it's pretty good even so and the jam is rich.

I should phone Thaxted with this information, or tell Jock to. But I recall the inspector's supercilious, curt tone to me earlier, and I nurse my grievance as I finish the cake and drink my coffee. I'm sure that he won't want me bothering him again at present, interrupting his busy day, being a hindrance. For now, I'll follow up this matter myself.

* * *

I'm due some time off, having covered extra hours for Vera in recent months when she's been visiting Ray. On Wednesday morning I cycle to Goswick, having failed to cadge Felix's car again because he has to go to Oxford. It's a dry, cloudy day and the road doesn't have too many upward gradients, so I squeak the miles away easily enough to bursts of 'Molly Malone'.

Goswick museum is off the main street, which is quiet in the overcast morning. Just a horse-drawn coal cart and a plumber's van to be seen. The museum is in a Georgian terraced house with three well-worn steps to the front door. Inside, I'm greeted by a small man with a long, full white beard, a mop of snowy hair, a large belly and half-moon glasses. Put him in a red outfit and he'd make a good Father Christmas.

'Morning, my dear. Have you come to spend time in our modest treasure house?'

'I will, thanks, but I wondered if you might be able to help me first.'

'If I can.' He hitches his bottom onto the reception desk and adjusts his glasses. 'Henry Claremont, by the way.'

'I'm Daisy Moore. Have you heard about the murder near Bidwell?'

'I did. Dreadful business.'

'Mr Ronald Carpenter, the man who was shot, was a guest at the hotel where I work. His wife is terribly upset.'

'Oh, heavens! How appalling, my dear.' Mr Claremont recoils, shuffling back a little on the desk. No doubt he'd been planning a peaceful morning pottering around the museum's riches, not in a discussion of violence just up the road.

He's so kindly and approachable, I don't like lying to him, but it's for a good cause. 'His wife believes her husband did some business at the museum and I said I'd come and ask for her. He worked for Strallen Insurance.'

'Yes, that's correct.'

'He visited you here?'

'He did, twice as a matter of fact, and very thorough and helpful he was too. I was so terribly sorry to hear the news of his death. Poor man!'

'Indeed. You made a claim on your policy?'

'That's right. We had a break-in late last October. The rotters stole some silver, porcelain and glass items and broke cabinets. Made quite a mess in the process. Worst of all, they took a Tudor wall hanging, a beautiful tapestry of a jousting scene. Priceless, really, and we were terribly upset. That's why Mr Carpenter came, to discuss the situation. He was efficient and the claim was settled by New Year.'

'I'm glad that you were compensated.'

'Yes, but money doesn't really make up for what we lost. Honestly, I never imagined that our little museum in this backwater would attract thieves, but I suppose I was naïve. We take so much pride in our collection and the tapestry had been in this village for centuries. The police have never found it and then lightning struck twice.'

'How do you mean?'

Mr Claremont sighs. 'We had a rare seventeenth-century Charles I memorial ring. Gold with a hand-painted portrait of the king and very valuable. I was so thankful that the thief missed it in October. Then we had another break-in in early January. Maybe the first thief returned, or it was a different one. So, back came Mr Carpenter and he sorted us out again.'

'You have been unlucky.'

'Yes. It's awful when thieves take heritage pieces that belong to us all. I have to admit, I've found the whole matter quite a strain and I feel that I've let people down. The museum has been a labour of love for me for a long time now. I considered relinquishing my role here, but I've put so many years in, I decided not to throw in the towel. I don't expect we'll ever get the items back. The police told me that with the chaos here and in Europe at present, it's all too easy for stolen goods to be traded across frontiers. The authorities are finding it hard to keep up with criminals. Breaks my heart, to be honest.'

I dislike upsetting him by making him recall it, but not enough to cease my questions. 'I suppose you got acquainted with Mr Carpenter a bit during his two visits.'

'Well, it was mainly business, but we had a cup of tea. He told me that he was married and his wife was rather delicate. I got the impression he was under some strain to do with that. Of course, lots of marriages suffered with the long absences of war. Being apart like that places a huge burden on folk. I was in the Great War, and when I came back, it was a good while before my marriage came right again. But it did, and we've been a great support to each other through the years.'

He smiles, which makes me feel less of a heel. This is too important to keep from Peter Thaxted. I presume that he'll contact Ronnie's employer and find out that way, but he should hear about the museum sooner rather than later.

'You do need to phone Oxford Police about this.'

Mr Claremont moves off the desk and folds his hands on his rounded stomach in a way that reminds me of Vera. 'Really? You believe it might be relevant?'

'I've no idea, but they need to be aware of any association Mr Carpenter had with the area.'

'I see, yes. Well, I'll take your advice and ring them. I'm sure he mentioned that he was seeing some other clients around the county as well.'

'Did he say who?'

'Not that I remember. He'd have to keep professional information like that to himself. Now, do let me show you around.'

I'd prefer to look for myself, but he insists on accompanying me and going into lengthy explanations with the verve of the true enthusiast. We examine Saxon, Roman and Victorian artefacts, a room of agricultural implements and a section devoted to butter and cheese making. The museum is lovingly arranged and cared for, and it's obvious that Mr Claremont lives and breathes it. I rarely visit museums, finding them tiring. Maybe it's the dry air, or the deadness of the exhibits, but I'm always overcome by weariness as I traipse around display cases.

A slim woman is affixing labels in the corner holding Georgian glassware. She's under five feet tall, in a sugar-pink polka-dot dress with a white lace trim at the collar, cuffs and hem. She looks startlingly young and fresh amid the displays of timeworn curios.

'This is Beverley Fanshawe, my dedicated assistant. You put your heart into this place, don't you, Bev?'

She blinks earnestly at him. Her fine blonde hair frames a pretty, angelic face. 'I do my best, Henry.' She turns her gentian-blue eyes to me. 'Very pleased to meet you,' she says shyly.

'This is Miss Daisy Moore, from Fernfield. She met Mr Carpenter, our poor deceased insurance man. I've been telling her how helpful he was in our time of need.'

'Oh,' she breathes. 'Were . . . were you a friend of his?'

'We met once, briefly. He checked in with his wife at the hotel I work at.'

'The hotel . . . How is his wife?' With her tiny stature, pink dress, lace, and white Mary Jane shoes, she's like a decorative figure on top of an iced cake.

'Mrs Carpenter is in a bad way.'

Her eyes water. 'It's so awful, unbelievable.'

'Did you meet Mr Carpenter when he came here regarding the insurance?'

'I did,' she whispers, putting a hand to her mouth. 'He was such a nice man.' A few tears roll down her cheeks.

Mr Claremont pats her arm. 'Don't take on now, Bev. We'll have a cuppa in a minute.'

We move on to another room featuring folk crafts, but I attempt to seize a chance to shake him off.

'I don't mind carrying on alone, if you want to check that Beverley's OK.'

'She'll do until we're finished. Bev's so soft-hearted, too much for her own good, in my opinion.' He clucks his tongue. 'She's a reserved kind of girl, stays in her shell a bit with customers, but she's dedicated to the museum. She's only just recovered from a nasty tummy bug too, quite knocked her sideways. It's good to have her back, she's my right arm here!'

I buy a couple of postcards I don't want. As I'm paying, a well-built man with a tight mouth, jutting jaw and sleeves pushed up his freckled forearms comes in.

'Ah, Alan, good to see you!'

'I got the timber, Henry, so all ready to go when you give the nod.'

'Miss Moore, this is Alan, Beverley's brother. He does various bits of maintenance for us here.'

'How do,' Alan says.

'Mr Carpenter was staying at the Dolphin in Fernfield before he died. Miss Moore works there. I was telling her about our thefts and how helpful Mr Carpenter was.'

'He sorted you out good and prompt,' Alan agrees. 'I need to do some measuring up for these shelves, Henry, then I'll cut the wood. I've brought my tools, so I'm all ready to go.'

'Go on through, I'll be with you in a minute.'

Mr Claremont fusses over my change and insists on giving me a free bookmark, but at last I manage to get away, shaking his hand while he says he must find the number for Oxford Police.

I've brought a sandwich and a bottle of orange in my basket. Halfway back to town, I pull off the road into a field and eat my late lunch sitting on the grass. I realise that some men don't tell their wives much about their work, but it does seem odd that Ronnie wouldn't have mentioned travelling to Oxfordshire on several occasions, especially as he had a friend living in the county. Did he meet Charles while he was driving around? A detour to Oxford wouldn't have taken too long. The tensions in the marriage interest me — the very fact that Ronnie revealed them to a stranger suggests that he had things weighing on his mind.

These are various strands of information, but I'm not sure where any of them lead me.

CHAPTER EIGHT

That evening, JB is out socialising and it's time I dealt with the latest fan mail. There's a small pile of envelopes on top of the piano, sent on by JB's agent. I sit by the fire and read through. They're all from women and all fairly standard adulation, except for one with a Southend address that grabs my attention.

Dear Jeffrey,

I've been an admirer of you and your work for ages. Since 1936, in fact, when I saw you on stage in The Country Wife. *You are so talented and witty. I confess I have written to you in the past and you've sent lovely replies. Also, I got your autograph at the stage door of the Adelphi when you appeared in* Follow the Sun. *You were so polite and kind, a true gentleman. You wrote, 'For Libby, best wishes, Jeffrey'. I've always felt that we have a <u>deep</u> connection and an under-standing. It's hard to explain, but it's as if something <u>unspoken</u> passes between us.*

I am writing to you now because my husband was killed in Africa. We weren't blessed with children, so I am alone and single again, with no one to care for. I read that you and your wife are separated. Maybe, like me, you are lonely and time hangs heavy. Could we meet up? It would be

lovely to talk to someone on my wavelength and I just <u>know</u>
that we would hit it off. I have such an appreciation of your
work and I never miss a production you're in.

I work as a secretary during the week, but my evenings
and weekends are free.

I do hope to hear from you soon.
Yours sincerely,
Libby (Felton)

I read it twice, torn between laughter and tears. JB's warmth, decency and wit evidently communicate to his fans. I often have fun when I'm responding to them, but this grieving, deluded woman will need careful treatment. Best to keep the reply brief but kind. I uncover the typewriter and write a reply on notepaper that JB has pre-signed.

Dear Mrs Felton,

Thank you so much for your kind letter and your comments on my work. Please accept my condolences regarding the death of your husband. You must have suffered a great deal.

I'm afraid that you've been misled by information you've read about my personal life. Best not to believe the gossip columns and remember that they often get their facts wrong.

I hope that you meet someone very soon. I'm sure you will, and I wish you every happiness in the future.

I usually enclose a signed photo, but I won't this time. JB is a handsome man now, but the photo, taken when he was younger, is very appealing and I don't wish to inflame Libby's obsession even further, or offer any encouragement. I dash off replies to the rest of the mail and leave it ready to post. Then I head for bed and lie propped on pillows with Oberon at my side, reviewing and updating my case notes.

CARPENTER
RC arranged to meet someone, probably the car driver, at Larch Bridge. Must have known them. Didn't tell wife.

Reason? Affair/ secret business deal of some kind that went wrong. Marriage was troubled?

No similar crimes recorded around the area recently.

Broadmeadow Farm. Mr Armitage was keen to get rid of me. Worth another visit.

RC had been to this area at least twice before, for work. Why keep it secret? Was wife lying, ditto Charles H? If so, why? Was the meeting that led to shooting linked to previous visits?

Claremont said RC was seeing other people around here. Who and for what?

Might be useful to speak to Linda, CH's fiancée.

The phone starts ringing. I'm warm and cosy and debate not answering, but it might be JB. I shift Oberon's paw from my neck, climb out of bed and head to the hall.

'Hello, Brize Lodge.'

Thaxted's scathing voice makes me tense. 'Miss Moore. I'm surprised to find you at home.'

'Why's that?'

'I assumed you'd be out with your torch and magnifying glass, seeking clues.'

'Very funny, Inspector. Did Mr Claremont contact you?'

'He did. He said that you were a very smart young lady and you'd told him to.'

'Have you seen him? He resembles Father Christmas.'

'We've spoken by phone for now, so I haven't been able to appreciate his festive aspects. What took you to Goswick museum? Random tourism, a fascination with ancient artefacts?'

I rise above the sarcasm. 'Why didn't Ronnie tell his wife that he'd visited around here before? Or did he and she's lied? What would her motive be, and did he see Charles Harrington on the two occasions he went to Goswick? Have you contacted Strallen Insurance yet? They're Ronnie's employer.'

'Miss Moore, stop posing questions and avoiding mine. Why did you decide to go to the museum?'

'I was in the Napolina café. Jock said that Ronnie had called in there during November and mentioned that he'd been to Goswick.'

'You should have passed that information on immediately, or told Jock to.'

'You seemed so busy, Inspector, and not keen on being disturbed. I had some time off, so I decided to check it myself.'

There's an indrawn breath. 'Miss Moore, I realise that you don't have enough to interest you in Fernfield, and I do sympathise with the lack of incentive for a good brain. Perhaps you should continue your education, or seek more challenging employment. Please, keep your nose out of police matters!'

'I don't need your career advice, thanks. I can shift for myself. And no need to thank me for an important lead. Goodnight.'

I have the satisfaction of putting the phone down first. Back in bed, I snuggle down and as my eyes close, an idea forms, to be pursued in the morning.

* * *

JB doesn't like early morning conversation, so I wait until he's finished eating his breakfast and reading *The Times*.

'JB, you've been to the Marquis, haven't you?'

'Frequently. Why?'

'What would be the least expensive dish on their menu?' I'm aware that restaurants have controlled prices, with an upper limit of five shillings for meals.

He folds the newspaper and replaces the lid of the marmalade. 'I'm not sure. I suppose the lunches would be less costly, but even so, there'd be little below, say, three shillings.'

'Ouch.' That's half a week's wages for me. My notion of eating at the Marquis and speaking to Linda Merchant is fading fast.

'Why are you interested in their menu?'

'I'm keen to go there and see if I can spot Linda Merchant, maybe talk to her. She's Charles Harrington's fiancée. Her parents run the Marquis and she works there. I don't want to rub Peter Thaxted up the wrong way. If I happen to be eating at the restaurant and chat to her, he can't find fault.'

'You would spot her, because she meets, greets and schmoozes the diners with the wine list as well as serving table.'

'That's music to my ears. I can't afford it, though, unless they'd do me a sandwich.'

'D'you think she can tell you anything useful?'

'I'm not sure, but I'm interested in the state of the Carpenters' marriage and she might have a view.' I tell him about my visit to Goswick museum and what I learned.

JB reaches for a cigar, lights up and takes a few puffs. 'Tell you what, petal, I haven't had the beef at the Marquis for a while. I'll treat you to supper. Shall we say Saturday night?'

'I wasn't angling for an invitation, JB.'

'Nonsense. Every esteemed factotum deserves an occasional treat.' He waves his cigar. 'I'll book an early table. I doubt that it will get too busy, but best to be on the safe side. You can hopefully snag Linda's attention. Word to the wise — don't turn up in trousers, it's a very county-and-conservative venue. Do you possess a reasonable skirt or dress?'

'I'm sure I've a skirt somewhere. I'll scrub up.'

* * *

In fact, I discover that I have no skirts, so I borrow a simple blue A-line from Sharon, who says it's one she hasn't worn for a while because it's too tight on the hips.

'Don't you ever want to come across as a bit more feminine?' she asks when I try it on in an empty room at the hotel and decide that it will do.

'I started wearing trousers during the war and I prefer them.'

'Don't take this the wrong way, but with your flat chest, they make you look a bit like a schoolboy. If you made an effort, wore some make-up and styled your hair, you'd be quite pretty.'

'I'll bear that in mind.'

'Where are you going, anyway? Have you got a date?'

'Just out, nothing special.'

'You're a dark horse, Daisy.' She flicks her lighter to a cigarette. 'I reckon you play your cards close to your chest.'

My flat chest, I almost correct her, but catch myself. 'You make me sound mysterious.'

'Well, you're an ordinary Londoner, but your accent's a bit swanky.'

'That'll be JB rubbing off on me.' I'd worked hard at upgrading and polishing my accent for my job in Whitehall so that I fitted in better with my Oxbridge colleagues.

'He's dead posh,' Sharon agrees. 'Like one of those BBC announcers.'

The skirt might be too tight on Sharon, but it's on the roomy side on me, so I pull it in with a belt and wear a jacket over the top to conceal the bunching.

JB tells me I'll pass muster, and on Saturday evening we're seated in the Marquis at six thirty. It's situated in a hamlet on a grassy slope opposite a pond and a cricket pitch. Inside, it's rather dark, with low ceiling beams and wall lights draped in fringed shades.

Linda Merchant has greeted us and shown us to our table. She has a lively smile, hair drawn back with a red ribbon, and an efficient manner. She addresses JB as if he's an old friend. 'Lovely to see you, Mr Berrow. We've even managed to get some beef for you tonight, which took a bit of effort! We didn't want to disappoint you.'

'Much appreciated, Linda. Let me introduce my friend, Miss Daisy Moore.'

We smile and say hello. Linda offers us the wine list. I let JB choose, as I'm ignorant on the subject.

He orders a bottle of burgundy and says, 'I was terribly sorry to hear that what happened with Mr Carpenter spoiled your engagement party.'

Her face darkens briefly. 'It was awful. Charles couldn't really relax, worrying about Ronnie and where he could be. We'd spent ages organising the evening, with a singer and pianist, but it didn't quite come off as planned. And then the awful news the next morning . . .' Her tone suggests that she was irritated by the cloud cast over her celebration.

'Did you know Mr Carpenter well?'

'We'd met just the once in London, when we saw him and his wife and had tea at their home, but he was an old friend of Charles.'

'That's a lovely ring,' I tell her. 'How did you and Charles meet?'

She holds out her finger, admiring the diamond. 'He was home on leave during the war and came here with a group of friends. It was love at first sight. When he was demobilised last December, we decided we'd get married as soon as we could.'

'When's the happy day?' JB asks.

'The sixteenth of August. I can't wait!'

She heads off to get our wine. So far, we're the only diners and the place has a slightly forlorn air. When Linda returns we order soup, roast beef for JB and chicken fillets for me.

Once she's gone back to the kitchen, silence envelops us.

'It's a bit creepy in here. Must be hard, catering for so few people,' I say to JB.

'I admire them for staying open, although I'm not sure how they keep going. They do get more of a late-night crowd coming out from Oxford.' He leans a little closer. 'When we've finished the main course, I'll head to the facilities and you can engage Linda while you order dessert.'

The soup is tinned oxtail, quickly followed by our beef and chicken. My fillets are fine, but not much better than Leslie would have cooked, and I decide that the Marquis is trading on its pre-war reputation and decent wines. Two older women arrive as we're eating, and sit whispering while they peruse the small menu and order sherries and mains. I note one of them glancing sideways in our direction.

JB inclines his head at them and murmurs, 'One of the *kommandantin*'s bridge cronies over there. She'll be informed toot sweet that we were seen dining, and what we were both wearing, drinking and eating.'

The two women share a certain style with Rosalind: good quality yet spartan clothing, sensible shoes and no-nonsense hair.

'Will she disapprove?'

'Oh, yes. She'll make sure to mention it and observe that one shouldn't dine out with *staff*. She'll advise that an appropriate form of thanks would be a small bonus, or a box of chocolates.'

'How come she invited me on Christmas Day?'

'That was different, a domestic invitation and therefore in keeping with the season. Complex rules apply in these matters, Daisy. I'm still learning some of them.'

'Doesn't it bother you that Rosalind comments on what you do?'

JB takes a sip of wine. 'Water off a duck's back these days. As long as I can retreat to the lodge, I'm content.'

When Linda has cleared our plates and asks if we'd like dessert, JB excuses himself.

'The special of the day is gooseberry tart with *real* cream,' Linda tells me.

'Sounds lovely.' I smile at her. 'It was kind of your fiancé to drive Mrs Carpenter back to London, especially as she suffers with her nerves.'

'Oh, do you know Tommie?'

'A little. I work at the Dolphin and I showed Mr and Mrs Carpenter to their room when they arrived. He was very keen that she should rest. I was able to offer some support after her husband went missing.'

'Ah, I see. Charles said that one of the staff there was helping her.'

'I did what I could,' I say modestly. 'She said a little about her anxiety and sleep problems. I suppose you're aware of that.'

'Really, I'm not that close to her.' Linda glances around. Rosalind's chums are busy with their main courses. She pulls out a chair and sits, folding her hands on the white cloth. 'Ronnie worried so about Tommie's health. It was quite difficult when we visited them in London, because she was silent and pale, hardly uttered a word. Ronnie had to make all the conversation for them both, and he kept fussing around her as if she was an invalid. I didn't take to her much, I have to admit, and I said to Charles that she could have made more of an effort. She's terribly self-absorbed. Does that sound awful, given what's happened?'

'Not at all.'

Reassured, she continues, 'And it's a beautiful house, just by the river, with a gorgeous garden. I couldn't help looking at Tommie and thinking, your husband has come home safe and sound and your home wasn't bombed, yet you're down in the dumps! As far as I can make out from Charles, Tommie spent the war hiding away in the house with her head under a cushion, and made no attempt to help in any way. She'd have been better off if she'd rolled her sleeves up and made herself go out and meet others, taken her mind off her own problems. Every woman likes a man to be attentive, but Ronnie smothered her.'

I can't picture Tommie with rolled-up sleeves. 'Perhaps she was lonely during the war.'

Linda polishes a spoon on a napkin. 'Maybe, but as I said, she didn't have to be. According to Charles, Ronnie always liked mollycoddling Tommie from the day they met. He treated her as if she was crystal glass, always insisting that she rest and not overdo things.' She examines the shine on the spoon and replaces it, satisfied. 'Charles is popping in to see Tommie again this evening. He goes to London on business frequently, so he'll check that she's all right. He says he owes it to Ronnie to take care of her.'

'Did Mr Carpenter ever have business trips around here?'

'Not to my knowledge. He visited Charles in Oxford now and again, and cheered him on at polo. Charles plays regularly, but I rarely get a chance to watch as weekends are our busiest times. Most of the players go on to the Barn Owl pub afterwards, but Ronnie didn't because he wouldn't touch alcohol.'

'I wondered if he'd fallen out with anyone.'

'Charles said that the police were asking that. Understandable, but honestly, he told me that it would be hard to pick a quarrel with Ronnie.' She sees JB returning and stands, pushing the chair in neatly. 'Well, this isn't getting dessert underway!'

We order gooseberry tarts and coffee to finish with.

'Any luck?' JB asks.

'Mainly more about Tommie Carpenter's nerves and her husband's attentiveness. Linda doesn't like her much. I can see why. Linda's got plenty of oomph, while Tommie's a wilting violet. But I might take a trip to Oxford soon.'

'For what purpose?'

I tap the side of my nose. 'I'll tell you if anything comes of it.'

The two older women are leaving. I catch the eye of the *kommandantin*'s friend and wave. She tucks her head down in alarm and hurries out. JB guffaws and slides a cigar from its gold case.

CHAPTER NINE

The next few days are hectic at the hotel, with an influx of guests that means all the rooms are taken. When I can get some time off, I borrow Felix's car early one evening and drive to Oxford. The Barn Owl is situated in the city centre and painted mustard yellow with black-timber trim. Above the door is a large sign featuring an owl with a heart-shaped face and an unnerving stare. I have no particular plan, I'm just going to see what I find, so I take a breath and push the swing door.

It's just after six when I enter the pub and order half a shandy. There are lots of photos of polo players framing the oak bar: action shots on gleaming horses, players receiving trophies, teams lined up with arms draped around one another's shoulders. I can't glimpse Charles Harrington in any of them.

The barmaid slides my glass to me. 'Haven't seen you here before.' She seems a bit wary. Maybe she's not keen on an unaccompanied woman in her pub.

'I was doing some shopping and I popped in to see if Charles Harrington's here.'

'Charlie boy? He's not been in today.'

'Never mind. I just wanted to congratulate him on his engagement. I did send a card, but hoped I might get the chance to do it in person.'

'Friend of the family, are you?'

'Not as such. I met him and Linda through the Marquis restaurant.'

'Oh, I see. Linda's a lovely girl.'

'She is, isn't she? I was chatting to her recently. I've been threatening for ages that I'd get to see a polo match.'

'Fan of the game?'

'To be honest, I'm not a big sports fan, but on the basis that you should try new experiences . . . I can see from all the photos that this pub is popular with the players.'

The barmaid casts her eyes upwards. 'I'm like you, I don't really take much interest, but the landlord's a big supporter.'

A couple more customers have arrived and she points to a low doorway as she moves away to serve them. 'Jago Villette was in the snug earlier, he's a mate of Charlie's. I expect he could tell you about upcoming matches.'

I take my drink through to a narrow, windowless room where two men are sitting separately, one elderly with a dog at his feet, and one in his twenties reading a newspaper. The older man flicks me the 'lone woman might be a floozy' glance while I approach the reader.

'Excuse me, are you Jago?'

He looks up and says in a cut-glass accent, 'That's my name.'

'Hello, I'm Daisy. The barmaid said you might be able to tell me about polo. I know Charles Harrington and Linda.'

'Oh, righty-ho. Take a pew.' He rises and pulls out a chair for me. He's stocky, with a high complexion, huge ears and a receding hairline.

'Thanks. Sorry to disturb your reading.' The paper is *Cherwell*, the student publication at Oxford. I've seen it in Felix's house. 'Are you at the university?'

'Was. I'm in banking now, but I still keep up with the alma mater.'

'Is that where you met Charles, at Oxford?'

'No, we met through polo.' He taps the newspaper. 'Have to confess, I was indulging in hubris, reading my own article. They cut hardly anything out, which is amazing.'

'What's it about?'

'Polo, naturally. What else is there?' He titters and makes a swinging motion with his arm.

'I'm completely ignorant regarding the sport, but I might attend a match and see what it's all about.'

That's a terrible miscalculation on my part, because Jago turns out to be a man in the grip of an obsession. I sit as he talks animatedly at me about polo, hardly pausing for breath.

'Really, you'd need some understanding of the game before you pop along to watch us, although we always welcome lovely young ladies to brighten our day and cheer us on! Polo originated in Asia, and the name derives from "pulu", the Tibetan willow root used to craft the balls. It's one of the world's oldest team games and British soldiers brought it here. In India, the game's played with seven on each team, but here we play with four . . .'

I fix a rapt expression on my face and empty my shandy as I listen to a litany of terms: mallet, chukkas, arena, knock-ins, infractions, changing horses, player positions, penalties, line of ball, cut shot, neck shot, handicap, trajectory, ride-off, hooking, tack. A flicker of panic seizes me as I envisage myself still pinned to the chair at closing time by this barrage of information. I study Jago, wondering what special alchemy makes a man simultaneously sporty and drippy. Maybe it's down to his plump, wet lips. The old man and his dog leave and I wish I could tag along. Hours later, or so it seems, Jago starts to slow.

'So, at that point the defending team gets a free knock-in. It's a fast game and it's important to understand the rules, otherwise you'll be baffled.' He finally pauses to drink his beer and I seize my chance.

'Gosh, that's all so fascinating. I will have to make it to a match, especially after Ronnie Carpenter's death. He liked to support the Oxford Hares, didn't he?'

'Gosh, yes, I heard about Ronnie. Good chap, cheered us on. His absence blighted the engagement party a bit. Rotten luck.'

I agree that being shot in the head was rotten luck. 'Did Ronnie often come to games?'

'Well, we play the season from around mid-April to September — did I mention that?'

'You did.' *Several times.*

'Good, wouldn't like to have missed out that crucial bit of info.'

'And Ronnie?'

'He'd be at a game once in a while. Good of him, to come from London. Yes, decent fellow all round. Saw him after the match last time he was here, but didn't get time for a chat because he was busy with someone.'

'Another player?'

'No, the local chap who maintains our field, Bill Mackie. They were very hugger-mugger — hadn't realised they knew each other that well. I expect Ronnie was trying to sell him insurance.' He laughs at his joke, spluttering his drink.

'When was that?'

'Last month, shortly after the new season started. I had a terrific match just last week, pity you missed it. I was playing pivot, I bumped a chap and then later on I managed to ride him off. Did I explain that? It's quite a difficult manoeuvre, where you . . .'

I raise my watch, feign a gasp of shock. 'I'm so sorry, Jago, I hadn't realised the time, I must go. It's been fascinating and thanks for explaining so much.'

'Oh, gosh, you're welcome. Been a pleasure. Hope to see you soon, then. The next match is on Saturday, play starts at two thirty.'

'Terrific. I'll try to make it.'

'Maybe we could have a drink afterwards? There's loads I've missed, I haven't even mentioned the horses and their gear. The reins and bridles are hugely important.'

'Yes, maybe. Thanks again.'

I reel outside. Jago and half a shandy have made my head swim. I hear my mother's voice. *Serves you right for telling lies, my girl.*

It's getting dark and there are spots of rain. For a moment, I'm so befuddled, I can't recall which side of the road I parked the car.

'Miss Daisy Moore, loitering outside a public house! Are you lost and can't find your way home?' Peter Thaxted is crossing the street towards me, his open coat flapping in the breeze.

'Hello, Inspector. Not lost, disorientated. I haven't driven to Oxford before, and I've just been bored witless in the pub by an enthusiastic polo player.'

His lips quiver. 'Polo? Do you play?'

'No, although after the experience I've had, I could write a short book on it.'

'Why put yourself through such suffering?'

'I'm not sure. It's better than boredom. And then there's the interesting detail that Charles Harrington plays polo and Ronnie Carpenter supported his team, the Oxford Hares.'

He leans on his stick, regarding me with an expression I can't read. Exasperation? Regret? Guarded respect? I'll go for the latter.

'Go on,' he says. 'I can tell that you have something to impart.'

I spot a café across the street. 'I'm hungry. Can I tell you while I have a bite?'

* * *

Twenty minutes later, we're eating cheese on toast and sharing a pot of tea. Tomato ketchup for me, brown sauce for the inspector. He struggles to get it from the bottle and slams the heel of his hand against the base. A stream pours on to his plate.

He sighs. 'Drought or deluge.'

'I had a colleague in Whitehall, a woman who enjoyed calculating the probabilities of such events: how often the bread falls buttered side down, the likelihood of rolling four on a dice, et cetera.'

'And I was under the impression you'd done hugely important war work.'

'We had to have some distraction, and in many ways, it's the same mental process as . . . the other work we did.'

Thaxted cuts his toast in half. 'I do *know* what you did.'

'Perhaps, but I can't say. Official Secrets Act.'

'Absolutely.' He dips his head, a lock of white hair skimming his brow, and says teasingly, 'You're coming down in the world, Miss Moore, eating in a café.'

He's more light-hearted than usual this evening, and a little less pale and worn, a hint of colour in his complexion. I wonder if he's made progress with the murder.

'Meaning?'

'I heard you were fine dining in the Marquis recently.'

'Let me guess. Rosalind told your mother.'

'Got it in one. What were you doing there with Jeffrey?'

'I am allowed to eat out with him.'

'Indeed. I wondered if the choice of venue was in any way associated with Linda Merchant working there.'

'I did happen to speak to her and she referred to the Barn Owl as a watering hole for polo players.' I glance at him. 'It's difficult to do anything around here without people noticing and gossiping.'

'Can't say I've observed it holding you back, but it must be terribly hard for you when you're trying to go undercover.'

He says it with humour, so I allow the barb. 'It's strange, the way we occasionally eat together in comparative harmony, when most of the time we're at loggerheads, with you warning me to stay out of your way.'

'Are you familiar with Newton's third law of motion?' Thaxted neatly dissects his food.

'I'm afraid not. I've never studied physics.'

'Shame, I think the discipline would appeal to you. Newton stated, "When one body exerts a force on a second body, the second body simultaneously exerts a force equal in magnitude and opposite in direction on the first body."'

'You've lost me, Inspector.'

'In other words, forces result from interactions.' He taps his fork against his plate. 'Sometimes, our dealings are productive, but more frequently, they're unhelpful.'

'I'll review that information,' I tell him, trying to sound as if I'm keeping up.

'I have a book about Newton if you want to borrow it. Now, what would you like to tell me about your polo connection? I have to be back at the station soon.'

'I'm not sure it was worth the torture of having to listen to Ronnie's acquaintance, Jago Villette, although I did get one snippet.' I tell him about Ronnie's meeting with Bill Mackie at the polo match. 'Could be something or nothing.'

He slips tablets from his pocket and swallows them with tea. 'That name seems familiar, I'll check it.'

'Jago invited me to a polo match on Saturday. Maybe I should go. He said that they always welcome lovely young ladies to brighten their day.'

Thaxted rolls his eyes. 'Doesn't seem your sort of thing, but then you're full of surprises.' He stretches his injured leg, winces and rubs the knee.

'Have you any significant suspects for Ronnie's murder?'

'I can't tell you that.'

'What about his business meetings around here — did you find out where he went, apart from the museum?'

'I refer you to my previous answer. I can say that your assistance was helpful. Did you say you came by car? Have you acquired one?'

'It's Felix's, I borrowed it. He's got a place at Oxford in the autumn, so he's going to stay in Fernfield for now.'

'I'm very pleased for him, he's survived many difficulties.'

'Including being arrested by you.'

'Acknowledged. Just doing my job, Miss Moore. Do you see him often?'

'Quite a bit. He makes the most wonderful biscuits.' I spear my last piece of toast, coating it with a smear of ketchup. 'There's something about the Carpenters' marriage that bothers me.'

Thaxted picks up his hat and coat. 'I can hear your brain whirring, so I'll leave you to your ruminations. May I walk you to the car?'

'Thanks, but I'm fine. I might have a stroll around the city centre, take in the sights and the nightlife, pretend I'm in London.'

'You still miss it a lot?'

'Now and again. I miss the invisibility. With any luck, eagle-eyed county ladies will be at home tonight and nobody will be snooping on me.'

He raises an eyebrow. 'Snooping's *your* forte, surely?'

'It would be nice to be taken seriously sometimes,' I reply crossly.

He levers himself up, using the table to balance, falters for a moment and then grasps his stick. 'We all want that in life, don't we? Goodnight!'

What's that supposed to mean, I wonder, and I shake myself when the door closes behind him. Perhaps Thaxted fears that his disability causes him to be underestimated at work. I've heard police constables referring to his moods and reliance on medication to get through the day, and some members of the public worry he's not fit enough. It can't be easy, doing his job while he's in pain. Like Felix, he's a survivor.

I finish the pot of tea absent-mindedly, reflecting on all the damaged people wandering this post-war earth.

CHAPTER TEN

The next day, an anonymous letter arrives by post for me at the Dolphin. It's franked Oxford, and is brief and written neatly on a sheet of lined paper.

> *Dear Miss Moore,*
>
> *I admire your gumption and the work you did to help solve the Laidlaw murder. If I were you, I'd take a closer peek at Mr Armitage of Broadmeadow Farm. He had dealings with Ronald Carpenter about insurance and they had a falling out. It might also be worth your while considering the Goswick museum fairly carefully too.*

It looks like a woman's writing to me, but then whoever sent it might have disguised their hand. Have I missed something at the museum, or does that last comment refer to the thefts and insurance claims? I guess that Inspector Thaxted might already have established if Ronnie had problems with Armitage. The sender might have ulterior motives and the letter could be an attempt to confuse me, but I'll take it at face value for now and rise to the challenge my correspondent has issued.

Leslie's a gossip and, being a Fernie, knows pretty much everyone in the area, so I give him a hand with preparing leeks in the afternoon.

'I had dinner at the Marquis, Leslie, and I didn't rate their food as being a lot better than yours.'

He whistles. 'Posh nosh! What were you doing there?'

'Just keeping JB company.'

Leslie sidles over and digs me in the ribs. He has a number of annoying habits: smothering his hair in brilliantine, grinning at his own jokes and taking an interest in my love life. Poking me in the side is one of his most irritating. 'You realise you're flogging a dead horse there, don't you?'

'What are you on about?'

He sniggers. 'If you're after a sugar daddy, you need to set your sights somewhere else.'

I carry on cleaning mud from a leek, one of my least favourite jobs because of the chance of lurking snails and other bugs. 'I don't need a sugar daddy, thanks.'

'Just as well.'

'Can you move away a bit? You're breathing in my ear.'

He inches back. 'Just saying, Daisy. I can tell you like Mr Berrow, but he's not for you.'

I throw the leek down. 'Leslie! Stop being so small-minded! He's my employer, he's married and I happen to like him a lot *as a friend*. Got it?'

'Keep your hair on. I'll shut my trap.' He goes back to making gravy.

'Good. I was trying to give you a compliment about your food!'

'Right. Well, thanks. Maybe you could tell Vera, although we'd better not try to charge the Marquis' prices. I've always said they're overrated.'

I run water through the leeks, shaking out grit. 'Have you come across the Armitages of Broadmeadow Farm?'

'Where Mr Carpenter was found?'

'That's right.'

'They've had a tough time, like plenty of others. The two sons died in the war and it's just the father and daughter there now trying to keep it going. Word is that they're often at odds with each other. Postie told me they fight like cat and dog.'

'Why's that?'

'Families!' Leslie tastes from his wooden spoon. 'That needs more salt. Pearl, the daughter, hates farming, never wanted to do it, but what with the war, her brothers gone and her dad needing the help, she's a bit stuck. It can't be easy for her being trapped there, a young woman with no social life, and Tony Armitage for a dad.'

'He's difficult?'

'You could say that. Always been a tricky, bad-tempered sort. His sons didn't get on with him. Plus, they had a fire a while since, some barns destroyed, which was a setback.'

Leslie starts fussing with the oven, grumbling that it's so old, it's hard to get the right temperature. I chop the leeks and chuck them in a pot, while I envisage another trip to Broadmeadow Farm after I've visited Ray and attended my first polo match.

* * *

The pervading smells in Oxford Prison, of drains and sewage, remind me of Hailsham House, where I lived temporarily after I set fire to my home. But the worst thing about over-crowded Hailsham, far worse to me than the malodorous air, was the lack of privacy in the packed dormitories and teeming communal areas. From Vera's comments, Ray must feel the same craving for his own space in here.

I wait at a table in a badly lit, windowless room with grey ceiling and walls and matching lino. It's like being in a box. There are around twenty tables and all the visitors are women with anxious expressions, most of them smoking like chimneys. This will be the first time I've seen Ray since he was imprisoned, and the palms of my hands are damp. I presume that as he's agreed to my visit, he's not holding a grudge. On the other hand, I might have got that completely wrong, and he's about to give me his frank opinion of my treachery.

When the prisoners troop in, they're dressed in grey too, so we're all trapped in a monochrome world. Ray's at the back of the line, wearing his habitual glum expression, and I raise my hand to catch his attention. He attempts a smile as he sits opposite.

'Morning, Daisy.'

'Hello. I wasn't sure what to bring, so I stopped for a copy of the *Daily Worker*.'

His eyes light up. 'Thanks, I haven't seen it recently. There's been a mutiny at the RAF base in Karachi and, of course, the capitalist press don't mention it. Members of the Communist Party there have been leading the struggle. It'll be good to read the latest on it.'

'What's the mutiny about?'

'There's been a very slow rate of demobilisation, and in deteriorating conditions. Lots of the men are bored and angry and want to get home. Quite rightly, they say that they've been put on the back burner.'

Ray used to be beefy but he's lost weight — he's reducing while Vera's increasing. Does one of Newton's laws apply? His skin is dull and his receding hair has thinned even more, but I'm reassured that his Lenin-style beard is trimmed.

'Thanks for saying I could visit, Ray. I wasn't sure you'd want to see me.'

'Why wouldn't I?'

'Well . . . my enquiries about Miss Laidlaw's death led to your arrest. I'd understand if you couldn't stand the sight of me.'

He rests his arms on the newspaper. 'Actually, it's quite the opposite. You did me a big favour.'

'How do you work that out?'

'I was hiding my head in the sand, wasn't I? I had this niggling worry that I'd get found out one day, but I'd dug myself such a deep hole, I couldn't see a way out. I was a coward, terrified of confessing to Vera.'

'It must have been very hard, keeping a secret like that.'

'It was bloody agony.' He smooths his beard. 'Mind, not as much agony as being married to Maude. You met her, didn't you?'

'I went to visit her in Streatham. She told me that she'd never divorce you because she's a Catholic.'

'I shouldn't have done a runner, but we didn't get on and she hated my political beliefs. I felt trapped. Anyway, it's my own fault that it all caught up with me, not yours, and I'm trying to sort the whole mess out. It's not just up to Maude, is it? I've got a solicitor and I've started divorce proceedings, whether she likes it or not. I love Vee and she deserves a proper husband. I want our baby to be legitimate.'

'That sounds like a sensible plan.'

'How is Vee? Is she managing? She tells me she's doing well when she visits, but I worry she's putting on an act.'

'Obviously, it's a strain for her but yes, she's coping. We all look out for her at the Dolphin.'

'It hit her hard, finding out about me and then Dora. She's a tower of strength, that woman. I don't deserve her.'

'It won't be too long before you're back home and then you can make it up to her.'

'I aim to. In the meantime, I try to keep busy in here. I've organised an education group. We're discussing the deconstruction of the British Empire and nationalisation of the coal mines. Also, I've intervened in a few disputes between prisoners and warders. I try to explain to inmates that the screws are working men and unwitting lackeys of the capitalist system. The best way to deal with them is to try to open their eyes to the injustices of state oppression.'

'Have your interventions been successful?'

'Up to a point. Some small accomplishments. The enlightenment of the proletariat is a long-term struggle.' He looks around and leans forward, beckoning me closer. 'I reckon I'm going to recruit a warder to the party. We've been talking and he's certainly very interested. That would almost make my time in here worthwhile.'

I hope he doesn't tell Vera that, when she's traipsed here hefting her burgeoning bump on and off buses. I bet the warders have no idea what to make of Ray. We chat for a while longer. I resist telling him that I'm heading to a polo match this afternoon. I don't want to have to sit through a diatribe about the decadent goings-on of the moneyed classes. It's good to see him, though, and to put aside my worries that he might be harbouring dark thoughts about me.

* * *

Despite Jago Villette's extensive lecture on polo, I find that I can make very little sense of the match on Saturday. Horses thunder, men sweep their mallets, people clap and cheer or groan, and the teams keep changing ends. The field is deep green, part of a club on the city outskirts, which is handily close to where the bus dropped me.

I sit on one of the terraced benches, taking my cues from other spectators and clapping when any of the men in a blue shirt with Oxford Hares emblazoned on the back does something heroic. I spot Jago and Charles Harrington on the field, bending and twisting on their horses. There are worse ways to spend a Saturday afternoon than here, in the warm sun, among people who exclaim, 'What a ride-off! Terrific blocking!' and 'Shocking umpiring!' Most of the women are wearing smart dresses and hats, but there are one or two in trousers, so I don't stick out like a sore thumb.

After about an hour, there's a huge round of applause and I gather that everyone's having a break. The players vanish to two tents on the other side of the field. I follow spectators to a pavilion with a café called the Chukka Room housed in a long conservatory at one end. I join the queue at the counter, where there are jugs of Pimm's, tea, sand-wiches, ginger beer and lemonade. I buy a glass of ginger beer and stand to one side, observing. I dislike most large social gatherings and it's hard to see where I might slot in. There are a dozen or so tables and the place is thronged and buzzing with chatter. A plump teenage girl is sitting on her own at a two-seater table by the side of the counter, gazing out at the field, so I head towards her.

'Mind if I sit here?'

'OK with me.' She takes a huge bite from a pile of sandwiches. Her face is blurred by the soft contours of puppy fat and she has spots on her cheek, which she's inexpertly tried to cover with foundation.

'I'm Daisy. Are you here for the game?'

'No,' she says mulishly. 'I'm with my mum. She's in charge of some of the horses.'

'This is my first time at a polo match.'

'Lucky you.'

'You don't like it?'

She flicks one of her plaits, lifts a shoulder. 'Stupid, boring way to spend your time.'

An awkward, comfort-eating girl. I sense her pain. It's such a tricky phase of life. 'Why do you come, then?'

'Mum makes me help, every weekend in the season. I have to hang around waiting for her mostly. I wash up in here later, get free eats in return.' She stuffs another sandwich in her mouth.

'I can't say I find the game that interesting,' I tell her.

'Just leave, then. Wish I could!'

'I might. What's your name?'

'Phyllis. I hate it, so I use my middle name, Diane.'

'I agree, Diane's better.'

She guzzles lemonade and reaches for another sandwich. If she spends a lot of time loitering here, she might have picked up a fair bit about the place and its clientele.

'I've come today because I met a couple of the players. Charles Harrington is one of them. He was friendly with Ronnie Carpenter, who's been murdered.'

She becomes the tiniest bit animated. 'I heard about that. Gruesome. He was shot.'

'That's right. I suppose you saw him in here.'

'He used to be around sometimes.'

'And Charles?'

She can fit an amazing amount of bread in her mouth in one go. She chews, swallows. 'He plays all the time. Gives me threepence now and again to fetch him a Pimm's. I had a sip of it once, it was disgusting, like medicine.' She pulls a sour face.

'Charles and Ronnie got on well?'

'I reckon, they were like pals. There was one time, though, Charles was calling Ronnie a bloody bastard.' She covers her mouth at the swear word and checks my reaction.

'Not very gentlemanly. Sounds like his temper was up.'

'Ronnie was telling Charles to leave someone alone and he went to punch him, but then he saw me coming with the drink.'

'Crumbs, you don't expect a punch-up between chaps at polo.'

A ghost of a smile flickers on her face. Having demolished the sandwiches, she starts on a jam bun.

'Did Ronnie name this person he wanted Charles to leave alone?'

'No name, but it was a she.'

'When did that happen, Diane?'

'Can't remember. Couple of weeks ago, just after a match.'

'So, they were arguing about a woman?'

'I heard Ronnie say, "Bloody well leave her out of it." They were all worked up and red in the face.'

'Where were they?'

'Round the side of the pavilion. You're nosy, with all your questions.'

'I am. Nosy's my middle name.'

She giggles, licks a fleck of jam from her top lip. 'What's your *actual* middle name?'

'Haven't got one. Just Daisy. My parents must have run out of ideas.'

'I like Daisy, it's pretty.'

'Thanks. Can I ask one more question and then buy you another lemonade?'

'If you like.'

'What can you tell me about Bill Mackie?'

'Yuk! He sees to the field and equipment, but I keep away from him.'

'Why's that?'

'I just don't like him. He tugs my plaits and whispers that I'm a big girl for my age.'

'You should tell your mum.'

'She's too busy. She doesn't like him either, says he's vulgar.'

'Is he around?'

'No. He had a fall or something and he's in hospital.'

'Let's hope he's in a lot of pain.'

'You're funny! Can I have ginger beer instead?'

'I'll get it for you now.'

I buy her a ginger beer and another bun, and take them to her as the spectators are leaving for the second half of the game.

'It's been great to meet you, Diane. I'm going to head off now.' There's someone I need to see, and I've no wish to hobnob with Jago, Charles and their chums after the match.

'Wish *I* could. I'm stuck here for ages yet.'

I leave her licking jam from the bun. I want to reassure her that things will improve, but she'll believe that I'm just another adult who doesn't understand.

* * *

The hospital is twenty minutes from the polo field. I walk fast along sedate, tree-lined streets, wondering who Ronnie and Charles had been arguing about. Did Ronnie suspect that his friend was having an affair with Tommie? Linda mentioned that Charles was going to see Tommie in London, and I recall how she'd clung to him when he arrived at the hotel and taken him up to her room. But why would he be having an affair with Tommie when he's soon to be married? People can behave foolishly and inexplicably, but limp Tommie seems such an unlikely inspirer of passion and Linda is a personable woman. Whatever the two men were arguing over, it had been settled, or at least a truce had been called, in time for the engagement party. Unless . . . unless Charles had pretended that things had been resolved and had lured Ronnie to his death. On the day he vanished, Ronnie might have responded to Charles's invitation to meet at Larch Bridge, go for a drink and let bygones be bygones. Charles could have stolen a car in case his own was recognised and, having fought in the war, he might easily own a gun.

I turn into the entrance for the hospital and enquire after Bill Mackie at reception. I'm directed to a surgical ward on the first floor, but before I go up there I browse the meagre offerings on the snack stall and buy a small bag of barley sugars to ease my introduction.

As I push through the swing doors to the ward, I see Peter Thaxted standing in the corridor, in conversation with a nurse. Luckily, he has his back to me, because it won't go well if he catches me here. I can hear his exasperated tone: *Please stop interfering, Miss Moore.* I nip into the ladies to my left, keeping the door a fraction open.

After a couple of minutes, I hear him tapping the tiles as he passes by. I glimpse his pale profile and the gleam of his bony knuckles as he grips his stick.

Bill Mackie is sitting on his bed in checked pyjamas, his neck in a collar and his left arm encased in plaster. He's absorbed in a *Reader's Digest* and doesn't see me until I say hello.

He grins. 'Afternoon, sweetheart.'

'I hope you don't mind me calling by. I was just at the polo and Jago asked if I'd pop in with these.' I hold out the sweets.

'Fancy him being so caring! Well, thank you kindly, Miss.' He pops a sweet in his mouth and proffers the bag.

I take one and pull up a chair. He's in his thirties, with coarse features, narrow, almost black eyes and slicked-back hair the colour of the sweets.

'I'm popular today,' he says. 'Just had a visit from the local plod. He looked as if he needed to get off his feet and consult a doctor. I told him, watching you makes me feel fitter!'

'Are the police making welfare visits these days?'

'Don't make me laugh, I hurt my ribs when I fell. And who might you be? Don't remember seeing you at the club.'

'My name's Daisy and it was my first match today.'

He sticks out his hand. 'Bill. You're much easier on the eye than the plod, darling.'

I shake hands. His lingers on mine a little too long. A forest of hair curls around his pyjama collar and I picture Little Red Riding Hood and the wolf.

'How's your neck and arm?' I ask.

'On the mend, they reckon. I can go home next week.' He winks at me. 'Want to come and be my nurse, plump my pillows and give me a bed bath?'

I twinkle back. 'I'd be hopeless.'

'I reckon you'd have an idea or two about keeping a man happy. Oops, made you blush!'

'How did you injure yourself?'

'My own stupid fault, messing about with a ladder. Anyway, how's Jago and all at the club?'

'Fine, and they sent you best wishes. There's a bit of upset because of Ronnie Carpenter.'

'Poor old Ronnie, eh? Very strange business.'

'Is that why the police were here? I suppose they must be making the rounds of anyone who knew him.'

'They have to keep busy, don't they?'

I nod in agreement. 'They've spoken to Charles Harrington recently. Did you spend much time with Ronnie?'

'The odd chat if we happened to trip over each other. I don't generally socialise with the chaps, darling.'

'Oh, right. Someone said you might have bought insurance from him.'

'I suppose I might. That was his line of business.'

'It is awful, Ronnie's wife is in a state.'

'That so?' He winks again. 'I've not met her, but when the noise has died down, she might be relieved.'

'That's a strange thing to say.'

'Is it? Old Ronnie was a secretive bugger behind the bluster.'

'Sounds fascinating. What was he keeping secret?'

'That would be telling, and I'm no snitch.' He leans forward, grazes my finger with his. 'You got a beau, then? You walking out on lover's lane? Any chance for me?'

I fold my arms. 'I'm spoken for.'

'Shame. Ah, well, you win some . . .' He taps his magazine. 'Fascinating article in here about how the Americans and Russkies are going to square up now. I'd like to get back to it, if you don't mind.'

He spars well verbally, and I can tell I'll get no more from him. As I'm leaving the ward, a nurse asks me if I'm Mr Mackie's family.

'No, it's the first time I've met him.'

'Awful man,' she glowers. 'Hands everywhere with the nurses. He's really upset several of them. Almost as bad as some of the doctors.'

While I'm waiting for the bus back to Fernfield, I consider Ronnie Carpenter, who is becoming a more complex figure, turning from the bluff, uxorious loss adjuster into a man whose marriage was strained, who had secrets and argued with his close friend. I'd love to discover what alibis Peter Thaxted has established and what he's found out from Bill Mackie. Maybe I can acquire some information to trade with him.

CHAPTER ELEVEN

I cycle to Broadmeadow Farm again after work with two large balls of wool in my basket as an excuse for my visit. There's no answer when I knock, so I push Lucinda around the back of the house, trying to keep to the less muddy areas. I can hear hammering and I follow the noise to a fence, where I find Pearl bashing nails into a post.

'Hello, didn't expect to see you again,' she says. 'I still haven't got any eggs.'

'I brought you some wool.' I take the paper bag from my basket.

'Oh.' She's taken aback, rubs her brow. She's wearing the same clothes as before, but today she has a blue silk scarf decorated with pink roses twisted around her hair. It's a delicate piece of material, at odds with her workaday, rough-and-ready appearance, and it lifts her sullen expression. She puts the hammer down, takes the bag and fingers the wool. 'It's good quality, I'll pay you for it.'

'No need. Guests leave stuff behind at the hotel and I found it in the cupboard. I remembered you said you'd run out.'

'Nice of you to come all this way with it, thanks.'

The evening sun's in my face, so I move sideways and she's in clearer focus. There's something different about her.

Last time I was here, she was jaded, but today her voice is duller and there's a hint of misery in her eyes.

'How are you? You might suffer with delayed shock, after finding a body.' And I doubt that her father would supply much empathy.

'Delayed shock?' She holds the wool against her chest. 'Maybe I do have that, yes.'

'Can I help?' Truth is, I wonder if she sent me the anonymous letter because she's had enough of being stuck here with her father. A call for help.

'Doubt it.' She leans on the fence, rests her chin on her forearm.

I lean beside her. The air is moist and heavy, and there are puffy cinder clouds banking overhead. We both stare at the tussocky field covered in cowpats while crows create a racket in a nearby tree. A couple of cows lumber towards us, heads lowered to the grass. One lets out a deep moo and is answered by another, out of sight.

'Moving here from London, the countryside seemed deeply silent at first, but now I realise it's full of noises that take time to register with me.'

After a long pause Pearl says, 'How can you stand living here after London?'

'It's a struggle sometimes, but I had no job or home at the end of the war and I got an offer at the Dolphin. It's not so bad and I like my employer. I might go back to London though. I'll see.'

'It must be nice to have options. This is all I've ever known and I hate it.' She kicks the fence and it shudders.

'Sounds as if you've had bad luck as well. Someone in town said you'd had a fire.'

'Last autumn, that was. We lost three barns and a load of silage.' She doesn't sound as if she cares much.

'How awful. Were you covered by insurance?'

Pearl works her jaw as if she's chewing and turns her head sideways, peering at me. 'Are you a gossip?'

'I've been accused of asking too many questions at times, but never of gossiping.'

'Well . . . I might as well tell you. It'll get out anyway. That man, Carpenter, he'd been to the farm after the fire. Came about the insurance claim. I didn't recognise him when I found him in the car — I didn't look too closely, and anyway, his face was a mess. When we were told his identity, Dad informed the police that he'd been our loss adjuster, and he said not to tell anyone else because all kinds of rumours would start. But like I say, nothing stays secret for long around here.'

'Did you meet Mr Carpenter when he visited?'

She fiddles with her scarf, tucks it under at the neck. 'Dad dealt with him, sorted it all out.'

'It was all agreed, then, no problems about the claim?'

'Far as I could tell. Don't pass on what I told you.' She bends to pick up the hammer and straightens, her face guarded. 'I'd best get on. I need to finish here before it starts to get dark.'

There are unsaid words hanging in the air. 'If you'd like a drink any time, give me a ring at the Dolphin.'

She nods. 'I'll see. Thanks again for the wool.'

Rain spits at me on the way back to Brize Lodge. Being with Pearl has lowered my mood, as if her desperation and moroseness has infected me. I launch into 'A North Country Maid', but singing does little to shift the pall of gloom that Broadmeadow Farm has draped about me.

I speculate as to where Pearl got the pretty silk scarf.

* * *

I'm sitting in my Noel Coward dressing gown late that night, amusing myself with a couple of replies to the latest fan mail, when I hear the front door opening and JB's resonant tones.

'Thanks for the lift, I'd have got drowned in that downpour. Come on in and take a snifter. Daisy and I often have one this time of night. Are you there, petal?'

'Present and correct, JB,' I call.

'Hope you've lit the fire. See who I've kidnapped!'

He hurries in, smart in a mossy-green tweed jacket with leather elbow patches and a red cravat. Behind him and looming over his shoulder like a pale heron is Peter Thaxted.

'Good evening,' he says from the doorway, scanning the typewriter.

'Hello. Have you been out together?'

'We attended supper chez the *kommandantin*,' JB says. 'The famous sculptor was there. Thank goodness Peter came along! It took the heat off me in the cultural stakes. Sit, Peter, take the weight off.'

Thaxted sits on one side of the fire and leans down to stroke a dozing Oberon. He's in a turquoise shirt, open at the neck under a navy wool waistcoat. Maybe it's what he wears for arty suppers. JB busies himself with the whisky decanter.

'I got a couple of new typewriter ribbons, Daisy, did you find them?'

'Thanks, yes.'

'What are you writing?' Thaxted asks. 'Your memoirs? Detective fiction?'

'Most amusing,' I reply. 'I've been answering JB's fan mail.'

JB hands us glasses of whisky. 'Daisy does sterling work, keeping my avid supporters satisfied. Pull your chair over, Daisy, there's a sneaky draught tonight. May is the most treacherous month for changeable weather.'

I gather up my dressing gown and bring my chair to sit between them.

'This is our routine most nights, Peter. Me and Daisy sit by the hearth with a nightcap and chew the fat. Sometimes we dance, or she helps me rehearse my lines, or describes my fan mail. Sometimes we discuss murder most foul.'

'Domestic bliss,' I add.

'May I hear a fan letter?' Thaxted asks. 'I've never been privy to one.'

'I don't suppose detectives get them,' JB laughs.

'No, only abusive or threatening notes occasionally.'

'There is a corker that I've just answered.' I fetch the letter and my reply and sip my whisky. 'This is from Debra Lane, who lives in St Albans.'

Dear Jeffrey,

I love all your work and I love you. I'm single, blonde and very attractive, and I truly am devoted to you. Would you be my beau? We could meet on the steps of the National Gallery, Trafalgar Square, where you kissed your dying fian-cée in The Light of Love. *Such a moving film. I wept buckets.*

Lots of love and I hope to hear from you soon.
PS I've been told I'm very like Carole Lombard.

JB holds out his hands. 'It's humbling to inspire such passion.'

'I haven't seen *The Light of Love*,' I tell him. 'Did you play a big part?'

'I was in a fair few scenes. It was an awful melodrama — a women's weepie — lots of sweeping violins. 1937, if I remember correctly.'

'I've seen it, lost an hour and a half of my life sitting through that.' Thaxted leans back with his long legs extended, holding his glass on his chest. 'My mother insisted that I accompany her. For an otherwise sensible woman, she indulges a craving for romantic tosh. You're right, it was awful, but you did your best.'

I enjoy this glimpse into Thaxted's home life, with the dutiful son reluctantly viewing a soppy love story. 'Well, JB, you certainly worked your magic on Debra.' I consult my typing. 'This is my reply.'

Dear Miss Lane,

How kind of you to write to me. Thank you for your comments regarding my work. It's always good to hear that my performances touch people.

I am most humbled by your suggestion of romance, but I'm afraid that my wife wouldn't approve. Also, the steps to the National Gallery can be quite slippery, so do be careful if you go there.

I wish you very well for the future and I am pleased that Carole Lombard's flame still burns in St Albans.

Thaxted laughs loudly, astonishing me and waking Oberon. 'You have a talent for being insolently polite — or politely insolent,' he says.

'Thank you.'

JB rattles the fire with the poker and puts two logs on. 'That's terrific, Daisy. I will never let you leave me. You're doomed to be my factotum for eternity. Now, if you'll excuse me for a moment, I have to phone Declan about lunch tomorrow.'

He takes his whisky, Oberon stalking after him. I've been debating a trade with Thaxted and decide to seize my chance in this unexpected social meeting, while he's thawed by drink and an evening's socialising.

'I have another letter, Inspector, that I'd like to show you. One that concerns the murder investigation, and maybe a bit of a fan letter to me in a way.'

'I'm intrigued.'

I take the anonymous letter from the mantelpiece. 'This came for me at the Dolphin, postmarked Oxford.'

He reads while the fire crackles and hisses.

'Before you ask why someone wrote to me, I visited Broadmeadow Farm, just out of interest. Well, in fact, I've visited twice.'

He hands the letter back and sips his drink. 'Twice.'

'Yes. On my first visit, I had the impression that Mr Armitage wanted to get rid of me.'

'You don't say.'

'All right, I can hear your silent laughter. Ronnie Carpenter went there last autumn because their barns burned down and they made an insurance claim.'

'That's correct.'

'What about the alleged falling out that the note mentions? I talked to Pearl Armitage today, trying to find out about that, but she clammed up.'

There's no response and when I glance at him his eyes are half closed, the way Tybalt's are when he's snoozing, but alert.

I press on. 'Maybe she isn't aware that there was a spat about the claim.'

Thaxted opens one eye. 'Miss Armitage is a moody, disenchanted woman living with an overbearing father. Maybe she craves a bit of melodrama, as in *The Light of Love*, and who could blame her? I am aware of the temperature of Mr Carpenter's dealings at the farm. Did you attend the polo match?'

'I did.'

'Find out anything of interest?'

'Yes, but first of all, what can you tell me about Bill Mackie, apart from the fact that he's a horrible lecher?'

'May I have another splash of this fine whisky?'

I top up his and then my own.

'Cheers,' he says. 'So you've met Mr Mackie as well? How *do* you ever get any work done at the Dolphin?'

I make up my mind to go for it. I've nothing to lose, except my dignity. 'Inspector, I met several of your constables last year and I have a much sharper mind than any of them. You yourself referred to their lack of wit, so why not utilise my skills? Do a good deed, help a woman who did her bit to save us from the Nazis and who's trying to keep her brain honed.'

'I was anticipating a spot of emotional blackmail.' He leans forward, elbows on knees and stares into the fire. The flames illuminate the stark angles of his gaunt face. 'Very well. First of all, give me a summary of what you've learned.'

I focus on the fire and concentrate. 'Ronnie Carpenter was a bossy man who fussed over his wife, but found his marriage a strain. No matter if he loved her, it must have been hard to return from war to such a needy woman. He'd visited this area several times before, but seems not to have told Tommie. On the day they arrived at the hotel, he told her he was going for a walk, but he met someone at Larch Bridge who was driving a stolen car. Mr Claremont at the museum told me that Ronnie was visiting other people around here. Jago Villette saw Ronnie with Bill Mackie at the polo club. Ronnie and Charles were supposedly good friends from way back, but not always, according to Diane, a young girl who helps out at polo matches. She saw Ronnie and Charles arguing, and I quote, "Charles was calling Ronnie a bloody bastard. Ronnie was telling him to leave someone alone and he went to punch him, but then he saw me coming." Diane's impression was that the someone referred to was a she. And yes, I visited Bill Mackie in hospital and had to suffer his luxuriant chest hair while he implied that he might have been discussing insurance with Ronnie at the club. He also said that Ronnie was a secretive bugger, but wouldn't elaborate. No crimes similar to that shooting have been committed in the area during the last six months.'

Thaxted straightens, his knee cracking. 'That's good, yes, and I see you've done your research. Now, Mr Mackie, he's a canny, small-time crook. He's been arrested before, but never charged due to lack of evidence. Suspected of burglary, handling stolen goods, that sort of stuff. I wondered if he was involved in one or both of the museum thefts, but he has watertight alibis for both of those dates.'

'What about the Friday Ronnie was murdered?'

Thaxted rotates the ankle of his injured leg. 'Hard to pin that down. It was Mackie's day off. He lives alone and he claims that he was at home, catching up on sleep and walking his dog. He produced a ticket for the late afternoon showing of *The Ziegfeld Follies* at the Oxford Odeon, but that doesn't actually mean that he was in the cinema.'

'That's such an unlikely film for Mackie to sit through. I'd have expected him to want a war story or something with gangsters.'

'Be careful of assumptions and personal prejudices regarding hairy chests. People are surprisingly multifaceted. I once put away a vicious criminal who loved to sketch flowers and was extremely talented with his charcoal. And what's Mackie's motive? Can't see one.'

I can't imagine Mackie having a soft side and there's something off about him, apart from his leching. 'Now that we're aware of the row between the two men, it sounds as if Ronnie was warning Charles to stay away from a woman. Has Charles Harrington got an alibi?'

'He had the day off work to run around and do last-minute things for his engagement party. He was out and about from 8 a.m. We're still following up his movements as best we can. There were no identifiable fingerprints in the stolen car, other than the owner's and Ronnie Carpenter's. The owner is squeaky clean.'

'It does seem odd, doesn't it, that Ronnie's body was left at a farm he'd visited before. Maybe the murderer was trying to cast suspicion on the Armitages, so it would be worth checking if someone had a grudge against them.'

'Hah! There'll be a long queue. Tony Armitage has had run-ins with just about everyone local over the years.'

'Another question — how did the killer get away from the farm? What if they planned ahead and left a bike hidden in the hedge?'

'Possible. Or there was an accomplice. There are a number of outstanding questions. Was the murder linked to Carpenter's previous visits in this area and did he see people as yet unidentified? Who were Harrington and Carpenter arguing about — was it Mrs Carpenter, or did Carpenter believe that Harrington was betraying his fiancée with another woman? Did Carpenter have a secret connected to this area that he was keeping from his wife? I talked to Mrs Carpenter and Harrington again. She repeated that she'd no idea that her husband had done business around here and he never bothered her with those kinds of details. Harrington claimed that Carpenter hadn't mentioned his work visits locally.'

'Charles Harrington might have a motive for murder. Is there anyone else?'

'Mr Armitage and Carpenter fell out over the insurance claim. Carpenter wasn't convinced that the fire at the farm was accidental and queried it with the fire brigade.'

'Ronnie believed that Armitage had set the blaze?'

'No accusations were made, but the issue was left dangling. There was a settlement in the end, but because of ongoing, unproven doubts, not as much as Armitage had hoped. However, it's hard to see how Armitage could have been stealing a car with intent to murder when, according to him and his daughter, they were busy on the farm all of Friday. Who might have sent you the letter?'

'I had Pearl Armitage in mind, but when I saw her today I wasn't so sure. She seemed genuinely surprised that I'd turned up again, but it's hard to read her because she's very morose. She didn't mention that there'd been a dispute about the insurance claim — perhaps her father didn't tell her.' I take a drink of the peaty whisky. 'I had an idea I'd like to run past you.'

'Oh yes?'

'Yes. I want to help. I could visit Tommie Carpenter in London and have a friendly, sympathetic chat, see what more I can learn about the marriage and Ronnie's character.' I'll revisit Goswick museum as well, but I'll keep my powder dry on that.

'Hmm.'

'I'd love to take a trip to London anyway, I've been promising to call on Father Hickey. You're going to be busy following up on Charles Harrington and trying to trace anyone else Ronnie was with. What's his employer told you about his work around here?'

'They have only two visits documented in this area, Goswick and Broadmeadow Farm. My goodness, is that the time! I must get home to my bed.' He gets up stiffly, gripping the side of his chair. 'Where's Jeffrey? He can't still be on the phone.'

I go to the hall, but JB isn't around. Then I hear a rumbling snore coming from his bedroom and I tiptoe back to the sitting room.

'JB's fast asleep.'

'He did enjoy a lot of wine with supper.' The inspector shrugs his coat on and snaps the rim of his hat.

'He says that Rosalind's cellar makes up for having to toe the line and present himself at the manor when instructed.'

Thaxted grins and takes his car keys from his pocket. 'If you choose to visit Mrs Carpenter in Chiswick to offer further condolences, that's entirely up to you.'

'Thanks.'

'But please, don't get Declan Hickey involved in this investigation as well. The last thing I need is that actor-cum-priest — and I'm never sure if he is actually a priest or playing a role — assuming a Father Brown persona.'

I understand what he means about Father Hickey. He's always a bit over the top and there are times when his brogue sounds almost Hollywood. 'I won't offer him any active role.'

'Night, Miss Moore.'

I watch him duck his head under the tumbling rain as he manages a lurching run to his car. The engine turns, lights wink and he's gone.

CHAPTER TWELVE

Tommie Carpenter is in a black-and-grey dress, with a single string of pearls at her neck. She's less agitated than the last time I saw her, but the vacancy in her eyes and listlessness of her speech suggest the effects of medication and she confirms this.

'It's so kind of you to drop in, Daisy, but you must excuse me if I don't chat for long. The doctor has prescribed a strong tranquilliser and I find that conversation tires me.'

I wait in the sitting room while she makes tea. It's a drab medley of faded green wallpaper and carpet, with heavy, brocade-covered furniture. Dotted around are many figurines: shepherds, ladies in crinoline, pirouetting ballet dancers and peasants carrying sheaves of corn. The air is warm and musty, as if a window is rarely opened. There are a handful of magazines and leaflets on the coffee table, including a Women's Voluntary Service one with the message, *Even if tied to your home, you can help street wardens and your neighbours.*

When Tommie brings in a tray of tea I tell her, 'I won't stay long. I was visiting town and I just wanted to see how you are. I've been concerned about you.'

'I'd be comforted a little if the police told me they'd found whoever did this awful thing.'

'I'm sure they're working hard on it. I believe that Charles has been to see you.'

She adds milk to her tea. 'Dear Charles, yes. He sits and listens to me ramble on. He's been helping me with some of the paperwork, which is beyond me. Ronnie used to deal with all the practicalities — banks, the house and so forth. Charles is such a support.'

'How did you manage during the war, when your husband was away?' Most women, however dependent, had had to learn some self-sufficiency during those six long years.

'Ronnie sorted everything when he was home on leave. He realised I was hopeless with those details and he didn't want me to fret about them. He understood my anxieties and how overwhelming I could find the world. That dear man was always careful never to mention any of the nastiness he was involved in, and he forbade me to listen to the news on the wireless.'

'Nastiness' is something of an understatement when describing a world war. 'Well, Charles and your husband were such good friends, I'm sure it helps him to be of assistance. I believe they never had a cross word.'

'Oh, never. They got on so well — almost like brothers, really.'

'By the way, I met Linda, Charles's fiancée.'

'She's kind too, she sent me a lovely card. Everyone is so kind.'

Yet Tommie seems to me the sort of woman who expects kindness as her due. The world muddles on around her and she creeps through it, hiding from reality, brittle and unaffected by its woes. Until now.

'Linda told me that your husband attended polo matches in Oxford now and again. Did he ever play?'

'No, he wasn't sporty, apart from a bit of angling. Charles has played for years, so Ronnie went to watch occasionally during the season. I didn't like him disappearing at weekends, but I realised he needed some relaxation and he could easily get to Oxford and back in a day.'

'I suppose he had to travel for work, so you wanted him at home in his leisure time.'

'Exactly. Some of the claims he dealt with were outside London.'

'Did he have to stay away overnight at all?'

'Oh no! He sometimes left terribly early, before I was awake and then he'd get back late at night. I told him that I'd endured years not knowing where he was, or if he was still alive, so I couldn't bear it if he didn't come home every evening. Even then, he had to finish off work sometimes. He had a little office in the basement.'

Her anxiety is so all-encompassing and exhausting to be around. Maybe Ronnie Carpenter had found the war something of a liberation. I imagine him closing the front door on his claustrophobic domesticity and exhaling with relief.

'Do you mind me asking — have you always been a nervous person?'

'I have, yes. As a little girl, I sleepwalked and had the most awful dreams. I still get nightmares regularly, especially if I don't take my medication. When I met Ronnie, it was as if he folded me in a lovely warm blanket.' Her eyes fill. 'And now he's gone. I'd only just got him back from the war and he's gone.'

'I'm so sorry, I didn't mean to upset you.'

She wipes her eyes with a hanky. 'I cry all the time, it's not you. Oh, who could have done this to him?'

I finish my tea while she blows her nose. 'Perhaps something went wrong on one of his trips to Oxford. Was Ronnie ever upset when he came home?'

She shakes her head. 'I'd better lie down, I'm woozy now. Thanks for coming, I appreciate it.'

I say goodbye and stand for a moment outside the door with the sun on my face. A woman is washing the steps down to the basement, clanging her mop against a metal bucket and humming 'Puttin' on the Ritz'.

'Hello!' I call to her bent back.

She turns, blows her fringe back. 'Can I help you, Miss?'

106

'I've just called on Mrs Carpenter.' I cross to the top step. 'She seems to be bearing up.'

'Awfully sad for her. She leaned so on her hubby.'

'She's not a strong person.'

'No. Are you a friend of hers? She doesn't have many visitors, so I'm glad you've been round.'

'We met in Oxfordshire when her husband went missing.'

'Well, she'll have appreciated you coming.'

I've noticed that the basement door is open. 'Would you mind if I pop down to Mr Carpenter's office? Mrs Carpenter asked me to post some letters, and she said I'll find stamps in there.'

'You go ahead, Miss. The police were in there last week, but they've done whatever they needed. I've finished the cleaning, so it's just airing.'

The square basement room has iron bars at the window and is poorly lit. There's a massive walnut office desk with a reading lamp, large blotting pad, a covered typewriter and pens in a wooden box. I pull out the tall green leather chair, which moves smoothly on castors, sit down and try the first of four deep drawers on the right-hand side of the desk, hoping it's not locked.

It opens, revealing writing paper and envelopes, stamps, pencils, pens, a ruler, a stapler, and an ink pad and stamp that says PAID. The second drawer contains several buff folders labelled in a sloping hand: OPEN, SETTLED and DISPUTED. I riffle through the papers inside, all of which appear to concern insurance claims. I skim-read dry phrases: *policy liabilities, ongoing validity of business, extent of damage, conditions and endorsements, emergency repairs.* None involve clients in Oxfordshire, but there are details of claims in Surrey, Kent and Berkshire as well as London suburbs. I glance up, but the cleaner is still busy outside, her humming — she's switched to 'Red Sails in the Sunset' — not too near. The third and fourth drawers hold folders with personal details about banking, the house, utilities and paid bills. Ronnie has used his red stamp across the bills, a satisfied flourish. Then, amid all this dry, ordered record-keeping I find a note slipped between electricity and rates demands. It's a stunningly emotional declaration.

> *Darling, writing this in haste. I do adore and love you and I agree that our time together is all too brief. Please be patient. I realise that I'm asking a lot of you, but my home situation is complicated and I have to tread with care.*
>> *Your love means everything to me.*
>> *Always, Ronnie xx*

No date, no indication who this was intended for. And why is it here, rather than sent to the object of Ronnie's affections? Perhaps he didn't have time to post it before he left for Fernfield.

I tuck the note into my bag and close the drawer, push the chair back neatly and head out.

'Find what you wanted?' The cleaner is pouring her bucket of greyish water down the drain.

'Thanks, yes. See you again, maybe.'

* * *

An hour later, I'm sitting with Father Hickey in the kitchen of his presbytery in Walthamstow, drinking tea and eating scones. I've given him a quick run through the investigation and he's just read the note I found in Ronnie's office.

'A man in the throes of love and not with his wife. Not a new story by any means, Daisy me darlin'. But who is *la femme* he was *cherchez*-ing?'

'I met Ronnie Carpenter only briefly, but he seemed such an unlikely Romeo and devoted to his wife.'

'Maybe he was so attentive because of guilt mingled with affection and duty,' the priest declares sagely. 'Was he really devoted or was he trapped? We can spin webs for ourselves, and I'd wager that's what happened to him. He started off liking and indulging his unworldly wife's quirks, but then they became a burden. There could be a fine colleen he met in the war and fell head over heels for. I see it now, clear as the Slieve Bloom Mountains when the mist has lifted.' He spreads jam on his scone, licks his knife and puts a hand over his heart. 'He was in uniform, so was she. Their eyes met across a crowded NAAFI canteen. He was about to leave on a dangerous operation, maybe his last. A piano player was tinkling "We'll Meet Again". She was so beautiful. They moved towards each other and danced as if it was the last time. Then they embraced . . . Ye can fill in the rest.'

'Haven't I seen that film?'

'A version of it with Trevor Howard or Robert Taylor. Sometimes they make the hero a Yank to mix things up a bit. Vivien Leigh might be in there and possibly Jeffrey in a small role.'

'He'd play the cheery sidekick or the wronged husband.'

'Ye've got the idea. But sure, a lot of these romances did take off in the dark days of Adolf's terror.'

'Your theory would mean that the woman this letter addresses could live anywhere and be impossible to find.'

'Are we wondering, did her wronged husband shoot yer man?'

'It has to be a possibility.' Yet I keep coming back to the idea that the murder must have been connected to Broadmeadow Farm. And if this killing is about Ronnie's adultery, why was he warning Charles to stay away from a woman? 'I'd better tell Inspector Thaxted I've found this note. Can I use your phone?'

But when I call him, he's unavailable, so I leave a message, asking him to ring me at home tonight.

'Are ye and Thaxted getting on?' Father Hickey asks. 'He has a fine brain, but he's a dry old stick, that's for sure. Almost died after that injury, the poor crathur. 'Twas touch and go in the hospital, I understand. Another walking casualty. Sure, it can't be much of a life for him, living with the mammy and depending on painkillers.'

'He's alive, which has to be better than the other option. He improves on acquaintance and he's a good detective.'

'Ah, I'd say ye've a soft spot for him.'

'I'm not sure I'd go that far. There are times when he irritates me so much I dislike him.'

'Whatever ye say, Daisy darlin'.' He whistles softly and pours more tea.

'How are you, Father? Is Abe back in London?'

Abe is his friend, a stage designer who's been away working in regional theatres.

He brightens. 'He'll be back soon from the wilds of Northamptonshire, thank God and all the saints in heaven. He's going to help me with decorating the church hall for the big victory parade in June.'

'Is that why you've got Union Jacks in the porch?'

'We're putting them up around the church and the hall. It's a strange flag for an Irishman to be raising, but when in Rome . . .'

'I might pop down for it, join in the celebrations.'

The priest rocks his chair back. 'Ye hanker after London, don't ye?'

A sudden and unexpected wave of misery sweeps through me. I associate Father Hickey with my mother — she worshipped the ground he trod on — and with both my parents dead, he represents a rock-solid presence from my past. Our burned-out house is only half a mile away and I'm aware of its ruins, a shadow flickering at my peripheral vision. On the bus, I'd travelled wrecked roads full of brick dust and piled debris, thinking, *These are my streets*. I nod, fighting to stay dry-eyed.

'Listen, Daisy, there's always a room here if ye want to stay a night or two. Aren't I rattling around in this place like one dry pea in a pod? Ye could stay over and jaunt around yer old haunts. But if ye take me up on the offer, reassure Jeffrey ye'll be returning. He dotes on ye.'

'Thanks, Father.'

'Could we dispense with the whole "Father" moniker now? It's Declan.'

I smile at him. 'It's impossible, I'm afraid. My mother would haunt me if I started to call a priest by his name. She'd see it as tantamount to heresy.'

'True enough. We wouldn't want to rub yer mammy up the wrong way. She was a woman of definite opinions.'

As he sees me out he says, 'Give Jeffrey my best and tell him there's a knees-up at the Chelsea Arts Club in late June that'll be too good to miss.'

CHAPTER THIRTEEN

'How was your trip to London?' Vera asks the next day. 'I'm glad you're back in one piece.'

Vera's a true Fernie, in that she doesn't hold with people venturing too far from the town and, in particular, going to London. It's tempting fate, asking for trouble and no good comes of it.

'Lovely, thanks. There are lots of preparations going on for the victory celebrations on the eighth of June. There'll be a march from Buckingham Palace to the Mall and fireworks in the evening. It should be amazing. I bought a programme at Paddington.'

'That's all very well, but some of us haven't got time for partying nonsense. Ray was saying that it's an awful waste of fuel and rations when ordinary people are struggling, and it's just an opportunity for the top brass to indulge themselves. He read that they didn't even invite the Poles, who contributed so much to the war. Anyway, when you've got your head out of the London clouds, maybe you could check the bar stock and complete an order.' She pauses, holds up a finger. 'I suppose you'll be wanting to have that Saturday off, so you can tear down to London and act the giddy goat.'

'I wouldn't mind.'

'Oh . . . very well, I'll make a note. Load of nonsense, if you ask me. By the way, that Inspector Thaxted left a message for you.' She sticks her thumbs in her belt. 'I hope you're not poking your nose into police business again. Don't forget you got your fingers burned last year.'

'You don't need to worry about me, Vera.'

'I should hope not. I've quite enough on my plate, thank you very much!'

In the bar, I read the message from the inspector, written in Vera's spiky hand.

He's sorry he hasn't had a chance to call you. Can you pop into the station at lunchtime.

In the bar, I start checking the various spirits, sherries, wines, beers and fruit juices, ticking them off against the stock list. While I work, I run over the Carpenter case. Charles Harrington and Bill Mackie don't have alibis for the day Ronnie was shot. Mackie appears not to have any motive for killing him, whereas Ronnie and Charles had argued about a woman. There'd been bad blood between Tony Armitage and Ronnie, but the farmer and Pearl had alibied each other for the day of the murder. Who was Ronnie's lover, and would he really have had the bottle to abandon Tommie? Unless she's a consummate actress, I don't believe that she had any inkling that he was playing away. And who sent me the anonymous note?

During my lunch break, I walk to the police station and I'm directed straight to Thaxted's office. He's sitting in shirtsleeves with his back to the window, hands resting in his lap, his bare, blue-veined feet planted on the worn carpet.

'Hello,' I say. 'Are you all right?'

'I was just taking a few minutes. I practise the Alexander Technique every day now. I sit here so that I'm facing the sea.' He nods towards the painting on the wall opposite, of a wild stretch of coast with an empty, shingled beach and white-capped waves. 'Someone posted a pamphlet about the technique to me, which was a kind gesture. I've taken lessons and I do believe it's helping my posture and my muscle strength.'

I'd put the pamphlet through his letterbox. I learned about the technique while working in Whitehall, where most of us ended up with cricked necks and back pain after hours spent crouched over desks.

'Oh yes, I've heard of it. I'm glad it's helping.' I produce Ronnie's note from my pocket with a flourish. 'I've brought you Ronnie Carpenter's love letter.'

'His *what*?' Thaxted's face is a picture as he drags his chair over to his desk and gestures for me to sit.

I'm only human, it's good to catch the inspector on the back foot now and again and I revel in my moment of revelation. 'I visited Tommie yesterday. That woman is such a bag of neuroses.' I explain about my exploration of Ronnie's basement office. 'Your colleagues who searched there missed this.' I hand him the note.

'How did those idiots not find this? I'll have to request another search. These are strong emotions. This was how you found it — no envelope?'

'Just that sheet of paper, tucked between a couple of bills. Maybe Ronnie wanted to add to it, or write another version, or just didn't have time to post it.'

'Or wasn't sure if he should send it.' Thaxted taps a finger against the paper. 'He had doubts? You would, if you were considering leaving a marriage.'

'And especially if Tommie's your wife. Leaving her would have been very difficult. He'd have worried how she'd cope. This is a woman who takes various medications for anxiety, doesn't like engaging with the world and refers to the war as "nastiness". Ronnie managed all the bills and household affairs, seems to have treated her as if she were an invalid.' I pick up a pen and click the nib in and out. 'It must have suited him, mustn't it?'

'Perhaps he enjoyed having a dependent wife. He felt strong and capable around her. The big man.'

'Really? Is that what men want in a marriage? Could you imagine yourself with a wife like that?'

Thaxted is bent below the desk, putting his socks and shoes back on. He raises his head, considers the question. 'I've never imagined myself with any kind of wife. I can't see you taking on that kind of role in marriage, Miss Moore.'

'Like you, Inspector, I've never imagined myself with any kind of husband.' My mother used to allege that no man would put up with my "take me or leave me" attitude. While I don't want to believe she's right, I'd rather spend my days as JB's factotum than shackled to the likes of domineering Ronnie Carpenter. 'If the woman Ronnie adored was also married, we could be pursuing a jealous husband who'd found out about them.'

'It's a reasonable premise. I spent some time with Charles Harrington. After a fair amount of bluster, he admitted that he and Carpenter had had a disagreement.'

'How did he explain it?'

'He claimed that he wanted to have sex with his fiancée, who was insisting on waiting until after the wedding. He'd mentioned this to Carpenter, saying he hoped to persuade her into bed. He said that he was taken aback when Carpenter saw red, and that's why he was telling Harrington not to be a cad and to leave Linda alone.'

'Did you believe him?'

'When he told me it seemed plausible, because Carpenter was an old-fashioned, protective sort with women. But now that we've learned that he was cheating on his wife, it sounds preposterous.'

'Unless it was one rule for Charles and one for him. Why would Charles lie? Even if he wasn't aware of Ronnie's affair, he'd surely been friends with him long enough not to misgauge his reaction that badly.'

'That thought did cross my mind, but Harrington wouldn't budge. I'll go back to him with this note today, see what he has to say. If they were such old, close friends, I'd have expected Carpenter to confide in him about an intense affair that might blow up his marriage.' Thaxted eases his shoulders back, lengthens his neck.

'I'm glad to see you're being mindful of your posture.'

'One tries. Who's the woman Carpenter was in love with? It could be someone he met in the forces, which casts the net so wide, it's dispiriting to consider.'

I'd best not tell him about Father Hickey's imagined meeting in the NAAFI. 'It has to be a possibility, though.'

'If he didn't meet her during active service, then their paths must have crossed during his work. The fact that he was murdered around here suggests she might be a local. He'd met Pearl Armitage. She's lonely, miserable and frustrated, possibly ripe for romance.'

'She did seem terribly down last time I saw her and I noticed she had a pretty scarf. A lover's gift? But . . . I can't see Pearl as the other woman. She's robust, earthy, speaks her mind and she's got a temper, rows with her dad. Surely not Ronnie's type.'

Thaxted's phone rings, and while he's talking, an idea worms into my head about the kind of woman Ronnie was attracted to. It's worth airing.

When he's finished the call, I ask, 'Did you meet Beverley Fanshawe at Goswick museum?'

'No, Henry Claremont was there on his own.'

'She's his assistant, and it strikes me that she might well be Ronnie's type.' I describe Beverley's pocket-sized figure, her shy manner and her sweetness. 'I could see her being attracted to a decisive man, and we gather that Ronnie liked delicate women. With hindsight, she did seem rather upset about his death, given that she'd only met him briefly.'

Thaxted steeples his fingers under his chin. 'Your anonymous note directed you to Goswick, and perhaps that was nothing to do with the thefts.' He regards me for a moment. 'I propose that we visit the museum together tomorrow morning, and see how the land lies.'

I couldn't be more astonished if he'd produced a rabbit from a hat. 'This is unexpected. Usually you're telling me to keep my distance.'

'I'm not inflexible. You've met Miss Fanshawe, you can smooth the way.'

'I'm glad I have my uses.'

'Is that a yes?'

'I'm game.'

'I hardly expected that you'd refuse.'

'I'll have to square it with Vera, as it's short notice.'

He starts flicking through papers on his desk. 'Well, if you'd rather dust and make beds than join me in this episode of the investigation, that's fine.'

'I don't dust or make beds. I'll sort it.'

'Excellent. Meet me here at ten. Cheerio for now. Please tell the constable on reception that I need to see him. And if you see an apple cart, tread carefully.'

'Pardon?'

'In case you upset it.' He picks up the phone and starts dialling.

I leave him to savour his witticism and hurry back to the Dolphin, steeling myself to negotiate a morning off with Vera.

* * *

The inspector is in a jovial mood in the car the following morning. I'm keeping my eyes averted from his awful top, a creation in green, yellow and purple stripes. A knitted man-ifestation of a bilious attack.

'So, Miss Moore, there's progress. Charles Harrington was extremely cooperative when I caught up with him yesterday. I showed him Carpenter's *billet doux* and he crumpled, agreed that his tale about wanting to get Linda into bed before the marriage was made up.'

'I've been considering that, and the more I did, the more I was convinced he was lying. I'd say that Linda would be perfectly keen to sleep with him before the wedding day. She struck me as an independent woman and deeply in love, so why wouldn't she?'

'Yes, well, we don't need to dwell on their personal arrangements.'

'What did he tell you about the love letter?'

'Your hunch yesterday was right. Carpenter was conducting an affair with someone he'd met locally. Frustratingly, he didn't reveal the woman's identity — or so Harrington insisted. He confided in Harrington after a polo match last month, told him that he'd met a wonderful young woman during the course of his work and fallen in love. The ensuing argument was in fact entirely the other way around from Harrington's first version — it turns out that Harrington was the moralist. He was appalled and concerned about Tommie. He told Carpenter that he must be mad, risking his marriage, and he asked who this other woman was, so that he could give her a piece of his mind. That's why Carpenter was telling him to leave her out of it and it almost came to blows. Harrington claimed that he lied to me because he didn't want Tommie to discover what Ronnie had been up to.'

'The two men must have made peace before the engagement party.'

'Harrington said that once he'd reached home and calmed down, he decided that he had no right to interfere, whatever his estimation of Carpenter's behaviour. He realised that living with Tommie must be difficult and a burden at times — even if, as he put it, it was partly one of his friend's own making. He phoned Carpenter and reassured him that he wouldn't attempt to intervene, but told him in the strongest terms that he should break off the relationship. He claimed that it wasn't mentioned between them again, so he had no idea what Carpenter's intentions were.'

'That seems to rule out Charles as having any motive for murdering his friend.'

'I agree. It'll be interesting to see what the shy Miss Fanshawe has to say. If she is the woman Carpenter was seeing, why hasn't she come forward?'

'Terrified, I should imagine. When you're tucked away in a tiny backwater like Goswick, you don't expect to be connected to a murder.'

When we reach the museum, Henry Claremont tells us that Bev isn't in today.

'She's under the weather again. Her brother called in and said she's peaky, but hopes to be back tomorrow. It's most unlike her to have time off, so I hope she's taking care of herself.'

'Does she live with her brother?' Thaxted asks.

'That's right, it's been the two of them since their mum died. Alan's found it hard to get work since he was demobbed, but he's got some hours at the stables and other bits and pieces now, and he does various maintenance tasks for me here. Is there a problem? Can I help?'

'Just something we need to check with Miss Fanshawe. Nothing to worry about.'

'Oh, I see. When the police turn up, I start hoping that our tapestry or precious ring have been found!'

Claremont gives us Beverley's address, which turns out to be a small end cottage at one side of the road we came in on. Thaxted turns the car and we're there within minutes.

'I met the brother briefly when I was at the museum. Am I allowed to ask questions, Inspector?'

He raises an eyebrow. 'Do I hear Daisy Moore seeking my permission?'

I shield my eyes from the garish vest. 'I'm trying to be polite.'

'Then you may, but allow me to get started.'

Alan opens the door when Thaxted knocks.

'Good morning, I'm Inspector Peter Thaxted, Oxford Police, and this is my associate, Miss Daisy Moore, whom I understand you've met previously. Are you Mr Alan Fanshawe?'

'That's right.'

'I'd like to speak to your sister, Beverley.'

He shifts his feet apart and folds his arms. 'Bev's not too good today.'

'So I understand. We called at the museum. It is important and I won't keep her long.'

'I've got to get to work, and like I said, Bev's not—'

'Who is it, Alan? Is it someone for me?'

Beverley appears behind him, holding a glass of water. She does have a sickly complexion, the shade of old candle wax.

'It's the police,' her brother tells her.

'Oh,' she says. 'I wasn't expecting—'

'We'll come in, if we may, Miss Fanshawe.' Thaxted smiles. 'I believe you're not well, so I'll try to make it quick.'

She gives me a puzzled glance and then taps her brother's arm. 'You get off to work, you mustn't be late.'

He hesitates, gives her a long look. 'Are you sure?'

'Yes! Go on, I'll be fine.'

He snatches a coat from a hook and edges past us. The front door leads straight into a sitting room. We sit on a small, low sofa while Beverley takes an upright chair, still gripping her water. She's in a plain dark blue dress, which is neat but fairly worn, and faded slippers — an outfit for staying at home and not entertaining unexpected visitors. Her hair is combed and held back in two yellow grips.

Thaxted makes the introductions again. 'I believe you've met Miss Moore.'

'Yes, at the museum,' Beverley agrees in a voice so soft, I can barely hear her.

'Sorry to bother you when you're not well,' I tell her.

'Oh, it's just a headache I couldn't shift.' She finishes the water and puts her glass down on a little table. 'I'm sorry, would you like some tea?'

'No, thank you.' Thaxted takes out a notepad. 'Miss Fanshawe, I'm here regarding a rather delicate matter concerning Mr Ronald Carpenter, who was murdered recently. You met him.'

'Yes, when he came to the museum about the thefts and our insurance.'

'And did you meet him on other occasions, away from your workplace?'

'No, just when he visited.' She runs her tongue across her lips.

'Are you quite sure about that?'

'Y . . . Yes.'

Thaxted clears his throat. 'I suspect that you and Mr Carpenter became very close.'

She's sitting on the edge of her chair, her hands clasped tight. 'I don't understand what you mean.'

Thaxted takes out the letter and passes it to her. 'I believe this was intended for you.'

It's a masterstroke. She stares, reads silently with her lips moving, and bursts into tears. We sit while she kisses the letter and weeps quietly but steadily. She searches in a pocket, then in another. Thaxted produces a hanky and reaches across to her, placing it in her hands.

'Why didn't he send this to me?' she asks. 'He must have planned to. I wonder if he wrote it after . . .' She stares at the note as if it might speak to her.

'I'll fetch you more water,' I say, wanting something to do. Watching Beverley is painful. She's like a wounded animal with nowhere to hide.

The kitchen is through a narrow space lined with shelves, a small, cheery room with a view to a thriving vegetable garden. I can see rows of beans, onions and potatoes. I find a glass and fill it, noting with interest the embroidered sampler hanging on the wall by the cooker.

In the sitting room, I put the water beside Beverley, who has her face buried in the hanky. She's still clutching the letter in one hand. Thaxted is doodling in his notepad. The silence is heavy with emotion. I gesture to the inspector for the notepad and he hands it to me. I scribble.

There's a sampler in the kitchen, of a lighthouse with the motto, 'Where There's Drink There's Always Danger.' Maybe she's a Rechabite too?

He purses his lips, nods and taps his pen on the notebook. 'Miss Fanshawe, if you can please try to compose yourself, I do need to discuss your connection to Mr Carpenter.'

She raises her head. Her eyes are like two huge wounds.

'Were you both in the temperance movement?' I ask. 'Is that how you got chatting? Ronnie was a Rechabite.'

She snuffles. 'Yes . . . that is, he wore a little enamel badge on his lapel. I recognised it and we discovered that we shared a belief in abstinence from alcohol. Oh, I miss him!'

'At least you can talk about him now. That must be a relief,' I say soothingly. 'Did anyone else find out about you?'

'No! I can't imagine who told you.'

Thaxted lifts himself from the sofa. It's so near the floor, it must be killing his leg. He moves to stand by the fireplace, leaning an elbow on the mantelpiece.

'Miss Fanshawe,' he says in a neutral voice, '*you* should have told us as soon as you heard the news.'

'I just . . . I realise, but I couldn't face . . . I've been in pieces.'

'That's why you've been off work, isn't it?' I ask. 'Not because of stomach upsets or headaches.'

'Some days I can't face it. It's so lonely, having no one to talk to about what's happened.' She dabs her eyes.

'Dry your tears, please,' Thaxted says. 'I need you to tell me more about your relationship with Mr Carpenter. But first, do you have any hard wooden chairs?'

'Yes, in the kitchen.'

'Thank you, I need one.'

While the inspector goes to fetch a chair, Beverley peers at me through swollen eyelids.

'Is he very cross with me?'

'He has every right to be. Answer his questions truthfully, it will put him in a better mood.'

Thaxted carries a chair in and sits. 'Right, now, take me through this relationship.'

Beverley makes a little sound like Tybalt mewing. 'I met Ronnie after the first break-in, when he came to the museum about our claim. I made tea and we started talking while Henry was preparing some paperwork. That's when I saw his badge and I asked him about it. I told him that my family have been involved with the temperance movement for many years. Ronnie left as we were closing and he offered to walk me home. We talked easily. If it was as if we'd known each other a long time. I didn't expect to see him again.' She takes a gulp of water.

'But then there was a second theft from the museum in January,' Thaxted prompts.

'Yes, and Ronnie came back. I was so pleased to see him — he'd been on my mind, but I'd seen that he wore a wedding ring. When he'd finished dealing with the claim, Henry had to get back to his son, who isn't at all well, and Ronnie and I stayed chatting for a while. For ages, actually. Ronnie was so unhappy in his marriage. He explained that Tommie, his wife, was nervy and deeply reliant on him. He said that since he came back from the war, he'd felt trapped and couldn't face spending the rest of his life with her. I listened to some of his war experiences and he said it was such a relief to talk about them, because he couldn't mention any of it to his wife. Then he asked me if I'd like to have lunch one day and I agreed. It was wrong of me, but I wanted to see more of him.'

She pauses. A horse trots by outside, pulling a scrap cart, the driver calling, 'Any old iron?'

'I half-expected that he'd think better of meeting me again, but he sent me a note a week or so later. We had lunch in a café in Oxford one day. I caught the bus in and Ronnie met me there. It was lovely. We didn't have a lot of time together, but we went for a walk, held hands. That was when we said we loved each other.' She holds her throat, head down.

'It can't have been easy for you to meet, given that he was in London,' Thaxted observes.

'It was difficult. Ronnie made it to Oxford when he had visits in Berkshire, or he drove there straight after work and we snatched some time. We don't have a phone, but I went to the phone box and rang him at his office at times we'd agreed. I wrote to him at his work and he sent letters to me here. It was painful, being apart when we longed to be together. He told me that he wanted to leave Tommie, but he had to be careful because of her health. He worried so terribly about hurting her and I understood that. We promised each other that we'd work things out. We were really in love, and then I heard he'd been found dead and I worried I'd go mad.'

Thaxted rubs his hand through his hair. 'Did Mr Carpenter tell you about the trip to Fernfield?'

'Yes, when we spoke on the phone. It was for his friend's engagement. I realised I wouldn't be able to see him, because his wife would be there. He said that he wanted to get the weekend over and done with, and he was going to tell Tommie that he was leaving when they returned home. Then he'd get in touch with me to plan the future.' She says meekly to the inspector, 'I suppose you have a poor opinion of me.'

He ignores that. 'Miss Fanshawe, where were you on the Friday when Mr Carpenter was shot?'

'Oh . . . I was at home here, doing housework. The museum is closed on Fridays.'

'And your brother?'

'I'm not sure . . . I expect he was at the stables for part of the day, or doing some farm work.' She opens her blue eyes wide. 'You can't suspect that we had anything to do with this!'

'I just follow procedures. I'll leave you my number. Please ask your brother to call me.'

'I will, yes. Can I keep this letter?'

'Not just now. I might be able to give it to you at some point. Please consider this next question carefully: did Mr Carpenter indicate that he was troubled about anything or anyone?'

'No, Inspector. Only his wife, because of the shock she'd have when he told her about us.'

As we're about to leave, I turn back to Beverley.

'I'd try and go to work, if I were you. It's not good being here on your own.'

She doesn't respond, just sinks her head in her hands.

In the car, Thaxted says, 'I can see why you said she's Carpenter's type. That sensitive, pliable quality.'

'And she's younger than him, and eager to fall for the brave, unhappy naval officer with the neurotic wife.'

'There were lies in there somewhere, hidden among what she told us, but I can't put my finger on them.'

'Is she concealing the fact that she's pregnant?'

Thaxted was about to start the engine but his hand freezes on the key. 'What makes you say that?'

'Her face is so washed out. Vera's complexion was like that in the early months of pregnancy. Also, the stomach trouble might be real, not just an excuse.'

'Morning sickness?' He taps the wheel. 'The meetings in Oxford might well have involved hotel rooms that she chose not to mention. Well, if she is, time will tell and she'd hardly have wanted the baby's father dead. But if the brother had twigged what was going on . . . he'll bear scrutiny.'

'If Tommie ever finds out about this, it'll send her into a spin. I'm sorry for all three of them.'

'Even for the two-timing Carpenter?'

I choose my words carefully, aware that I'm talking to a man who has been on horrific battlefields. 'Engaging in war must change you and broaden your horizons, for good or bad. He wouldn't have come back the same Ronnie. I can understand why he might have reckoned life was passing him by, stuck with a timid wife who never wanted to go anywhere or do anything. Then he met a pretty young woman who hung on his every word. Suddenly, life would have seemed full of possibilities. Lots of marriages haven't survived the war.'

Thaxted has a faraway, slightly misty expression. Did he have a relationship that couldn't last the conflict? I find a bag of mints, shake it to bring him back to the moment and offer it to him. He takes one and starts the car.

'That's the problem with murder,' he says briskly. 'It tends to expose all the victim's failings, hopes, dreams and secrets.'

CHAPTER FOURTEEN

I'm shopping in Fernfield High Street, a dreary activity, given that there's so little to buy. I'm managing to get some of life's essentials with my ration card — toothpaste, a comb and soap — when I bump into Linda Merchant.

'Hello!' she says. 'How are you? I heard that you called in to see Tommie. That was sweet of you. How did you find her?'

'Exhausted and a bit adrift. She's glad that Charles is helping her with all the red tape and paperwork.'

'There's loads to do, but she has no one else to give her a hand. It takes up quite a bit of his time. I hope that Charles can sort most of it soon, so that he can concentrate on our big day.' She gives a sour laugh and holds onto her hat in a sudden breeze. 'Some weeks, he seems to spend more time with Tommie than he does with me!'

Once again, I sense that Linda is irritated by her fiancé's needy friend. 'How are your wedding plans going?'

'Very well, thanks. In fact, I'm just on my way to a fitting for my dress. I managed to get some lovely satin and my mum bought lace curtains. Mrs Boswell, the dressmaker, is working wonders with a Simplicity pattern. I told her that I wanted a frothy dream of a dress and she's pulled out all the stops. It has a Sabrina neckline, princess seams and bracelet-length lace sleeves, and the veil will be lace too.' She claps her hands together. 'When I try it on, it's as if I'm floating!'

I've no idea what a Sabrina neckline or princess seams are, but I nod enthusiastically. 'It sounds wonderful.'

'Yes, at least that side of things is going smoothly. Sadly, Charles has to find a new best man now that Ronnie's passed away. He's going to ask his friend Jago.'

We move into a shop doorway to make way for a woman pushing a shopping trolley.

'Jago Villette? I met him in Oxford. I attended a polo match. He's a keen player.'

'Oh, Jago's mad about the game. He's a darling. I keep trying to matchmake for him, but haven't succeeded yet. I expect that's because he's still moping after his village sweetheart.'

'It didn't work out?'

'His parents stuck their noses in and said she wasn't the right sort. They're minor aristocrats with a high opinion of themselves and who Jago should associate with. So, I suppose he had to cave in. His parents hoped that he'd meet someone at Oxford. Sad, really, but it wouldn't be a good idea to fall out with his family, and I'm sure he will meet someone else, especially as he doesn't languish around Goswick so much these days.'

A little jolt, like a buzz of electricity, runs through me. 'Goswick? Who was Jago's sweetheart there?'

'Her name's Beverley. Why d'you ask?' She touches my arm and giggles. 'You've gone a bit wide-eyed. Oh, do *you* like Jago, is that it?'

'Oh, no!'

'Are you sure? I could make a proper introduction!'

Even if I had fallen for Jago and fancied playing gooseberry to his passion for polo, it's hard to see how his family would approve of him romancing a woman who works in a hotel. I'm surprised at Linda's suggestion. Then I remind myself that my association with JB affords me a certain social cachet around here that makes allowances for my station.

'It's not that at all. I'm sure Jago's very nice, but I just wondered. It's a touching story.'

'Well, if you change your mind . . . I must get on for this dress fitting. Lovely to see you again. Give my best to Mr Berrow.'

I turn into the Napolina, needing time to sit and digest this new information. Over a cup of bitter coffee — Jock has run out of sugar — I wonder if Jago might be capable of murder. If he'd found out that Beverley was seeing Ronnie, he might have acted in a fit of jealousy.

Rindi hops into the chair opposite me, fixing me with his bright, impish eyes. He adjusts his fez, takes a nut from his bag and rolls it in his paw.

'I come here because it's the only café in Fernfield, but I wish there was a monkey-free one,' I tell him. I brace for him to throw the nut at me, but instead he pops it in his mouth and chatters loudly before scampering away.

I finish my unpalatable coffee. I need to speak to Charles Harrington as soon as possible.

* * *

Felix is going to wait for me outside Charles Harrington's flat in Oxford. It's just gone 5 p.m. When I phoned, Charles said he'd be back from work by then. Felix and I are heading to the cinema afterwards, to see *Murder in Reverse*.

'I won't be long,' I tell him.

'What's your excuse for visiting Mr Harrington?'

'I don't really have one, so I'll need to tread carefully. I might pretend an interest in Jago Villette and take it from there.'

Felix frowns. 'It sounds very underhand.'

'Yes, it is. But I can't come up with any other reason for asking questions about Jago.' My boss in Whitehall had observed that a capacity for deviousness was useful in decryption — *'It helps to have that sort of wily mind.'*

Charles lives very near Inspector Thaxted and I find myself scanning the street as I ring the doorbell. He answers promptly and shows me into an airy ground-floor flat. The table in the sitting room is loaded with ledgers and folders.

'Do take a seat. I'm just having a beer, would you like one?'

'No, nothing for me thanks. I'm sorry to bother you, I'm sure you're terribly busy with wedding arrangements and supporting Tommie.'

'I am pretty flat out and I'm wading through Ronnie's affairs with the help of his solicitor. Luckily, he was an organised chap, kept everything up to date.' He gestures to the tabletop. 'It's so odd, dealing with his stuff. I still can't get my head around it all. But always happy to help.' He raises his glass. 'Cheers, anyway.'

'Yes, and I do hope all goes well with your wedding plans. I wanted to pop by because I met your friend Jago Villette recently.'

'Did you? Where was that?'

'In the Barn Owl. We chatted for a while. Then I bumped into Linda in Fernfield — she was on her way for a dress fitting.' The more distracting flannel I can wad around this conversation, the better.

'The dress!' He clamps his hand to his forehead. 'There are so many dramas about that garment! Linda and her mum must have spent weeks on it. They don't seem to talk about anything else. Much easier to be a chap and stick a suit on.'

'I'm sure it will be worth all the fuss, and she'll be stunning on your big day. Linda mentioned that Jago used to be very fond of someone in Goswick.'

Charles takes a slow draught of his beer. 'That's right, a girl called Beverley. Seems to have developed a big crush on her in his teens but . . . well . . . his parents said she wasn't really up to snuff socially and reined him in, so it didn't go anywhere. Her family put their oar in as well, reckoned she was getting ideas above her station and it would all end in tears. Poor old Jago tends to get a bit maudlin about her at times, especially when he's had a few. Goes on about her. Drives past her house when he visits home, that sort of thing. He's a bit of a romantic, you see. His parents were right, though, it would never have worked out.'

'They don't meet up?'

'Seems unlikely. I'd imagine she might have married by now. Did Jago yarn about her to you?'

'We did have a long chat.' Before it occurs to him to ask why I'm interested, I steer us back to the safe topic of the wedding. 'I believe Jago's going to be your best man.'

'Yes, he's agreed to step in for Ronnie. It'll be so strange, not having him there. We went back a long way.'

'It must be very hard for you. Well . . . I've a friend waiting, best not to keep him hanging about and I should let you get on with all your work. I'm sure Linda has lots of jobs for you to do as well.'

'Don't remind me,' he groans. 'I have to help decide on menus this week. I honestly don't care what we eat, as long as there's enough of it and plenty of champagne!'

Felix puts down the book he's reading when I rejoin him. 'How did it go?'

'You'll be pleased to hear that I hardly had to practise any deception. Charles had too much on his mind to focus on the reason for my random questions. I did establish that Jago still has nostalgic yearnings for Beverley. What if he saw her with Ronnie around Goswick when he was visiting home, or maybe spotted them in Oxford and decided to do away with him?'

'On the basis of, "If I can't have her, no one else will"? Isn't that a bit far-fetched after what was effectively a teenage crush?'

'I'm not sure that it is. Some people stay deeply attached to their first loves. And Jago would know that Ronnie was married. He could have seen it as a way of protecting Beverley and saving her from the clutches of an adulterer. Charles described Jago as a romantic. He's a man with frustrated, unfulfilled longings. Also, Ronnie would have been happy to meet Jago, who could have pretended that he wanted to chat about polo or something to do with Charles's wedding. I'd better contact Inspector Thaxted tomorrow. He needs to check Jago's whereabouts at the time of the murder.'

For a man with an unworldly manner and the abstracted air of an academic, Felix transforms into a racing driver behind the wheel of a car, zipping around bends as if someone is trying to overtake him. We zoom into the city. I find myself pressing down on an imaginary brake.

'Does it annoy you, Daisy, that you have to defer to the inspector?'

'Yes and no. I note your expression of disbelief. Sometimes, it's really maddening. I pretend that we're a partnership, with me as the sleeping partner. I'm fooling myself. I'm sure that Thaxted sees me as an annoying rash that keeps coming back.'

'I expect he values you more than you realise.'

'I wouldn't place any bets on that. "Intermittently tolerates" would be a more apt description.'

There's a billboard outside the cinema with a poster advertising the film. It depicts a horrified man with staring eyes, his face tinted a sickly green. In the bottom left-hand corner is a woman in a clinging red evening dress — or possibly a negligée — standing by as two men fight on the ground below her.

'He looks as if he's eaten bad fish,' Felix says. 'It claims to be "an unusual British thriller". I hope it lives up to the publicity.'

'The clue's in the title. It's about a man who's released from prison after wrongfully serving time for the murder of his wife's lover. He discovers that his victim faked his death and is very much alive.'

Felix isn't burdened by leaps of imagination. 'Sounds absurd, but I'll suspend disbelief.'

The queue moves forward and Felix and I have an important discussion about whether to buy sweets at the kiosk or have an ice cream in the interval.

* * *

131

The following evening, I'm about to fetch my bike and cycle home when Pearl Armitage turns up at the hotel, sidling in with hands in pockets.

'I was passing by, been out fetching supplies, wondered if I might catch you,' she says off-handedly.

'Well, you have. How are you?'

'Fine, thanks. I made you this.' She rummages in her bag and shoves something at me.

It's a beret, beautifully crocheted in the ruby-flecked wool I gave her. 'Thank you, that's very kind.' I try it on in front of the mirror in the hallway. 'Perfect fit!'

'It's just a thing. You don't have to wear it.'

'Really, I like it.'

Her hair is loose around her shoulders, a dark chocolate colour and she's wearing a skirt and thin sweater, teamed with her pretty scarf. She seems a bit perkier. Maybe it's because she's away from the gloomy farm and her autocratic father.

'Anyway,' she says, turning as if to go.

'Do you fancy a drink? We could go in the bar. It was quiet earlier.'

'I don't want to be a bother.'

This self-deprecation is tiresome. 'You're not. Let me buy you a drink as a proper thanks for the beret. No one's ever made me one before.'

We have the bar to ourselves. Pearl says she'll have a gin and orange and I pour myself a whisky.

She glances around, fiddling with her scarf. 'This is nice, isn't it? I've not been in here before.'

The bar is at its best in the evening, with a fire flickering and the low lamps concealing the wear and tear, although I always find that it smells as if the boozy breath of hundreds of guests is lingering in the air.

'It's not bad. The hotel is going to be redecorated soon. It does need refreshing, the paintwork's terribly scratched.'

'That's always been my dream, to have my own place that I could decorate. I'd paint it white and green, and crochet the cushion covers and bedspread. In the evening, when

I came home from work, I'd have cheese on toast and listen to the wireless. I might even manage to keep a boyfriend!' She downs some drink. 'Pigs might fly.'

It's a modest enough ambition. 'What's stopping you having a boyfriend now?'

'My dad!' She flips up a coaster and slaps it back down. 'Any chap comes anywhere near me, Dad frightens him off, gives me all that rubbish about "He's not good enough for you." More like he's terrified of losing his free farm labourer.'

I recall Mr Armitage's grouchy manner. 'I can see your problem, but a man might come along who's crazy about you and willing and able to stand up to your dad.'

She smiles to herself, trails a finger along her scarf. 'Funny you should say that. There might be a . . . no, I won't say anything more and jinx it.'

'You're keen on someone?'

'Maybe. How about you?'

'No, I'm footloose. I like it that way. What job would you do if you could choose?'

'Work in a wool shop,' she says with a flash of spirit. 'I love wools — the different hues, textures and strengths. And I could do demonstrations for people and help them with their difficult patterns.' She taps a foot on the dingy carpet. 'I bet you think I'm pathetic.'

'Why would I?'

'You've got a job in town and you can go where you like. You've probably got somewhere decent to live.'

'I have struck lucky with my accommodation, but I'm not always convinced that I'm where I should be, doing what I want.'

'What about your parents?'

'They're both dead.'

'Oh, sorry.'

We both concentrate on our drinks. When Pearl gives me a sidelong glance, she reminds me of one of her cows, interested but hesitant. At last she shifts nearer and says, 'What would you do if you were worried that someone might have done something wrong, but you didn't want to cause a load of trouble for them?'

I put my glass on the table and cup my hands around it. 'I suppose it would depend on the nature of what this person had done. Whether or not it was serious or illegal.'

'What if it was illegal?'

'I'd have to consider reporting the person.'

'Even if you knew them well?'

'I'm not saying it wouldn't be difficult, but yes.'

'Right.'

'Are you referring to your dad?'

'I can't say.' Her lips are sticky and shining from the orange juice.

'If you tell me more, I might be able to help.'

'I told you, I can't.'

'Did you send me an anonymous letter?'

'Me? No!'

I believe her. 'It's difficult to help you with your question without more detail.'

She shrinks back at that and fumbles for her bag. 'I'd best get home and unload the stuff in the jeep.'

'You haven't finished your drink.'

She knocks it back. 'Thanks. See you.'

And with that, she's gone. Did she mean that her father had set the fires in their barns? But why bring that up now, when the insurance is settled and it's old news?

I hold the beret up to the light. It has a delicate lacework pattern. Something's eating Pearl and she wants to open up about it, but I'm not sure that I can find a way to help her unburden herself.

CHAPTER FIFTEEN

JB is visiting the Dolphin to discuss the refurbishments with Vera. The *kommandantin* has taken an arms-length interest in the plans, keen to stress that the décor must be *'seemly'* and *'nothing flashy or common'*. She's stipulated the — in her eyes — tasteful wallpapers to be used throughout, which will be supplied by a London company. It's amusing to watch Vera's butter-wouldn't-melt manner with JB. Ray wouldn't approve; he'd accuse her of being a lackey to the capitalist boss. JB, who is apologising for the proposed wallpaper in the dining room, which features birds of paradise, is an unlikely oppressor of the workers. He's in full dandyish mode, wearing sand-coloured cords and a lemon shirt with a red scarf knotted at the open neck. He opens doors for Vera as they tour the hotel and has her all of a flutter.

'You do have a way with the ladies,' I tell him when they've concluded their discussions.

He twirls an imaginary moustache. 'Dunno watcha mean, me old china. Shall we have a cuppa? We can go to that rather low café you patronise.'

We walk to the Napolina, JB informing me that he has an audition next week for a part in *The Glass Menagerie*.

'So I gotta practise talkin' American, honey.'

JB drops into so many accents, I live with many versions of him. For most of February, he spoke in a Welsh lilt while he was recording a part in *The Corn Is Green*.

'Look-it here!' he continues in his American persona. 'If it ain't the local sheriff! Howdy, pardner, what brings you to our part of town?'

Inspector Thaxted is coming towards us, a canvas knapsack over one shoulder. He wrinkles his eyebrows. 'Inhabiting a role, Jeffrey?'

'Sure am. Good to see you, Peter. Join us for a cup of the Napolina's finest.'

Thaxted checks his watch. 'I can spare ten minutes. Lead on. Did you enjoy the film, Miss Moore?'

'Were you at the cinema? I didn't see you.'

'Heavens, I don't have time for such amusements when I'm investigating a murder.'

I refuse to give him the satisfaction of asking how he's found out I was there. We reach the café and place our orders, coffee for the inspector, and tea and a slice of apple tart for me and JB to share.

'Is that dratted monkey around?' JB asks.

'Having a kip at present. He had a busy night of it,' Jock replies darkly.

Thaxted takes off his hat and fans himself. 'You can breathe, Miss Moore, you weren't being tracked by the county Gestapo. I met Mr Koller outside the station and we passed the time of day. He said you'd been to the cinema and he found the film cheap and ridiculous.'

'Just how I like them,' JB butts in. 'Was this *Murder in Reverse*?'

'Yes,' I reply. 'It wasn't so bad. A bit hammy.'

We sit at a corner table. It rained heavily earlier in the day and the café smells of damp cloth and stale cigarettes.

JB sniffs. 'Ah, eau de Fernfield. How shall I divide this tart, Daisy? Down the middle or across? These life decisions are so harrowing!'

'Down the middle, then there'll be no quibbles.' I turn to the inspector. 'Any update on Jago Villette?'

'Yes. On the Friday in question, he was off work with a head cold. He told me that he stayed in bed all day because he wanted to be fit for the evening's celebrations. He shares a flat with a friend, who left for work without seeing Mr Villette, who was there when he arrived home at five thirty.'

I eat a spoon of apple tart, which is much too sour, but the pastry's crisp. 'What did he have to say about Beverley?'

'He was refreshingly forthright and admitted that he still misses her and, yes, he drives past her house when he visits his parents. He stated that they haven't met for a long time. I decided not to name names for now, so that Mrs Carpenter *might* be spared hearing about her husband's infidelity, but I asked him if he'd seen Miss Fanshawe with another man. He said not. He told me that he hadn't seen Carpenter since April, when he attended a polo match. He has no alibi, but he doesn't strike me as a killer.'

JB dabs his lips with a napkin. 'Anyone can become a killer, surely, if the circumstances are right,' he says. 'One of my intense lady fans might take exception to Daisy's letter of reply and, enraged by unrequited yearning, come after me with a hatpin. *Murder at the Stage Door.* Crime of passion and all that.' He gestures at his remains of the tart. 'Those apples needed to be introduced to the sugar bowl.'

'True, any of us is capable of murder and Villette might have been enraged at another man usurping him,' Thaxted agrees. 'However, I have other suspects in my sights. This coffee's flavourless.'

'Felix makes an excellent cup,' I tell him. 'He adds a pinch of cinnamon to warm milk, Austrian style.'

Thaxted inclines his head. 'A man of many talents, indeed. I must away and chase villains.'

I open my mouth to query who his other suspects are, but he's easing towards the door with his stick and greeting the vicar, the Reverend Lipton, who's arrived clutching a pile of church magazines.

'Sounds like he's ahead of you with the case, petal.' JB smiles impishly. 'Have you got a move up your sleeve?'

'I'm a bit stumped, to be honest. Maybe I'll talk to Beverley Fanshawe again.' I watch Thaxted pause outside the window, leaning against it for a moment. 'Has the inspector ever had a romance?'

'Oh, Peter had quite a swagger to him before the war. Personable chap, athletic — played tennis extremely well — sociable and popular with the ladies. I saw him with a few on his arm. He lost a fair bit of spirit as well as his health in Egypt. His mother told Rosalind that he's had to go on stronger medication because his leg muscles are so damaged.' JB returns the vicar's greeting. 'Good day to you, Reverend! Yes, we'll take a copy of your magazine. How much?'

I wait while the vicar chats about the church spire and how grateful he is that Mrs Berrow has made a generous contribution. It's hard to imagine the gaunt inspector with a swagger. These days, a lady on his arm would be propping him up.

* * *

A couple of days later, I borrow Felix's car and drive back to Goswick. I'm all at sea with the nuances of this case and convinced that I'm missing something obvious. It's best to continue asking questions, hoping that they'll lead me somewhere. I've checked that the museum is closed today, so I hope to find Beverley at home.

It takes a few minutes for her to open the door. I'm about to give up when she inches it back. She's perspiring and deathly pale.

'Oh, it's you.' Her breath is sour with a tang of acid drops.

'Is there something wrong?'

She stares at me, her face working, and then reaches out and grips my arm. 'I've lost my baby.'

That's when I notice the rivulet of blood on the inside of her bare leg. 'I'd better come in.'

Inside, she collapses on the sofa and I sit beside her.

'There's blood on your leg.'

'Oh, I didn't see . . . I must have missed it.'

'When did this happen?'

'Not long ago. I had cramps and then a lot of blood came. There was such a mess.'

'How many weeks pregnant were you?' I've no idea why I'm asking, as my grasp of miscarriage is minimal. My mother had two before I was born. I recall her telling a neighbour that it was as if her insides had dropped out and she was as weak as water.

'About two months. I'd only told Ronnie. He was over the moon.' She starts weeping.

I take in her greasy hair and inflamed eyes. She had a wholesome appearance the first time I saw her, but this morning she looks shop-soiled. 'I'm terribly sorry. I'd better drive you to hospital.' The nearest is the cottage hospital at Fernfield.

'Oh, no! I can't go to hospital. They'll find out. I can't face it.' She's scrunching the hem of her skirt, digging her fingers in the folds.

'Beverley, you have to. If you hadn't miscarried, you'd have had to seek medical help at some point. You can't keep this to yourself and deal with it alone, you need to be checked over.'

'I can't bear it, I can't!'

'I'm sure that Ronnie would want you to look after yourself. If he was here, he'd say the same as me.' I listen to myself spouting nonsense, hoping that it will be effective.

Beverley slumps against me. 'Oh, this is awful. I've no idea what to do!'

'You can't stay here alone in this state. Where's Alan?'

That makes her shoot upright. 'He mustn't find out! He's at work.'

When was she planning to tell her brother? When a large bump appeared, or was she going to present him with a bundle containing a nephew or niece one day? 'Come on, then. If we go now, you can be back at home before he is. You must — it's important, Beverley.'

'All right. Please, can you just go to the bathroom first? I tried to clean up, but I'm not sure . . . The cramps were so awful. I don't want Alan to see . . .'

I climb the steep stairs to the tiny bathroom. There are some red trails on the toilet seat and in the sink. I wash the blood off and scrutinise the floor. There's a glob of something I'd rather not examine on the lino by the bath, so I pick it up in toilet paper and flush it away. I grab a towel from the rail as I exit. I don't want to have to explain to Felix why there are blood smears in his car.

It's a warm day, but Beverley is shivering. I give her a glass of water while I find her a coat and make sure she has her bag. I spread the towel on the passenger seat of the car, glad that there's no one about, and settle her inside.

She sighs and snuffles beside me. 'Ronnie had always wanted children, but he said his wife was too fragile. He was so thrilled when I told him. We were going to be together before the baby was born. Ronnie said he'd rent a flat and it would be just the three of us. Now I've lost them both.' She cries again, that hopeless, drained kind of weeping that's worse than enraged howls.

I drive fast along the country lanes. This miscarriage has to be for the best in the long run. Beverley's life in Goswick with her illegitimate baby would have been no bed of roses. I've admired Vera's courage in handling Ray's bigamy and her consequent unmarried status, as well as his imprisonment while she's pregnant. But she's older and more mature than Beverley, and has her mother as well as her baby's father for support. Beverley has had to keep her mourning and this child a secret. The strain must have been awful and might even have caused the miscarriage. I'm furious with Ronnie Carpenter for leaving her in this predicament. And if he hadn't been shot, would he have abandoned Tommie for her? The jury's out, as far as I'm concerned. There's a lot of mileage between wishing, making promises and taking action.

To distract her, I ask, 'What time will Alan be home?'

'Teatime, he said. He's helping Tony with his roof for the next couple of weeks.'

I glance across at her. 'Do you mean Tony Armitage at Broadmeadow Farm?'

'Yes. Alan does some days there now and again. I wish he could get something regular instead of having to do all these here-and-there jobs, but he says beggars can't be choosers.'

When we reach the hospital, I tell Beverley that I'll wait and drive her home. I'm not sure that she's heard me as a nurse leads her away. She's gone into shock, walking with a heavy tread, her eyes vacant. She's nothing like the pretty, carefully dressed young woman I met at the museum. I can't help recalling all those folk songs about girls discarded by careless lovers, often with a baby on the way.

To pass the time, I read the parish magazine that JB bought from the vicar and stuffed in my bag. It's called *St Clement's Chimes* with half a dozen pages produced in patchy ink. There's a timetable of services, news of a June bring-and-buy sale, articles about social events in the parish, an update on the fund to restore the spire, some recipes under 'How to Make the Most of Your Ration Book', notices of births and deaths, prayers for the sick, and a section headlined 'Supporting Our Returning Heroes'. This discusses the challenges facing demobbed troops, and details charities that can help those who are struggling as well as fundraising activities. I note a paragraph expressing appreciation.

Our thanks are due to Mr and Mrs Henry Claremont, who have taken time from caring for their own son to organise a very successful concert in the church hall in aid of injured and disabled service personnel. Miss Emily Lowden played her flute beautifully, Alfred Harker gave us some rousing tunes on his mouth organ and the children's choir sang with spirit. We wish Michael Claremont well in his ongoing recuperation. He is in our daily prayers.

I remember Beverley's comment that Henry Claremont's son is unwell. I start on the 'Know Your Scriptures' crossword, which will be something of a challenge as I'm only nominally religious and I've never read the Bible. I've filled in one across ('Armageddon'), but I'm puzzling over two across ('The wife of Moses') and wishing that Father Hickey was on hand, when Beverley reappears, walking carefully.

'Well?' I ask.

'The doctor said I can go home. There are no complications. He gave me aspirin and told me to rest and relax with a hot water bottle.'

'That's good. I'll drive you back. It's just three o'clock, so you've plenty of time before Alan gets in.'

In the car, Beverley's silent for a while, her hands covering her abdomen. Then she blurts, 'What will I tell people? They'll wonder why I'm poorly. The doctor said it could be a week or so before I'm well enough to go to work.'

'Say it's personal, women's troubles. Keep it vague, and mention that you've seen a doctor about it. It's almost the truth, and people will be too embarrassed to pry. The same goes for Alan. Most men are terrified by female plumbing, so he's unlikely to ask questions.'

'Thanks, yes, I'll do that.' She turns to me. 'You won't tell Inspector Thaxted about this, will you? I'd be mortified if he found out. He might mention it to other people. I can just about bear it if I'm sure that it's not general knowledge. I'd never live it down.'

I can't see why Thaxted should be informed. He's already aware of the possibility that Beverley was pregnant and factoring it into his investigation. 'I won't tell anyone.'

'Thanks. It means a lot that I can rely on you.'

'How are you feeling now?'

'Nothing much. Numb.'

'I'm not surprised after what you've been through.'

'D'you mind if I don't talk about it?'

'No problem.' I'm relieved to drop the subject. 'Actually, I wanted to ask you about Henry Claremont's son, Michael. Did he sustain bad injuries during the war?'

'Awful, yes. He was in a tank regiment and he was badly burned, lost both legs and his lungs were damaged. He's at home now, but poorly. Henry told me he has awful nightmares every night. Oh, goodness, Henry will be so disappointed that I'm missing work again. I hate letting him down, and I've already had time off.'

'Would you like me to call on him and explain that you're unwell? I'll phrase it carefully.'

'Oh, that's good of you. Please, yes. I just can't face any questions. He lives across from the school house, number eighteen. Tell him I'll be back as soon as I can.'

In the cottage, Beverley goes straight to bed while I make her a mug of tea and fill a hot water bottle. Her bedroom is as I expected, a little haven of pastel colours and flowered prints. She has two dolls and a teddy on her dressing table. I'm pleased to see her enjoying the tea because I have a final question, the one I came to ask before events took over.

'I've discovered that we have a mutual acquaintance, Jago Villette. Do you see much of him these days?'

'Dear Jago.' Her voice is fond. 'Hardly ever. We were sweet on each other one time, but it didn't work out. I haven't seen him for ages. Another bit of my life that didn't go well. I expect I'll be left on the shelf and turn into an old maid.' She sinks back into her pillows.

'You're shattered, so I'll leave you now. I'm sure sleep is what you need.'

'Thanks again. I'm so sorry to have been such a bother.'

She sounds remarkably like Tommie. 'No bother, I'm glad I turned up when I did.' And Beverley has given me background that's filling in uncharted landscape in the map of this case.

'You won't . . . You won't tell anyone about this, will you?'

'Scout's honour. My lips are sealed.'

She pulls up the blanket, says bleakly, 'I'd chosen names: Ronald for a boy, Edith for a girl, after my mum.'

I say cheerio. I don't cry easily, but I'm rubbing my eyes as I leave the cottage.

CHAPTER SIXTEEN

The Claremonts' is a modest house with a front garden resembling a building site, with piles of bricks, a concrete mixer, a wheelbarrow and bags of sand covering the space. A man in spattered trousers and huge boots whips round the corner from a side gate and trundles the wheelbarrow away. The door is answered by a harassed woman in her sixties, her grey hair twisted in a loose bun.

'Is Mr Claremont in? My name's Daisy Moore and I have a message for him from Beverley.'

'Come in, dear, come in. You'll have to forgive the din, we have builders here, so we're all at sixes and sevens. I'm Eileen Claremont, by the way.'

She's thin and angular, not at all the well-upholstered wife that Mrs Claus should be. She takes me through to a cluttered back room, where Henry Claremont is sitting at a drop-leaf dining table, a lined notepad with headings and rows of figures open in front of him. There's a teapot with a knitted cosy and a plate of biscuits at his elbow.

'Henry, this lady wants to speak to you.'

He peers up at me through his half-moon glasses. 'Hello, Miss Moore, this is an unexpected pleasure. Do sit down, if you can find a space.'

'Here.' Mrs Claremont snatches a pile of laundry from a dining chair. 'Can I get you a cup of tea? The pot's fresh. The kettle's on all day for our workmen, I can't keep up with their thirst.'

'Thanks. What are you having built?' Through the back window I can see more piles of bricks and two men constructing a wall.

The couple exchange glances in a weighted silence. She disappears through a door and rattles crockery.

'I didn't mean to be intrusive,' I say.

Mr Claremont gathers his beard in one hand and squeezes it. 'No, no, my dear, not at all. We're having a ground-floor extension made for Michael, our son. He can't get upstairs these days, got badly beaten up in the war. It's important for him to have his own space, where he can move around in his wheelchair.'

His wife bustles back in with a cup for me. 'We've been on top of one another since Michael came home. He's been sleeping in the sitting room and then there's the equipment he needs taking up space. He's gone for his therapy today. At least that gets him out for a while.'

I imagine that it's a relief for both Michael and his parents. 'You'll be pleased when his extension is finished.'

There's a huge bang and thud followed by a loud burst of swearing. The window frame rattles and a man calls 'Timber!' amid laughter.

Mrs Claremont clutches her chest, pours tea for me and tops up her husband's cup. 'Some days, I'm sure they're trying to give me a heart attack! We certainly will be over the moon when it's done and we get our peace back. These things always end up costing more than you bargained for and everything's scarce or so expensive these days. And then there are the medical bills — we're paying for specialist therapy for Michael.' She gestures at her husband's calculations. 'Henry's always trying to balance the books, aren't you, dear?'

'Now, no need to bother Miss Moore with our troubles.' He moves the milk jug towards me. 'Do help yourself, and to biscuits.'

'I'd best tell you why I'm here. I called in to see Beverley because we have mutual friends. She's not terribly well, had to see a doctor.'

'I'm sorry to hear that,' Mr Claremont says. 'Anything we can do to help?'

'What ails her?' his wife asks. 'She does seem to have been poorly lately.'

'It's a bit delicate and she's embarrassed about it, that's why I said I'd pop by and tell you. *Female* problems.'

'Oh!' Mr Claremont blinks and fusses with his glasses. 'Well, I hope she's better soon.'

'She just needs to rest a bit and then she'll be fine.'

'Her mum had troubles down below,' Mrs Claremont says. 'I expect it can run in families.'

Thank goodness for euphemisms. 'That might well be,' I agree.

'I'll call and make sure Bev is getting enough rest,' she tells me. 'I'll take her some oxtail soup, that'll build her up. Alan's a decent chap, but I don't suppose he can find his way around the kitchen.'

'I'm sure that will help, but maybe not for a day or two. She's so tired, the doctor's told her to stay in bed.'

'And there I was, Henry, worrying that you'd caught some kind of bug from Beverley,' his wife says fondly. 'You've not been too bright yourself recently, have you?'

'It's nothing,' he says, 'just all this blasted chaos and noise going on all the time. Thank heavens it's nice and quiet at the museum.'

'Apart from the thefts,' Eileen says. 'Those haven't done much for your health, dear.' She shakes her head at me. 'I keep urging Henry to hand the museum over to someone else, but he won't listen. It's his baby and he can't cut the ties.'

'You know how important it is to me,' he mumbles.

'I do.' She puts a hand on his. 'I suppose at least you've got somewhere to escape to,' she adds with a hint of envy. 'I'm stuck with that lot out there.'

The concrete mixer shudders into grinding, deafening action. I take that as my cue to go. 'Thank you for the tea. I'll let you get on now, you've lots to cope with.'

As I'm unlocking the car, the vicar of St Clement's arrives, hurrying up to the door. This time, Mr Claremont opens it and they disappear inside, the Reverend Lipton gesticulating in the manner of a man in a flap.

I sit in the car for a while. A shower of rain passes, a brief burst of bullets on the windscreen. I picture all the people I've been contacting since Ronnie died and place them in their home and work locations. A pattern starts forming in my head. I've no idea if it makes any sense and some of it is based on supposition. Maybe Ronnie's murder is nothing to do with his affair with Beverley. Not a crime of passion at all, but a planned execution.

* * *

I'm at work the next morning, on my way to take Amelia Ward a tray of tea. Sharon stops hoovering to catch my arm as I pass her on the stairs.

'Did you hear that the police have made an arrest? They got Mr Carpenter's killer. That lanky inspector's got more to him than he lets on.'

'Who told you that?'

'Maggie at the greengrocer. It was in the *Oxford News* this morning.'

'Who's been arrested?'

'I can't tell you. Good news, though. Mrs Carpenter will be relieved.'

Mrs Ward wants to gossip, but I cut her short, saying I'm busy. She says that her Harry always had time to listen, and she's wailing if only she could be with him when I escape from her. Vera's in the kitchen badgering Leslie about recipes, so I use the office phone to ring Peter Thaxted in Oxford. I have to wait a couple of minutes before I'm put through.

'I heard a rumour that you've made an arrest,' I say as soon as he comes on the line.

'And good morning to you, Miss Moore. I can confirm that we're holding a suspect in custody.'

'Who is it?'

'It's not been made public yet, so if I tell you, you must keep it to yourself.'

'I have sworn lifelong secrecy to the state.'

'I'm still taking a risk if I inform you.'

'I can be as silent as the grave.'

A long pause, which I'm sure he's enjoying, and then he says, 'Bill Mackie.'

'What's his motive?'

'Mr Mackie's not saying much yet, except to deny murder, but I have evidence that he saw Ronnie Carpenter with Beverley in Oxford, so I'd say possibly blackmail that went wrong.'

'That must be the secret he was referring to regarding Ronnie.'

'Indeed. Also, we found a Browning pistol, the same make as the one used in the shooting, hidden in his flat.'

'Well . . . I suppose I should say congratulations.'

'You don't sound convinced.'

'Are you?'

'Not entirely, but there's enough to start building a case. I have to go. And cheer up, at least there's one less lothario on the streets.'

I replace the receiver and stare at the calendar of the Cotswolds on the wall. May features a bucolic scene of cows, milkmaids and milk churns outside a dairy, taking me back to my conviction that the unravelling of this murder lies not with a small-time crook in Oxford, but at Broadmeadow Farm.

Vera sticks her head through the door. 'Daydreaming? I need you to deal with the electrician, who'll be here any time now. He can have one cuppa while he's working, but keep Sharon away from him. When he came about the wiring, she was all over him like a rash, and he lapped it up. I'm not paying her to waste her shift on her love life.'

'Is he handsome?'

'So-so. I'm not sure that concerns Sharon. He's not married, that's his main advantage.'

'It's hard for single women. There aren't enough men to go around these days.'

'That's not my problem, I'm sure. She needs to keep her mind on her job.'

'I'll do my best to be a hindrance, but I can't promise to stand in the way of romance.'

'Hilarious. You could get a job as a comedian. Now, about the refurbishment — it'll start at the beginning of October, when I'm back at work, so we'll have to try and keep upheaval to a minimum. I went through all the costings with Mr Berrow and he's agreed. The price of things, it's just as well Mrs Berrow bails this place out when push comes to shove.'

'Do we rely on her money to survive?'

'I don't want to speak out of turn . . . Not quite, but the balance sheet's not always in the best of health these days. We did a good trade before the war, turned a tidy profit. I'm sure things will pick up when people start to get back on their feet and the economy improves. That's what Mr Berrow expects too, and he reckons we might as well get the place up to scratch so that we're ready. I'm drawing up a plan one room at a time so that we can maintain guest numbers.' She straightens the calendar, although it's perfectly aligned and then says with a classic Vera U-turn, 'Anyway, Dreamy Daisy, I can't stand around here all day chatting to you, I've things to do.'

'You started the conversation.'

'What? Yes, well . . . let's both push on and remember, only one cuppa for the electrician.'

CHAPTER SEVENTEEN

The postman is cycling towards me as I near the track to Broadmeadow Farm. He waves and slows, pulling into the verge.

'Not a bad day, weather might hold. You heading to the farm? Fancy taking a couple of letters, save my legs?'

He's a she, I realise, with a merry voice and strands of hair escaping from the back of her cap.

'Just pop them in my basket.'

'Ta, that's a real help. I'm running late.' She selects the letters, drops them in and rides away.

There are two ladders propped at the front of the farmhouse when I cycle into the yard and dismount. Alan Fanshawe is standing at the bottom of one of them smoking a cigarette and squinting at the sky from under a peak cap.

'Hello, I'm Daisy. We met at your house.'

'Right. You were with that policeman. Bev said he was asking about the thefts at the museum.'

I'm glad that she'd found a plausible excuse for our visit. 'He just had a few questions.'

'Uh-huh. What were you doing with him?'

'He's a friend of my boss, he happened to be giving me a lift.'

He weighs this up, tilting his cap back and sucks in some nicotine. It doesn't sound credible to me, but he appears to buy it.

'Has Beverley got over her illness now?' I ask.

'She's not so bad. Just some bug or other. What brings you here, then?'

'I've some more wool for Pearl.'

He has an impassive manner, the kind Peter Thaxted excels at. 'She said you gave her some before. Generous of you.'

'I work at the Dolphin and guests leave stuff behind. Pearl might as well make use of it.' I've actually bought these skeins myself to oil the wheels of this visit. I point to my beret. 'She made me this.'

'Did she? I'm surprised she found the time, the way she has to work her fingers to the bone for her old man. Are you a new friend?' There's a hint of antagonism in his voice, despite his smile.

'Perhaps. It's always good to find friends in life. Are you mending the roof?'

'That's the general idea. Pearl's fed up of the rain dripping in her room, says it keeps her awake nights. Her dad's finally come round to seeing sense and doing something about it.'

'I suppose the insurance money has come in handy around the place. Are they rebuilding the barns that were destroyed?'

'I don't ask Tony any questions. He doesn't take kindly to people poking around in his business. It's the one thing I agree on with him. We both like our privacy.' He adds with distinct dislike, 'Apart from that, I don't have much time for the man.'

'Still, best not to bite the hand that feeds.'

'What?'

'He's paying you to fix the roof.'

'Right.' He pinches his half-smoked cigarette, takes a tin from his pocket and tucks it in. 'You seem very informed about what's going on.'

'I get to hear things.'

'What do you do at the Dolphin?'

'Bit of this, bit of that.'

'Don't you have any guests at the moment? How come you're not at work?'

'Time off for good behaviour. Is Pearl in?'

He points a thumb at the kitchen. 'She's busy cooking something. Everything has to be ready to her dad's timetable.'

'I'll just say hello.'

'Don't keep her too long. She's got a lot on today, like every other day.'

He shins up the ladder as I knock on the door. Pearl opens it, holding a grater with strings of cheese hanging from the holes.

'Oh, it's you.' She leans forward, glancing up.

'I just said hello to Alan. He's gone back up to the roof. I brought you some more wool.'

'Come in, then.' She's dressed in brown breeches, belted at the waist with a dark green shirt tucked in. The silk scarf is at her neck.

The kitchen is awash with savoury aromas. 'What are you making?'

'Potato, leek and cheese pie. Nothing exciting.' She wipes her hands on a tea towel and looks out of the front window. 'I can't offer you tea today, I'm a bit rushed and this pie needs to be ready for dinner.'

'Sure, I don't want to hold you up. Here's the wool. That's a pretty brooch, is it new?' It's leaf-shaped and pinned at the neck of her shirt.

Her voice rises. 'It's just paste. I picked it up at a jumble sale a while back. This wool's new, though.' She sniffs it.

'Yes, whoever left it must only have just bought it.' I point upwards. 'I'm glad you won't be rained on in bed any longer.'

'About time!'

'Alan seems to have a fair few skills.'

'He can turn his hand to anything. He did a bit of roofing before the war.'

'Where did he fight?'

'All over. He was one of the lucky ones, came back without a scratch.' She takes a simmering pan from the hob and stands at the sink with her back to me, straining potatoes in a colander. Steam gushes up and she holds her head back.

'Have you thought any more about that problem you mentioned when we had a drink?'

She lifts the colander and shakes it. 'Forget I said anything. I've sorted it out.'

If the problem did concern her father, she might be too frightened of him to act. 'If you're sure. I'm happy to help if I can.'

Her rigid back speaks volumes. 'I was being daft, making something out of nothing. Dad likes dinner on the table at one, so . . .'

I'm not wanted and I sense that's it about more than the meal being on time. She's cheerier than when she came to the hotel, but also more guarded.

'Thanks again for the wool, I appreciate it,' she says at the door.

'Come and have another drink sometime.'

'I will if I get a chance.'

I mount my bike and cycle away. The sun is full, the air clear and bright, even if it does stink of rotting dung. One thing I'm convinced of, from Pearl's tone — she didn't buy that brooch for herself and I can guess who did.

* * *

That afternoon, Beverley Fanshawe phones me at the hotel.

'I hope you don't mind me calling you at work, I expect you're busy.'

'It's quiet at the moment. How are you?'

'A lot better, thank you. I slept for a whole day and when I woke up, I was much stronger.'

'I'm glad. I saw your brother at Broadmeadow Farm earlier. I hope he's looking after you.'

'Thanks, yes. I told him what you suggested, about women's troubles, and he didn't ask any questions.'

'I called on Mr Claremont and told him you weren't well.'

'Yes. Actually, that's why I'm ringing.'

'About what I told him? I mentioned female problems, that's all.'

Her voice is only just above a whisper. 'No, that's fine, it's . . . well . . . I popped to the museum yesterday. I needed some air and a bit of exercise, so I walked down, just to tell Henry I'd be back at work soon. I assumed he'd be pleased, but he was very odd, in quite a state. Sort of distracted and pacing up and down. I've never seen him like that.'

'Did you ask him if there's a problem?'

'I tried, but he was quite short with me. Really, completely unlike himself. In fact, it was as if he couldn't wait for me to go. Henry and Eileen are scraping money together to pay for therapies and equipment for Michael and it's all horribly expensive. She told me a while ago that they'd exhausted their savings and that they were both losing sleep over it. I mentioned it to Alan.'

'What did he say?'

'Just that Henry has a lot of things on his mind to do with Michael, and not to be a worrywart. But, you see, I'm sure it's more than that. Henry was terribly distressed. You're so calm and clear-headed, I decided to ask your advice. Should I speak to Eileen about it?'

'It's hard to say. You're friends with her and she's talked about their circumstances before, so why not?'

'Oh, Eileen's a bit like a mum to me. She brought soup round and made a fuss of me when she heard I wasn't well.'

'Perhaps you should broach it with her, then. I did gather that they're both quite worn out with the home alterations they're having done for their son. It might help if you raise it with her, as long as it wouldn't cause offence.'

'Yes, thank you, I will. I'm terribly fond of them both, and what's happened to Michael is so hard for them. There might be some way I can help.'

'Take it easy, don't return to work too soon.'

'Oh, you were right in what you said to me before, when you visited with the inspector.'

'What was that?'

'You told me I'd be better off at work, because it would take my mind off Ronnie. I won't be daft, but I will go back to the museum as soon as I can. At home, I just mope and dwell on regrets.'

'You're the best judge, but yes, that sounds sensible.'

We say goodbye. I sit at reception with pen and note-pad, bringing together details, making notes, scribbling them out and reshaping them. After a while they're in a form that satisfies me and indicates an interesting combination of information and links.

Henry Claremont, museum, two thefts. Financial difficulties re son/ building work. Charitable work via church. Stressed/ distressed.

Alan Fanshawe, works at museum & Broadmeadow. Friendly with Claremont & knows Armitages.

Ronnie Carpenter visited museum & Broadmeadow.

It might be time to speak to Peter Thaxted again, but not until I've checked in with someone else.

'Writing a love letter, Daisy?' Vera shoots past with a first-aid box. 'Chop-chop, Leslie needs some help because that's what he's done. He's managed to cut his hand and the potatoes can't roast themselves.'

* * *

JB has landed a part in *The Seagull* by Chekov. It's a tale of love and loneliness, he's informed me, and he's playing Trigorin, a self-obsessed author. I'm helping him with his lines, taking the role of Nina, who is an idealist and keen on

Trigorin. The characters seem to mope around a lot, saying significant things.

'*It was a curious play, wasn't it?*' I recite in a dreamy voice.

JB produces a pronounced Russian accent. '*Very, I couldn't understand it at all, but I watched it with the greatest pleasure because you acted with such sincerity, and the setting was beautiful.*' He pauses. '*There must be a lot of fish in this lake.*'

'*Yes, there are.* Are you going to play the part in that accent, JB?'

'No, I'm having a bit of fun and finding my way in.' JB takes a puff of his cigar and glances at his lines. '*I love fishing. I know of nothing pleasanter that to sit on a lake shore in the evening with one's eyes on a floating cork.*' He flips his copy of the play shut. 'What a sad case Trigorin is! I've had enough of him for tonight.'

'I think I'd fall asleep if I went to see this play. They don't *do* much, do they?'

'That's Chekhov for you. Lots of introspection and melancholic pauses. Let's take a turn around the dance floor.'

He winds up the gramophone and puts on his Duke Ellington record. Although the days are warm, it's still chilly enough at night to light a fire, and we execute a cramped foxtrot to 'Don't Get Around Much Anymore' while logs crack in the hearth.

'I'm glad that the dear old Dolphin is going to have a wash and brush-up, it's badly needed,' he says.

'Vera said it's costing a lot.'

'Yes, but don't worry, I can still afford your wages. Have you heard if Mr Mackie has confessed?'

Mackie's name has been made public now. 'No updates.'

'You're still not convinced that Peter has the right man?'

'No.' I stumble slightly on a chassé. 'I'm planning to speak to the Reverend Lipton.'

'You don't reckon he's the murderer, surely?'

'He might be able to throw light on something for me.'

'Ah, I see how the land lies, you're being enigmatic.'

'Yes, I'm taking a leaf out of the inspector's book.'

The next track plays, 'Mood Indigo', and we have a rest. JB pours whisky and hands me a glass.

'I was doing a bit of investigating myself, with the *kommandantin*,' he tells me. 'Peter did have a sweetheart called Matilda before the war, was pretty keen on her by all accounts. However, she was smitten by a pilot while Peter was hospitalised and married him. So, he nurses a wounded heart as well as a wounded leg.'

'That's sad.'

'You ever been smitten, Daisy?'

'No, can't say I have. Were you, with Rosalind?'

'I believed that I was. It's amazing how we can persuade ourselves of things when we try.' His eyes rest on the photo of Joe Casey, his previous factotum.

'Vera must be smitten with Ray, to stick by him.'

JB's smile is melancholy. 'Ah, Vera is one of those people with a conventional, single-minded view of life. There are times when I envy her. She doesn't question the way things are, she stiffens her spine and ploughs on.' He reaches a foot out, tickles Oberon under the chin. 'One last dance before the curtain falls on today?'

* * *

I've never been to evensong before. It's me and half a dozen people in St Clement's, listening to the Reverend Lipton recite psalms. The low spring sun is warming the stained-glass window behind the altar, creating a rainbow of colours around its depiction of the Miracle at Cana. The rest of the church is shadowy with silvered light and pockets of darkness. Candles glimmer around the front of the altar. The last time I was in the church was for Lucinda's funeral, so this service is more upbeat. It's a peaceful half hour and at least I remember the Lord's Prayer and can join in that towards the end.

I linger behind while parishioners drift out, speaking in those hushed tones that are reserved for death and church. The Reverend Lipton sees me still in one of the front pews and patters towards me. He has a doleful face and a care-worn air. 'Miss Moore, isn't it? How lovely to see you at a service.'

'It was very tranquil, thank you.'

'Evensong does always pour balm upon the soul. It's good to have that time for contemplation and rest as the day is closing. And we do all need that kind of peace with the world as it is.'

'How true. I'm sure that lots of ex-servicemen and women benefit from this kind of healing service.'

The vicar perches beside me, patting down his white cassock with fussy fingers. 'I do hope so. The church tries to help them corporally as well as spiritually.'

'Yes, I was reading your parish magazine and I saw the efforts to help those left in need, including Mr and Mrs Claremont's contribution. The concert's success must have been a great boost for them, especially as they have their own struggles, supporting their son.'

'There are so many left with injuries and other problems, but we must do what we can.' He clasps his hands. 'I do miss dear Lucinda Laidlaw. She was such a stalwart of the parish. I could always call on her and she responded.'

'I'm sure she's much missed. I was with Mr and Mrs Claremont recently. They certainly do their bit, although they have their hands full with building work.'

He fingers the cross round his neck. 'Poor Michael. That is indeed a tragedy. Yes, very sad.'

We sit in the hush, the only sound a guttering candle. I'm trying to find a way to probe without giving affront.

'Mrs Claremont seemed worried about her husband's health. They commented on how much their extension is costing.'

'Did they?' He runs a hand down his jaw. 'It's not easy for them.'

'The strain was obvious. Perhaps they've been able to borrow money to help them out.'

The vicar gives a little start, his head twitching. A candle flickers with a final burst of light around the blackened wick and dies.

Oh no, Henry, what have you done?

'Let's hope that's the case.' He stands and tucks his arms in his cassock sleeves. 'I must see to the vestry now, but do please stay as long as you wish.'

'Thank you. Oh, Reverend Lipton, before you go — who was Moses' wife? A crossword clue baffled me.'

He seems thankful to be on familiar territory. 'That was Zipporah, Miss Moore. She is described as a practical woman, taking action when needed.'

'It sounds as if Moses struck lucky, given that he had quite a lot on his schedule.'

The vicar gives a startled laugh and hurries away through a side door.

CHAPTER EIGHTEEN

On my way back from the church, I note that the police station light is on. I park my bike outside and approach the yawning, rosy-cheeked constable on the desk. He tenses when he sees me and glances around as if seeking somewhere to hide. I can't blame him for being wary, because I got him into trouble with a furious Inspector Thaxted last autumn. I'd lied my way past him to see Felix, who was in custody.

'Hello, is Inspector Thaxted here?'

'He is,' the constable agrees cautiously, 'but he might be busy.'

'Great. I'll be back in a minute.'

I leave him open-mouthed and cross to the fish and chip shop, buy two portions of cod and chips, and then present myself back at the station and ask to see Thaxted. The constable sniffs appreciatively, eyeing my newspaper bundles. He dials the inspector, using a pencil he takes from behind his ear.

'That Miss Daisy Moore is here, sir. Yes, certainly, thank you, sir.' He replaces the receiver. 'He says you can go through.'

'I've brought supper,' I tell Thaxted as I edge his door open.

He's at his desk, pen in hand. 'Should I beware of Greeks bearing gifts?'

'That implies that you're suspicious of me. Oh, hold on, do you eat fish?'

'I do, and I have to say, those smell like little parcels of delight.'

'I've salted them and added liberal splashes of vinegar.'

The inspector caps his pen and rubs his hands. 'I'm famished. For once, I am genuinely pleased to see you while I'm working.'

We sit at the desk and eat in silence for a few blissful minutes.

'Churchill calls fish and chips our "good companions",' Thaxted says, 'and he's spot on.'

'That's why he wouldn't let them be rationed during the war — too crucial to morale. Sometimes, I reckon that if the Nazis had introduced them to Germany, they might have won.'

The inspector chews with deliberation. 'If they had, you wouldn't have come into my life to annoy me.' He waves a chip at me. 'I'm sure that this supper, generous though it is and extremely welcome, comes with a hidden agenda.'

'Inspector, I'm like Zipporah, Moses' wife.'

He coughs. 'Pardon?'

'She was a practical woman who took action.'

He finds a hanky and wipes his fingers. 'There are some indications that Moses was polyamorous.'

'Such a busy man, what with the commandments and parting the Red Sea. Has Bill Mackie confessed?'

'On the contrary, he's loudly maintaining his innocence.'

I finish the delicious bits of singed batter, wrap up my empty newspaper and shove it to one side while I find my most recent notes. 'I've been talking to a number of people, Inspector.'

'Sadly, there's no law against you doing that.'

I place the notes in front of him. 'May I take you through some ideas I've had after these further conversations?'

'Please do.'

'There are interesting links between the people in my notes. Henry Claremont has a severely injured son, Michael. He and his wife are having expensive alterations made to their home to accommodate Michael, as well as paying for treatment. This is all causing them significant financial problems. Beverley Fanshawe phoned me to say that she's worried about Henry, who's distressed. His wife referred to him being unwell recently. The Claremonts organised a charity concert at St Clement's church hall to help raise funds for ex-service personnel. I saw the vicar visiting them and he seemed very tense. I wondered if Henry might have "borrowed" some of the proceeds from the concert. Are you with me so far?'

'I'm managing to keep up, yes.'

'Alan Fanshawe works at Goswick museum and at Broadmeadow Farm. What if one or both of the robberies at the museum was an inside job? What if Henry Claremont, needing funds, was inspired by the value of the Tudor wall hanging and the rare ring, and realised that their sale would help to solve his financial problems? He might have got Alan to steal them. They could then have shared the proceeds. Ronnie might have had suspicions after the second theft and started sniffing around. We've learned that he didn't hesitate to challenge if he suspected double-dealings. Maybe Henry and Alan decided to do away with him — or Alan did on his own — and he carried out the murder and dumped the body at Broadmeadow to cast suspicion on Tony Armitage. Alan probably knew about the bad blood between Tony and Ronnie, and he's ex-military, so might easily have a gun or access to one.'

Thaxted hooks his hands behind his head. 'That's a lot of conjecture. Also, if Claremont gained financially from the museum thefts, would he have needed to steal from the charity concert funds?'

'I agree. Perhaps he didn't want to spend too freely after the thefts in case he aroused suspicion. It's hard to believe that Henry would have robbed his own museum. He loves that place and he's devoted years to it, but if he's desperate enough financially, that could have made him impulsive. It's surely worth considering. Also, I'd bet that Alan Fanshawe is sweet on Pearl Armitage, and vice versa. He doesn't have much time for her father, or the way he treats his daughter and frightens off any suitors. Alan might have calculated that as well as disposing of the danger that Ronnie posed, he'd cause trouble for Tony, and maybe even get him out of the way for a while. That would clear the ground for him and Pearl.'

Thaxted uncaps his pen and circles Henry Claremont's name on my notes. 'You're right about one thing. The Reverend Lipton came to see me yesterday. He suspects that Claremont stole from the charity concert collection. The figures don't add up, and the vicar had what he called an embarrassing conversation with Claremont, who claimed he couldn't account for the anomaly.'

'Oh. I do like Henry, and he and his wife are facing such awful circumstances. I don't want to believe that he's been stealing or involved in murder. What are you going to do about the charity money?'

'I discussed the situation with the vicar who, like you, has great sympathy for the Claremonts. The reverend is keen not to cause them any further grief. He quoted the gospel to me: "For if you forgive others their trespasses, your heavenly Father will also forgive you, but if you do not forgive others their trespasses, neither will your Father forgive your trespasses."'

'That's a lot of trespassing.'

'Isn't it just? We agreed that I'll speak to Mr Claremont and suggest that if the money should reappear, no more questions would be asked about it. I imagine that will do the trick.'

'That's generous of you. Were you influenced by the gospel?'

'No,' he replies tersely. 'I believe in humanity, not heavenly fathers. I've met Michael Claremont. He's a brave young

163

man whose life has been permanently altered. If his parents didn't care for him, he'd end up in an institution. I admire their sacrifice. Also, I'm not interested in prosecuting a fragile man like Claremont, who has the odds stacked against him, when there are much worse villains around.'

The inspector rubs his brow, opens a bottle of tablets and takes a couple. Then he crumples our supper wrappings and aims them expertly in his bin.

'What about my other theory, about the burglaries and the murder?'

'You've presented an interesting scenario, and one that has already occurred to me. I've been considering it and making enquiries.'

'I don't want to be right.'

'No. I hope you're not too.'

'Maybe I'm completely wrong, and it will prove to be Bill Mackie or Jago Villette. When you asked about Alan Fanshawe, did he have an alibi for the Friday when Ronnie died?'

Thaxted waves a hand from side to side. 'It was vague. He was cycling between a couple of farms and working on his own at both of them on hedging and fencing. Several people saw him, but couldn't be sure about the times. I presume you haven't said anything to alert him to your suspicions?'

'No. He didn't like me turning up at Broadmeadow Farm, but that could be because he'd seen me with you. He realises that I've befriended Pearl, and if he's guilty, he has a lot to hide. Pearl crocheted me this beret.'

'Very fetching. If you're right, and Alan Fanshawe is involved in Carpenter's death, she might unpick it again, or stick her crochet hook in you.'

'Don't say that with such relish.'

He smiles weakly, his face grey and tired.

'Will you update me?'

'I'll tell you what I can.' He becomes the stern policeman again. 'In the meantime, stay away from all of these people.'

'Night, then.'

'And thanks again for the supper. It will keep me going while I burn the midnight oil.'

* * *

The Dolphin is buzzing, so I have little time in the following days to wonder where Thaxted's enquiries are leading him. Then, one morning, things take an unexpected turn. I'm emptying the waste-paper bin at reception when a piece of scrunched paper catches my eye. It's a shopping list. I smooth it out.

Aspirin
Hair clips
Shampoo
Calamine lotion

Nothing exceptional, other than the handwriting, which is identical to that on my anonymous letter. I take the list to Lesley and Vera, who don't recognise it.

'Why are you bothering with a bit of rubbish?' Vera asks.

'The writing's familiar.'

'Ask Sharon. Maybe it's Amelia's.'

But I know it isn't, because I've seen Amelia's lists before. I discover that Sharon is out on errands for her, so I have to wait until she returns and delivers two bags of shopping upstairs.

'Amelia's always buying sweets,' Sharon tells me when I find her having a cigarette in the bar while she unpacks new stock. 'They can't be good for her, but I suppose she's got no other comforts.' She twists her leg. 'Blast, I got mud up the back of my stocking. There was a puddle right outside the newsagent.'

'Do you recognise this?' I show her the list.

'I chucked it in the bin, didn't I?'

'Yes. Who wrote it?'

165

'Mrs Carpenter. She asked me to pop out for a few bits for her while she was here. I was getting stuff for Amelia anyway, so I said yes. I found that in my pocket this morning, so I threw it away. Why are you asking?'

'Just interested.'

'You and your mysteries! I'm just nipping to the bathroom to wipe this stocking clean, in case Vera reckons I'm skiving. That woman's always snooping around checking up on me.'

I remain in the niffy bar, breathing in Sharon's smoke trail and chewing a nail with elation. This raises so many questions. How did Tommie hear about my part in the Laidlaw case? Then it dawns on me that Amelia might have told her. Why was she guiding me towards Broadmeadow Farm and Goswick? Was it to divert me from other matters? She'd lied when she claimed that Ronnie never discussed his work with her. Does that mean that she has other information? Did she travel to Oxford to post the letter, or did someone do that for her? And what else might she have lied about?

I carry on taking bottles of gin and brandy from their boxes and line them up on the shelves, making sure to bring older stock to the front. Tommie Carpenter has an unexpected aptitude for deception and manipulation. I track back to my conversations with her, all framed by tears, sighs and weary fragility. Sad Tommie, helpless Tommie, medicated Tommie, who rarely leaves home and can do almost nothing for herself. Yet the same woman could store and use information she'd gleaned about me to pen an astute letter. I see her sitting opposite me in Chiswick, holding her forehead and explaining how Ronnie dealt with everything, and she did her best to avoid all that nastiness that went on for six years. Then I recall the coffee table and the leaflets I'd noted on it, including the one from the Women's Voluntary Service. I don't like having my strings pulled and it's dawning on me that there's far more to Tommie than meets the eye.

CHAPTER NINETEEN

I'm back in London, in a community hall in Acton, meeting Mrs Alice Weaver, a WVS centre organiser. A banner above the front door declares, *A LITTLE THING IS A LITTLE THING, BUT FAITHFULNESS IN LITTLE THINGS IS A VERY GREAT THING*. The centre is busy, with queues being served by women in dark green dresses. There's a wonderful smell of soup. Tea urns hiss beside tall enamel jugs of coffee. A group of volunteers sit at a table with a sign saying *Emergency Mending*. They're busy hemming and sewing buttons and patches. The place hums with calm efficiency.

Today I'm Lillian Walsh — my mother's name — and I'm a researcher, collecting information about Women's Voluntary Service activity during the war for a fictional author. I've dreamed up a nifty working title for her book, *The Subtle Army*.

We sit in Mrs Weaver's little office while another woman types away in a corner, stabbing at the keys with two fingers. Mrs Weaver has a purposeful gait, courtesy of stout, muscular legs, and is wearing a tweedy two-piece suit in a herringbone pattern. She's given me a comprehensive picture of the different kinds of activities her volunteers have been carrying out: assisting with air raid precautions, staffing rest centres, railway station canteens and field kitchens, operating car pools, escorting evacuees, mending service uniforms and knitting socks being just a few.

'We thought we'd only be needed for the duration of the war, but the government has decided that we're invaluable and still needed for another couple of years. And who are we to argue with that? We spend a lot of time these days helping bomb-damaged families, wounded service personnel and refugees. A dozen of us are taking part in the victory parade in June, so we're being drilled to perfection. Some people are of the view that we should wait until the war is over everywhere before we celebrate, but all I can reply is that it's a poor heart that never rejoices.' She adds in her no-nonsense, high-pitched voice, 'It's very nice to hear that someone wants to write about us.'

I'm making random notes. 'You do such important work behind the scenes.' I'd benefited from WVS canteens when I was a bus driver. Their tea and buns helped me through many a long night. I'd witnessed how they'd tirelessly cared for distraught and exhausted people. 'Actually, the author I'm researching for is friendly with someone who volunteered with you, a Mrs Carpenter. That's what gave her the idea for me to visit you.'

Her brow furrows. 'Carpenter?'

'She lives in Chiswick.'

'Tommie Carpenter,' the typist chips in without raising her eyes from her work.

'Oh yes, Tommie,' Mrs Weaver says. 'She used to come and help at the clothing centre once a week, assisting people who'd lost all their possessions.'

I suppress a shudder, finding that close to home. I'd lost everything in the house fire, and I'd had to wear ill-fitting clothes donated by an almoner at the hospital. The huge serge knickers are a particularly painful memory.

'Tommie never seemed in the best of health,' Mrs Weaver comments.

I'm sure that I hear a snigger from the typist, but when I glance across, her head is down.

'Mrs Carpenter doesn't help now?'

'She stopped once the war ended and her husband came home,' Mrs Weaver says. 'That's true of a number of our volunteers, who wanted to focus on their families. Quite understandable, especially where there are children to consider. Thankfully, many of them have stayed on, so we can continue to offer a robust service.'

There's a tap on the door, with someone needing Mrs Weaver, and she excuses herself. The typist continues picking out her letter.

'This blasted key keeps sticking,' she complains, flicking back the 'R'.

'Bit of oil might sort it.'

'I've tried that, and cleaning it. I hate typing, but someone has to do these reports. The government does love paperwork!' She swivels around. She has a long, intelligent face. 'I'm Norma: admin, secretary, accountant and whatever else needs to be done. Are you a friend of Tommie Carpenter?'

'Me? No, but I've heard a bit about her.' I inject a hint of snideness. 'Not all of it flattering.'

Norma pushes up the sleeves of her khaki siren suit and stretches her arms out, linking her fingers and cracking them. 'We get the odd volunteer who's more of a hindrance than help, and she was one of those. Mrs Weaver was being polite about her. That woman got on my wick!'

'How come?'

'Don't write this down or repeat it, for God's sake.'

I close my notepad. 'OK.'

Norma's definitely been waiting for an opportunity to open these floodgates. 'Tommie was such a moaner, always going on about her health. Fine, she wasn't called up because she had nervous problems, but the way she went on was off-putting. She was here to help people who'd been left with nothing except the clothes they were wearing. We all stick a smile on, no matter how down we are, to keep morale going. Most of us have lost family members, but we leave all that at home. I mean, that's one of the major reasons we're here, to bolster people when they're in a bad way. Not Tommie. She turned every conversation back to her favourite subject — herself. No one liked her. We were relieved that she only did one shift a week.'

'I've heard that she was a homebird and relied on her husband.'

Norma snorts. 'That's not the only man she relied on.' She pauses to check my reaction.

'Go on.'

'You definitely won't repeat this?'

'Cross my heart.' I make the sign across my chest while holding my breath.

'Tommie got very pally with Horace Russell, an ARP warden for this area. He'd direct walking wounded here and help us with the blackout. An older chap, very kindly. Lost his wife a while ago and lives on his own. He'd listen to Tommie wittering on about her palpitations and panic attacks. I saw them drive away in his car a couple of times.'

I want to embrace Norma and twirl her around the office. 'A romance, would you say?'

'No comment.' She widens her eyes.

'I presume that Mr Russell lives locally?'

'He does, just a couple of streets away in Lordship Road, next to the dairy.'

Mrs Weaver reappears, complaining about a shortage of men's trousers and asking Norma if she can phone Chelsea to track some down. I tell her that I have everything I need. Norma makes a zipped-lip gesture behind her and I nod, intending to break my promise straight away.

* * *

It's a blowy, moody day with scudding clouds. The wind whips up brick dust and ash from bomb sites, scattering it liberally. I have to stop to rub grit from my eye. The evidence of Tommie's deceptions is growing. Not only did she not spend the war cowering at home, but she's also not quite the devoted wife she's been keen to portray.

The house next to the dairy in Lordship Road has a silver birch in the front garden. Its branches creak and rattle, dislodging new leaves, which form a pale green carpet on the path.

A tall man, balding and broad across the shoulders, answers my knock. I've decided to stick to my researcher alias, as it worked well with the WVS.

'Hello, Mr Russell?'

'I am.'

'My name's Miss Walsh. I've been at the local WVS and they said you might be able to add to the research I'm doing.' I spin my story about a book. 'Would you be able to spare me half an hour?'

'It's not terribly convenient.' He has a mild but firm manner and he's blocking the gap in the door.

'Honestly, I won't take up much of your time.' I pretend to check my notes. 'They said that you've offered them so much valuable assistance, and they were sure you'd be happy to comment on their work. I've had a bit of a journey to come this way, so it would be handy to speak now.'

He rubs the edge of the door. 'Very well, you'd better come in.'

He takes me into a back room furnished minimally with a couple of armchairs. A blue curtain is drawn back across the stairs that lead up from it. A jug of dried grasses stands in the cast-iron fireplace and the mantelpiece holds a green china plaque commemorating the Great War. There's a tray on the table with a teapot and two used cups. I place him in his late fifties, with a pleasant face and regular features. He holds himself straight.

I open my notepad. 'Mrs Weaver at the WVS talked me through their work. She told me that your ARP role brought you into contact with them.'

'That's right. I had to ensure that their hall was properly protected and I carried out emergency drills with them, so

I got to meet everyone. I'd escort folk there after bombing raids, and get a cup of tea myself when I could grab one. Smashing ladies, all of them, and brave too, always going the extra mile. Great community spirit, kept us all going when things were bleak.'

A floorboard creaks above. Mr Russell clears his throat.

'I'm sorry if I've interrupted you.' I gesture at the tea tray.

'Not at all. A neighbour popped by earlier.'

'I suppose you got familiar with all the volunteers?'

'Yes, I'd say so.'

I riffle my notes. 'Let's see . . . Sorry, I jotted loads down . . . I asked for some individual stories . . . So much info. Ah yes, they mentioned a Mrs Carpenter, said she was particularly helpful with their clothing supply and they're sorry that she's not with them now.'

Mr Russell has a natural authority, but it wavers a little when I say Tommie's name and he can't help glancing upwards.

'I won't be recording anyone by name,' I reassure him. 'It's just good to have a few personal notes.'

That relaxes him a little. 'Yes, Mrs Carpenter was one of the volunteers. Another very nice lady, always lending a helping hand.'

'Even though she didn't enjoy the best of health, apparently.'

'So I believe.'

'It's just so impressive, that someone like that would still give up her time.'

'True, but so many people did and were extremely selfless. What did you do, Miss Walsh?'

'I drove buses.'

'Well done. Another very important job.'

'Thank you.'

Another soft sound from upstairs, like the click of a door. This time, Mr Russell makes a visible effort and keeps his eyes on me.

'Will you be taking part in the victory parade with the ARP? Some of the WVS ladies are.'

'Oh yes, I'll be there with my local contingent.'

'Will Mrs Carpenter attend?'

'I've no idea. I doubt it, as she doesn't volunteer these days.'

'Are you still in touch with her?'

'No,' he responds with quick annoyance. 'Why do you ask?'

'Someone mentioned that you gave her a lift sometimes.'

'I'm sure I've given lots of volunteers lifts over the years — too many to remember. It was all part of the job, you understand. Whatever needed doing got done.'

'Well, thanks so much, Mr Russell. This is a bit cheeky, but may I use your bathroom before I go?'

He stands, says politely, 'Through the kitchen and you'll see the door to your left.'

The bathroom smells fusty with a hint of scent, and is distinctly chilly. A facecloth is draped over the side of the worn enamel bath. There are two toothbrushes in a mug on the sink, next to a shaving brush, soap and razor. I open the small cabinet above and see a lipstick tube, a tin of talcum powder, zinc ointment, plasters, a rolled crepe bandage, a small spray of Blue Grass perfume, almost full, and a bottle of chloral hydrate pills. I open the lipstick, which is barely used, and sniff the Blue Grass. It's the same aroma as the scent in the air. I assume that Mr Russell isn't using women's cosmetics and they're surely too new to be his dead wife's. I flush the toilet and run water in the basin.

'Thanks again,' I say to Mr Russell. 'I appreciate you giving me your time.'

He nods and escorts me out, warning me to watch my step on the slippery leaves and cracked paving slabs.

I catch a bus to Chiswick and Tommie Carpenter's home. I'm convinced that she was lurking upstairs at Russell's house. I'd seen those prescription tablets on her dressing table at the hotel. As I expected, there's no answer when I ring the bell.

'She's not in, dear, I saw her going out this morning,' a woman calls to me from her doorstep several doors down.

'Oh, thanks. Never mind, I'll catch her another time.'

'It's nice to see her getting out a bit more these days. I expect she's taking her mind off her awful tragedy.'

'I'm sure she is.' *And maybe it's not such a tragedy after all, but an opportunity for a new life.*

I make my way to Paddington, anxious to discuss all this with Peter Thaxted as soon as possible.

CHAPTER TWENTY

I reach Brize Lodge just after six in the evening and phone
Inspector Thaxted. Fernfield station is still open, but I have
no luck when I ask for him.

'I'm sorry, miss, he's not here.'

'Is he at Oxford station?'

'No, miss. The inspector's not available and won't be at
present. Would you like to speak to someone else?'

'Not really. Where is Inspector Thaxted?'

'Sorry, miss, I can't comment. If it's important, I can
pass a message on to Oxford.'

'No, forget it.' I slam the phone down in frustration and
pace around. JB is away in Birmingham for two nights, in discussions over a film script, otherwise I'd ask his advice about
contacting Thaxted at home. Then I spot JB's address book
on the hall table and open it at 'T'. The inspector's number is
there. It would be a huge step to ring him at home, and I'm not
sure I have the courage to intrude. I pace a bit more, unsure
what to do, dithering up and down the hall. Tybalt scampers
in and sits, watching me wear tracks in the carpet.

'I shall follow Zipporah's example,' I declare to him,
picking up the phone again and dialling before I lose my
nerve. A woman picks up: a warm, tired voice.

'Good evening, is that Mrs Thaxted?'

'Yes.'

'My name is Daisy Moore. I work for Jeffrey Berrow and I've met your son.'

'I've heard Peter mention you, Miss Moore.'

'My apologies for bothering you at home, but I wondered if I could talk to the inspector. I tried the station and they said he's unavailable. It's rather important. I wouldn't impose otherwise.'

'I'm afraid that's not possible. Peter is in hospital.'

'Oh.' I catch my breath. 'I'm sorry, I didn't know.'

'That's all right, my dear. He was taken ill suddenly and he was admitted this morning.'

'How is he?'

'Not terribly well. They're running tests at present.'

'Can he have visitors?'

Her voice grows firmer, protective. 'Not just now. He needs rest and quiet.'

'Right. Well, please give him my best wishes when you see him.'

'I will. May I pass a message to him about the reason for your call?'

'No, no need.'

'Very well. Goodnight.'

I resume my pacing, confused and unsure what to do now. My brain is foggy. What if Peter Thaxted is seriously ill and unable to return to work for some time, if at all? I'm surprisingly bereft.

After a while I get a grip, feed and water the cats, and dispose of a mangled sparrow's corpse that one of them has kindly left by the back door. While I make a strong brew of tea, I reason that someone must be covering Thaxted's work during his illness, and especially a murder inquiry. I take out the typewriter and type a note with a carbon copy, taking care not to get the inspector into any trouble over my involvement.

To the detective overseeing Inspector Thaxted's investigation into Ronald Carpenter's death.

I work at the Dolphin hotel in Fernfield and I have spoken to Inspector Thaxted a number of times about this investigation. I have now discovered that Mrs Carpenter sent me an anonymous letter several weeks ago, suggesting that I focus on Broadmeadow Farm and Goswick museum regarding the murder. Mrs Carpenter has claimed that she rarely leaves home and spent the war years isolated and unwell. I have established that in fact, she volunteered with the WVS in Acton once a week. During this work, she became friendly with a Mr Horace Russell, an ARP warden and widower who lives alone. They were seen leaving together at times. I visited Mr Russell's home today and I believe that Mrs Carpenter was there, staying out of sight upstairs. In the bathroom, I noted two toothbrushes, a lipstick, a woman's scent and a bottle of sedatives, the same ones that Mrs Carpenter takes. I also called at Mrs Carpenter's house, but she wasn't at home and a neighbour informed me that she was out, and had been going out more often recently.

Mrs Carpenter has lied about a number of issues and I believe that the police need to enquire into her circumstances more closely.

Yours Sincerely,
Daisy Moore.

I slip the letter in an envelope, place it with the folded duplicate in my bag, and then switch on the wireless because the house is too silent. I wish that JB was here to dance with in our comforting ritual. In his absence, I pick up Oberon, who's replete with his rabbit supper, sleepy and docile. I hold one of his paws out and we sway around the room to 'I'll Get By'.

* * *

The following morning, I'm up early after a restless night's sleep and I call at Fernfield police station on my way to work. The red-cheeked constable is on reception again, scratching his ear and scanning cartoons in the *Daily Mail*.

'Bit early for fish and chips,' he remarks.

'I've heard that Inspector Thaxted is in hospital. Who's carrying on with the Carpenter murder?'

He rubs an eye. 'That would be Sergeant Crane.'

I write the name on the envelope I have ready, adding URGENT, and pass it to him. 'Is the sergeant here today, or in Oxford?'

He handles the envelope as if it might explode. 'The sergeant's not here. I've no idea what his plans are.'

'I have important information for him about the murder inquiry. Can you try phoning him for me at Oxford station?'

The constable folds his arms. 'No, miss, I can't. I can give him your note, if you like.'

'When will he get it?'

'I haven't got a crystal ball. I'll put it in his tray, so he'll see it when he's here.'

'It is urgent.'

'Yes, miss, so you claim. The way you carry on, you seem to reckon you're the bee's knees, if you don't mind me saying so.'

'You can say what you like, as long as you tell the sergeant that he needs to read that letter as soon as possible.'

'That'll be for the sergeant to decide, as and when.'

I leave him chuckling over his funnies and cycle to work. As soon as I've taken off my jacket, I phone Oxford Police and ask for Sergeant Crane, but I'm told he's unavailable. I explain that I've left an urgent note concerning the Carpenter case at the local station, and the receptionist says she'll pass on the message and my phone numbers.

The day passes in a busy whirl. I keep hoping that Sergeant Crane will phone me, but the only calls are hotel related. At six o'clock, I take Amelia Ward's evening meal to her. She's plonked in her chair, both legs resting on a stool.

'Oh, goody. What is it tonight, Daisy?'

'Lamb stew and tapioca pudding.' Leslie has run out of ideas today — *I'm a chef, not a blasted magician!* — and reverted to his standard wartime menu.

'I'm so hungry, I could eat a horse!'

I pull across the tray that sits over her chair and place the meal on it. She lifts the metal lid on her dinner plate and sniffs.

'Ooh, lovely. Now, tell me, what's going on in the world?'

This is a regular question whenever she sees me. I've grown used to being her walking news digest. 'Quite a lot. The Tokyo War Crimes Tribunal is underway, the Italian king has abdicated, the Bank of England has been nationalised, there was a dash to the fishmonger this morning when word got out that a fresh supply was in, India is going to be independent and grave robbers have stolen Mussolini's body.'

That last snippet interrupts her tucking into her stew. 'That's disgusting!'

'He can't smell too good. Hope I'm not putting you off your food.'

'Not me, dear! But why would anyone do that?'

'His fascist supporters took him, unhappy that he'd been buried in a pauper's grave. They left one of his legs behind.'

Amelia has a good hoot over that. 'Talking about bodies closer to home, have they caught whoever shot that poor Mr Carpenter yet?'

'Not that I've heard.'

She salts the lamb liberally. 'I wonder how his wife is getting on. I understand all about being left a widow — the loneliness and sorrow. My pillow used to be drenched in tears for months after my dear Harry left me.'

'She's managing, I expect.'

'Could you open the window a notch for me, dear?'

I undo the catch on the sash and lower the window a couple of inches. 'It's a lovely evening, beautiful sunset over the park.'

Amelia's mouth is full of lamb. She gulps the food down and licks her fork. 'It was so awful for Tommie Carpenter that day her husband went missing. She must have been out of her mind, searching the streets for him.'

I turn from gazing at the magnificent blood-orange sun, not sure that I've heard her correctly. 'Searching for him?'

'Yes, dear.'

'How do you mean?'

She scoops up mashed potato. 'I suppose she was out in the car, looking for him. I saw her parking.' She points her knife. 'At the side there.'

Hotel guests park in a bay to the right of the hotel, visible from Amelia's window. I sink onto the window ledge and watch her jaw moving methodically. 'What time was that?'

'Now you're asking, dear. I suppose it must have been around three. I'd had a nap after lunch and I was reading one of my magazines when I heard the car. Poor woman, no wonder she looked so anxious. She ran for the hotel!'

'Amelia, did anyone from the police come to see you after Mr Carpenter was found?'

'No, dear, why would they do that? I never met the man. This cabbage is fine, but Leslie never puts enough salt and pepper on for me. Maybe it's me getting old — they say that your sense of taste suffers.'

It's easy to discount Amelia, closeted away in her room, hardly ever seen or heard, but I'm surprised at Thaxted's omission. This turns everything upside down. I wasn't aware that Tommie could drive, but then the subject has never arisen. I'd have assumed she couldn't, in keeping with her passive reliance on others. Amelia's rabbiting on about her tapioca, but I don't hear a word. Why was Tommie out in the car and why did she never mention it, pretending that she'd been asleep all afternoon? Surely there can only be one reason for the deception: she was involved in her husband's murder and she's been busily misdirecting us all since.

'. . . and I've always preferred it with a bit of syrup on top, but this isn't half bad,' Amelia drones on. 'Can you draw the curtain a little, the sun's in my eyes now.'

I tune back in and pull the curtain across, hiding the dazzling glow.

'Thank you, dear. A cup of tea in a little while would be lovely.'

'I'll bring it soon, Amelia, when I fetch your dishes.'

I stand outside her door, resting against it, trying to order my racing thoughts. Tommie Carpenter now resembles an out-of-focus photograph, full of blurred shadows and distorted light.

There's still no message from Sergeant Crane late that night. While I'm brushing my teeth, I decide that if the police can't be bothered to respond to an urgent contact, I'll just have to pursue my own path.

CHAPTER TWENTY-ONE

I'm back at Tommie Carpenter's house. I can tell from her guarded expression that she and Horace Russell have worked out that I was the visitor who came calling in Acton. It's pouring down outside, so I traipse the damp in with me. Tommie offers to take my coat as if it might bite her, and hangs it in the hall.

When she offers me tea, I decline and produce the anonymous letter. 'Let's not pretend any longer. You wrote this to me. I've seen your handwriting. Maybe you forgot that you gave Sharon a shopping list.' I take that from my bag and place it next to her letter. 'Perfect match.'

She pulls at her bottom lip. 'Very well, yes. I wrote to you.' She's in a plain purple skirt and blouse today, very much the grieving widow.

'We'll come back to that. You've told a string of lies — so many, I'm not sure where to start. You were out in your car the afternoon your husband was murdered, not asleep in your room, as you claimed. There's a witness, so don't deny it. You volunteered with the WVS in Acton during the war and you've been having a relationship with Horace Russell. You were upstairs at his house when I called to see him. You weren't quiet enough, Tommie.'

'What's any of this to do with you?' She still has her frightened-mouse air, but there's a hint of defiance. Maybe Horace has coached her.

'You lied to me and drew me in with your letter, so I'd say it has plenty to do with me.'

Tommie takes out a hanky, lowers her head and dabs at her eyes.

'Don't try the waterworks,' I tell her. 'I've had enough of the "poor little me" front. There's a lot more to you than meets the eye.'

'You have no right to come to my house and speak to me in this way, no right at all.'

'But you let me in. You didn't have to, or you could have pretended to be out. I'd say you want to establish what I've found out. I have told the police about this, by the way. Have they been round?'

'No.'

'It's only a matter of time.' Although I'm beginning to doubt that. 'You might as well tell me what's been going on, and get a rehearsal in for when they come calling.'

She picks at an embroidered arm cover on the sofa and does a bit more eye business with her hanky.

'I'll get the ball rolling. Did your husband know about Mr Russell?'

'Absolutely not!'

'Did you and Mr Russell murder him?'

'No!' She twists the hanky to her mouth. 'You can't believe that, surely.'

'I'm not sure what to believe, except that you've been lying much more expertly than I'd have given you credit for. You've done a good job of concealing things behind your helpless act.'

'You're so confident in yourself,' she says waspishly. 'It must be nice to be so certain about everything.'

I prefer this more spirited Tommie, but I'm not filled with certainty at the moment. 'Don't make assumptions about me. And don't try to turn this conversation around.

I'm just someone listening to your story, and I reckon that it's a fascinating one. Start with how you got involved in the WVS, and why you kept that work a secret.'

She falls for that, needing her moment in the limelight. 'They put a leaflet through the door early on in the war. I'd pick it up now and then and wonder if I could help at all, but then I'd be a bag of nerves and decide I couldn't possibly. Then one day, I mustered my energy and I walked into the centre. They were so welcoming and clearly needed as many pairs of hands as they could get, so I joined up. I didn't tell Ronald about it. He would have been shocked and forbidden it. He was so protective and worried about my health, but I had to get out of the house now and again. I've never had friends as such, and the days were so long and empty.'

'Sounds like you made a good decision.'

'I wasn't at all sure about it to start with. It was noisy and demanding, but I began to enjoy going there. It did me good, talking to people. The hours just vanished. I wasn't taking so many tablets because I had to be alert. Then I met Horace and we hit it off. I did have a relationship with him. I was lonely, and he's reassuring and such good company.'

'Those broad shoulders would be appealing.'

'Oh, sneer if you like.'

'Actually, I wasn't. I can imagine that you needed his friendship.'

Her face softens. 'That's how it was for a while, a friendship, but then it grew. We fell in love. We stopped seeing each other before Ronald came home last year. I couldn't face breaking up my marriage. It was hard, because I do love Horace, but I still loved Ronnie too. It would have been so unfair to do that to him after he'd been away fighting for me and all of us. I didn't see how Horace and I could be happy if we caused such misery for Ronnie. Horace is a gentleman. He was distraught, but he understood. Ronnie came home and we settled back into our usual routine. At times, it seemed as if Horace was a dream, although I missed him every day.'

She takes a bottle of citrussy cologne from the table, pours a little on her hanky and pats her temples. 'Ronnie was working hard. Some weeks I barely saw him and the temptation to contact Horace was great, but I resisted. The days were so long again, here on my own. I missed the WVS at times, but I couldn't go back. That would have meant telling Ronnie, and he'd have been utterly against it. Then . . . then we arrived at the Dolphin and everything went wrong.'

I've been drawn in to her story and will her to carry on. 'What happened, Tommie?'

She shivers. 'Could you pour me a blackcurrant cordial? It's in the sideboard. Have one with me.'

I find a bottle of dark purple cordial and glasses and pour us a large one each. 'Here, this will help. You'd arrived at the hotel . . .'

'Thank you.' She takes a sip. 'I could tell that something was up with Ronnie. He'd been edgy all morning, but I put it down to tiredness and having a lot on his mind with work. After you left us in our room, he sat on the bed and suddenly started weeping with his head in his hands. I had no idea what was wrong. I'd never seen him cry. Then he blurted out that he was in love with someone else, a young woman he'd met through work and she was expecting their baby. I didn't understand at first. He was almost incoherent, saying that he'd made a terrible mess of things, he didn't have a clue what to do for the best, and he wouldn't blame me if I hated him. I burst into tears and my heart started to flutter. I was afraid I was going to pass out.' She drinks again and massages her throat. 'Then Ronnie grabbed his coat and rushed out. I was stunned. I simply couldn't make sense of it. I waited for a while, assuming that he'd come back. He could see I was unwell and usually he'd never leave me in that state — he'd bring me a cold flannel for my forehead and rub my hands. When he didn't return, I saw that he'd left the car keys, so I took them and drove around for a while, hoping to find him. I was shaking so much, I've no idea how I kept control of the car. I couldn't see him anywhere, so I returned to the hotel. I lay on the bed and I did doze for a while until I came down and found you. I couldn't say that I'd gone out to look for Ronnie, because that would have meant discussing the reason for his distress before he left. That was the last time I saw him. I had nothing to do with what happened to him, and at that point, I hadn't seen Horace for almost a year.'

I'm not mad about the sickly, slightly slimy cordial, but I drink it, needing the boost. 'Why didn't you explain any of this to the police?'

'I couldn't focus at all when that inspector talked to me. I was in shock. Once I had some time to myself, I became so angry with Ronnie. We were supposed to be having a weekend together, I'd made a big effort to accompany him, and all the time he'd been carrying this secret around with him. It was all a pretence and to tell me there . . . in a hotel bedroom, when he knew I was exhausted from the journey . . . and then he left me all alone. What business was it of the police and why should I expose us to the tittle-tattle? Whatever happened to my husband was nothing to do with this affair he'd been having.'

'You can't be certain about that.'

'Maybe, but it seemed unlikely, and I decided that if the police found out about the affair, I'd say it was the first I'd heard of it. I have the right to some dignity!' Her lips are wine dark from the cordial. 'I'd given up someone I loved dearly to stay with Ronnie, and then he announced that he'd been seeing another woman. A child expected! He told me that, ran away, and then he was dead. I was absolutely stunned. I didn't see why I should be a laughing stock.'

I'm fairly sure that I believe her, which brings deep disappointment as I'd been convinced I'd found our murderer.

'Why send me the anonymous letter?'

'I wanted Ronald's killer found. Mrs Ward had told me about the woman who was murdered last year, and how you helped solve that crime. When I returned home, I went down to Ronald's office and I looked through his recent work files.

If he'd met this other woman through his job, I might come across some reference to her. I had a terrible need to find and confront her, but I didn't see any women's names. I read documents about the insurance claims at the farm and that museum, and I wondered if one of those contacts had led to his death. I didn't want to tell the police and face more questions, but I had to do *something*. I realised that you were connected to Inspector Thaxted, so I wrote to you. I didn't want you to see a London postmark, so Horace went to Oxford and posted the letter there.'

I'm glad that she missed the love letter among the bills. It wouldn't have done her any good and she'd have been even more tormented. 'There are possible leads around those two places where Ronnie did business.'

'So you and the police have been asking questions.'

'Yes.'

She leans forward, plucking at her hanky. 'Have you discovered who this woman is, the pregnant floozy Ronald was seeing?'

'No.' I don't want to expose these two women to each other. What good would it do? There's no baby now. Beverley will surely meet someone soon enough, and Tommie and Horace can walk into the sunset. The past will settle, gathering dust.

'Just as well, I suppose. Horace has told me to let it go. He says that finding out who she is wouldn't be any good for my nerves. He's worried I might have a relapse.'

Tommie has certainly found an ideal replacement for her husband. 'What time would you say you started searching for Ronald on that Friday?'

'I suppose just before two o'clock.'

Amelia saw her return around three. During that hour when she was searching, she might have noticed people. 'When you were driving around, did you see anyone or anything suspicious?'

'Such as what?'

'No idea. Just cast your mind back.'

'Oh . . . I don't . . . I was in such a state. I can't even remember where I went. Around the town and along some lanes. I'm so tired now.' She dabs her forehead with the cologne again and holds the hanky over her eyes.

'I'll go in a minute, but can you recall anything?'

'Pedestrians . . . a green bus . . . and . . . yes, there was a cyclist going really fast on one of the lanes, sort of hunched over the handlebars.'

'Man or woman?'

'I can't say. A boy or a man, I presume, as he was wearing trousers and a cap of some kind.'

'Can you describe him?'

'Barely. He was a blur really. I'm fairly sure he was wearing a khaki jacket.'

'And the lane — can you recall which direction?'

'I've told you all I can. I was crying while I drove around in circles.'

'You started seeing Horace again after Ronnie's death?'

'Why shouldn't I?' A pink flush rises in her cheeks. 'I can rely on him. I've needed him and he's been such a comfort. We've had to be careful, because Charles has been helping me and I don't want to be the source of any gossip. When enough time has gone by, we'll marry. He'll sell his house and move in here.'

Amelia was right when she predicted that Tommie would be an eligible widow.

She leans to one side, head in hand. 'I want you to go now. Horace will be phoning soon, and I need time to recover.'

I leave her. The rain has lightened into a fine mizzle, soaking damaged bricks and mortar, bathing the city in a watery grey light. The bunting that's gone up in preparation for the June celebration hangs and flaps limply, but my mood is now cautiously optimistic.

* * *

Back in Oxford, I head straight to the hospital, buzzing with energy. I don't care if Peter Thaxted is sedated and bandaged head to toe, I need to see him and discuss the Carpenter murder from all angles. In the ward, I spy him sitting on the side of his bed, dressed and buttoning his shirt. From this distance, he's like an old man, with his snowy hair sticking up at odd angles. He's engaged in an argument with a doctor who's standing before him, gesticulating. It's startling to hear him with his voice raised. His anger is usually of the quiet, cutting kind. I hang back.

'. . . and I'm the best judge of that,' he's saying crossly.

'Very well, Peter, but it's foolish of you. I can only urge you to stay for another few days.'

'I've had my fill of hospitals. I appreciate what you've done. I'll take the medication.'

'You must promise to come back if you're unwell. Any dizziness or temperature.'

'Yes, yes.'

'I need you to sign a self-discharge form.'

'I'll sign whatever you like, just bring it here.'

The doctor shakes his head and heads to the nurses' station. I approach the bed hesitantly, given Thaxted's scowl, but when he sees me, his face brightens.

'A human being from the world outside!'

'Hello. Are you being an impatient patient?'

'Dratted place. I hate hospitals, I've had enough of them for a lifetime.'

'Have they diagnosed the problem?'

'Some sort of infection. I've got yet more pills to take. I can't sit around here. Can you fetch me my coat from the locker and hoist my stick over?'

'Yes, but don't forget you need to sign a form.'

'Traitor. Are you colluding with them?'

'It's only a signature, and there's no point in getting a hard-working doctor into trouble.'

'The voice of reason.' He adjusts a cuff. 'What are you doing here?'

'I need to talk to you urgently about Ronald Carpenter. I've left messages and a letter for Sergeant Crane but he hasn't responded.'

'Crane's all right if he has plenty of guidance, but he's got no initiative. That's why I have to get out of this antiseptic prison before he lets any more valuable time slip by.'

A flustered nurse brings a form for him to sign, which he does with good grace and takes her hand, thanking her courteously for her care, and apologising for being a crank. She gives a little bob like a curtsey and hurries away. He shrugs his coat on, pockets two bottles of tablets, grabs his stick and walks gingerly out of the ward with me following.

In the corridor, he takes a deep breath. 'I need to wash and change my clothes, shake the hospital smell off, and have a decent bite to eat. We'll go to my house and we can talk there. Can you forge ahead and whistle up a cab?'

'I'm on my bike, so I'll cycle after you.'

'Just as well, as I'll need to soothe my mother when she sees me at the door.'

CHAPTER TWENTY-TWO

I cycle slowly through the damp, misty evening, brushing away raindrops as they fall from the trees. I want to give the inspector time to get home and surprise his mother. I'd imagine that the last thing she needs at the moment is an unexpected guest.

The large, detached Victorian house is stately and set back from the road. Mrs Thaxted opens the door to me, a tall, slender woman with white hair in a centre parting, pulled back in a French pleat. She has a grave smile.

'You must be Miss Moore. The side gate is open, so you can pop your bike round there.'

I park the bike while she waits for me at the door and then extends her hand as I enter the house. When I shake it, it's cool and firm.

'Peter is having a wash and brush-up. Please, do come through.'

'You must have had a shock when he arrived home.'

'Yes and no. He's always been a law unto himself, so I was half-expecting that he'd turn up. I understand his dislike of hospitals, but I do wish he'd take better care and listen to the doctors. He said that you came at exactly the right time, like a summoned sprite.'

'I didn't persuade him to discharge himself, he was ready to leave when I arrived.'

'Oh, don't worry, I haven't cast you as the villain of the piece. Do sit down.'

The house is full of pale, polished wood, the furnishings in plain dark blue. It has a monastic ambience and there's a faint, pleasant smell like incense. Mrs Thaxted is wearing a homespun outfit of knitted grey dress with a cream cardigan. Her face is lined, but her skin has a peachy bloom. I'm aware that she's a member of the Peace Pledge Union, which promotes pacifism, and JB has described her as a woman who does charitable work.

'Now, I'm preparing supper for Peter, so you must join him.'

'Thanks, Mrs Thaxted, I don't mean to inconvenience you.'

'Nonsense, you're most welcome, and please, do call me Olivia.'

'And I'm Daisy.' It'll be peculiar to call her by her first name when I've never got past formalities with her son. 'Can I help at all?'

'It's kind of you to offer, but it's a simple meal.'

She has a contained, composed quality. This must be a reassuring bolthole for Thaxted when he arrives back from work.

The inspector appears in fresh clothes, his hair brushed and orderly. We sit in a small dining room with a few dishes on the table: potato cakes, lettuce and tomato salad, bread rolls and asparagus in a lemony dressing. There's a bottle of red wine open. Olivia pours us two glasses.

'I've eaten, so I'll leave you to your discussions. I have my tea waiting in the sitting room, but just say when you'd like coffee.'

'I'll make that, Mother. I'm sure there's a play you're dying to listen to.'

She nods. 'You're quite right. Enjoy your meal.'

We eat in a hungry silence for a few minutes.

'This food's delicious,' I murmur. 'I've never eaten asparagus.'

'Mother pretty much grows it all herself.' He drinks his wine, rolls the stem of his glass. 'We had to release Mackie. He gave us nothing and we didn't have enough evidence. The bullet used to shoot Carpenter didn't match his gun.'

'I'm pretty sure he's not the culprit.'

'So, what's your urgent need to speak to me?'

'There's lots to flag up.' I take the duplicate of my letter to Sergeant Crane from my bag and put it by his plate. 'I'll give you a minute to read this urgent note I left for your sergeant.'

He reads while I continue eating. When he throws the letter down with a groan, I carry on.

'As you can see, first of all, I discovered that Tommie Carpenter sent me the anonymous note, so that started me questioning why she wanted to influence me. Then I recalled that when I visited her, I saw information about the WVS in her house. I followed my nose and visited the WVS centre near her in Acton, where I was told that she volunteered there once a week until the end of the war.'

Thaxted has eaten little. He pushes aside his plate and leans forward with his elbows on the table. 'Contrary to the picture of the woman who's always been too frightened to stray far from home.'

'Yes. Do you mind if I finish the asparagus?'

'Be my guest.'

I take the remaining spears. 'From gossip at the WVS, I learned that Tommie had become very friendly with an ARP warden, a widower called Horace Russell. I visited him at home.' I explain about my conviction that someone was hiding upstairs and the woman's items in the bathroom. 'Then back at the Dolphin, Amelia Ward — our elderly resident who's a Tommie type, in that she rarely ventures out — told me that she'd seen Tommie park the car around three o'clock on the Friday afternoon when Ronnie vanished. So, Tommie was out and about, not asleep in the bedroom for hours.'

He massages the bridge of his nose. 'I told PC Emerson to speak to Mrs Ward.'

'Is he the reddish faced, sleepy constable?'

'That's him.'

'Amelia said that the police didn't question her.'

'He'll be lucky if he's even allowed desk duty by the time I've finished with him.'

'I'm not one to take pleasure in another's misfortune, but when I asked him to give Sergeant Crane that urgent note, he observed that I act as if I'm the bee's knees.'

'Spare me from idiots! So, Mrs Carpenter has been lying consistently from the start of this business. I'll take great pleasure in hearing what she has to say for herself.'

'I can tell you what she said.'

'You've seen her?'

'I was in London today. I came straight to the hospital from the train.'

Thaxted mutters under his breath and pours more wine, making ruby splashes in the lamplight. 'Have you seen those westerns, where Jimmy Stewart or Henry Fonda swear in a deputy and pin a badge on him?'

'Yes.'

'I've never sworn you in or given you a badge.' He's got his narrow-eyed glare. 'You shouldn't have contacted Mrs Carpenter once you discovered that she'd lied, and about so many issues. You *should* have left it to the police.'

I put my hands up. 'Hang on, I've been trying to leave it to the police, but there's been a resounding silence.'

He doesn't look at all well, and I'm not sure that he should be using wine to swallow medication.

'Very well, I'll allow you that. Give me the gist of your conversation with Mrs Carpenter.'

'I went to London with the notion that Tommie and Horace Russell had got rid of Ronnie so that they could be together. Tommie acknowledged that she's lied, but I believed her when she said the murder was nothing to do with her. Do you really want to hear the rest of this, or does my lack of a badge mean that you want me to shut up?'

'Oh, carry on.'

I give a resumé of my conversation with Tommie. 'She lied because of shock and confusion, and to save face. It made sense to me.'

'And the anonymous note?'

'Tommie went through her husband's papers and read about the insurance claims at the farm and the museum, so she wondered if his death was connected to one of those. She didn't want to contact you and have to answer difficult questions, so she wrote to me because she'd heard about my involvement in the Laidlaw murder. Also, she picked up that we're . . . acquaintances.'

There's a silence. One of the lamps flickers and I can hear the low drone of voices from the wireless in the sitting room.

'I need strong coffee,' the inspector says. 'Would you like some?'

'Please. I'll bring the dishes.'

I stack them and take them through to the kitchen, where Thaxted is fiddling about with a chrome percolator that's bubbling on the stove. He directs me to the cupboard with cups and saucers and walks up and down, massaging his leg while the coffee hisses. We drink it there in the kitchen at a small table with cushioned chairs.

'I met Mr Claremont,' Thaxted says. 'He owned up to siphoning money from the charity collection. Said it was a spur-of-the-moment decision because of his financial straits. The man was distraught and begged me not to tell his wife. I agreed, on the understanding that he'd repay it. He denied any knowledge of who carried out the burglaries. I'm inclined to accept that. I can't see him planning such a complicated manoeuvre. He's basically a decent man who gave in to temptation. Ronald Carpenter's paperwork doesn't indicate that he had any suspicions about the museum thefts.'

'There's one other thing that Tommie Carpenter told me. When she was out searching for Ronnie, she saw someone cycling fast along a lane. A boy or a man, she assumed, as the figure was wearing trousers. All she could remember was that he had on a khaki jacket and a cap.'

'Not terribly helpful. I'll need to speak to her myself. Now, I must track down Sergeant Crane to establish what he has been doing, or more likely failing to do in my absence, and you have to get home. I'll call the station and get someone to drive you.'

'But my bike . . .'

'It can go in the back or the boot. I'll take you through to Mother while I organise your lift.'

Olivia Thaxted is listening to the wireless, which is now tuned to classical music, and knitting a vermilion and pineapple-yellow garment with round needles. This must be how she expresses her defiant, adventurous side.

I take a chair near her. 'Thanks for the meal, it was lovely.'

'Did Peter eat much?' she asks in a low voice.

'A bit.'

'I do worry about him so.' She has soft amber eyes with fine wrinkles at the corners.

'He's determined, good at mind over matter.'

'That can only take you so far. Do you have anyone who worries about you, Daisy?'

The question catches me off guard. 'JB — Jeffrey — does.'

'Ah, yes. I hear he speaks fondly of you. Perhaps he's found—'

A ring at the door interrupts her. It's my lift.

'Thanks for this,' I tell Thaxted while a constable fits my bike in the boot. 'I hope PC Emerson doesn't find out I've been chauffeured home. It will confirm his worst suspicions about me.'

'Believe me, he'll have other things on his mind. Goodnight, Miss Moore. Safe home.'

He's gone by the time we're reversing down the drive, but his mother is at the window waving, her knitting secured under her arm.

* * *

'I'm a bit stumped,' I tell JB later, over whisky. When he saw me arriving back in a police car, he fretted that I'd been arrested and I had to convince him that all was well. Now I've brought him up to date.

'What's Peter's home like?' JB asks. 'I've never been inside. Olivia did once invite the *kommandantin* and myself for supper, back when we were together at the manor, but I'd committed some indiscretion which now eludes me — there were so many — and she went alone.'

'It's a handsome house. Tranquil, simply furnished, soothing. A bit of a haven for him.'

'He'd need that after his experiences. He's going to interview Mrs Carpenter?'

'Yes. I expect she'll weep and need her smelling salts.'

JB has a cigar going, his waistcoat hanging open. 'I can see why you rated Tommie and her beau as suspects, me old fruit. She's certainly a case of still waters running deep.'

'For the first time, I was truly sorry for her, although she's still annoying. Good luck to Horace Russell, facing a lifetime of putting up with the vapours. The cyclist she saw could be significant, but it's not much of a description to go on.'

We're both yawning through the haze of cigar smoke.

'How did your script discussions go, JB?'

'I said yes to it. It's a comedy caper. I'll be playing a head teacher. The director's an old friend of Declan's, so that clinched it for me. I hear that you called in on him.'

'We had a cuppa. He was very kind, and said I can stay over now and again if I want to spend a bit of time in London.'

JB points his cigar at me. 'He'd better not be trying to poach you from me.'

'Don't be daft. He doesn't need a factotum, and a priest would hardly be allowed to give house room to a female companion. If my mother had heard such a rumour, she'd have contacted the bishop and demanded excommunication.'

'Well, good. I don't want to have to fight a duel at dawn with him.'

He's chuckling, but I hear the undercurrent of anxiety. It's the lure of London for me that worries him, not the priest. I say reassuringly, 'He's a link to my mum, JB, a link to my past. I'm not packing a suitcase.'

'Excellent.' He stubs out his cigar and drifts his fingers through the smoke stream. 'I'm going to hit the hay.'

While I'm brushing my teeth, I reflect on Tommie's account of her husband's revelation in the hotel bedroom, her subsequent driving around in an emotional daze and the cyclist she saw through her tears. Then I recall the postman at the farm, who was in fact a postwoman. I pause, white foam on my lips, concentrating. Sharon's comment comes back to me, that I can sometimes resemble a schoolboy. I rinse my mouth and draw a shape in the condensation on the mirror above the sink, a trousered figure. Anyone and no one.

In bed, I lie awake for a long time with Tybalt on my stomach, turning over elusive snatches of conversation.

CHAPTER TWENTY-THREE

I'm deep in dealing with a sudden plague of ants in the hotel kitchen the next morning when Vera fetches me. Inspector Thaxted's on the phone.

'Are you in the office?' he asks me.

'No, on the reception phone.'

'You need to go in the office and close the door.'

I get Vera to replace the reception handset once I've gone in the office. She glances at me through the window with her not-best-pleased face.

'Hello, I'm in the office now.'

'I'm sorry, Miss Moore, but I'm the bearer of bad news.'

For a moment, it crosses my mind that he's about to tell me something awful about his health or that JB's had an accident, and I grip the receiver tightly.

'It's Mr Claremont, I'm afraid. He's been found dead. He took his own life.'

'What? How . . . how did it happen?'

'I can't say much. He was found in the river this morning. I wanted to tell you before you heard on the grapevine, and please treat this as private information.'

I sit down, stunned. 'His wife and son . . . This is dreadful.'

'Yes. I'm not dealing with the family, that's in the hands of other officers. I have to go, Mrs Carpenter has just arrived from London and I must interview her.'

'Was it because of the money he stole?' I ask. It has to be. He must have been ashamed.

'I can't speculate, and neither should you.'

'Thanks for telling me.'

'Once again, I'm very sorry. Goodbye for now.'

I stay sitting for a few minutes, recalling Henry Claremont's warm welcome when I visited the museum. Beverley will be terribly upset. Vera raps on the window, making me jump, and opens the door.

'You look as if you've seen a ghost,' she says. 'Bad news?'

'Oh . . . just something the inspector told me. I'd best get back to the marching ants.'

'Pardon me for asking, I'll mind my own business in future,' she says huffily, but I ignore her. I have too much on my mind.

* * *

After work, I decide to cycle to Goswick and call on Beverley. I've been wondering how she's coping after the miscarriage, and I've a niggling notion in my head from last night that I need to test out.

'Heading home?' Vera asks.

'I'm going to visit a friend in Goswick first, Beverley Fanshawe.'

Vera approves. 'I'm glad you're making some female friends in the area. A young woman like you should be social-ising with people her own age. It's good for you. How did you meet her?'

'At Goswick museum, she works there.'

Vera's response indicates that news of Mr Claremont's suicide hasn't travelled this far yet. 'I went there once with Ray. He was fascinated by the stuff they had about agricultural labourers and their working conditions. Enjoy your chat with your friend.'

Endorsed by Vera, I set off for Goswick, picturing the colour she'd turn if she discovered that unmarried Beverley had been having an affair with a married man, and had just suffered a miscarriage. When I arrive at the cottage I find Beverley cleaning, her hair wrapped in a scarf, her eyes tear drenched.

'Oh, I'm a sight!' she says breathlessly. 'I'm wearing Alan's old shirt and trousers and I'm all grubby. Have you heard about Henry?'

'Yes. I'm so sorry.'

'I always clean when I'm upset — it sort of helps, I've no idea why. Anyway, I've been working through the kitchen, all the cupboards, pans and crockery. I'll make a cup of tea.'

In the steamy kitchen, which smells of scouring powder and Jeyes Fluid, she blows her nose and puts the kettle on.

'When did you hear about Henry?' I ask.

'Mid-morning. A neighbour came to tell me. I called to speak to Eileen, but I didn't stay. She was too upset. Michael was there. I'm not sure that he'd taken it in. I just said if there was anything I could do to help . . . Henry was such a lovely man, and always so kind and understanding to me. He taught me so much about the museum, and never criticised when I started there and made mistakes. Why would he do such a thing? He doted on Eileen and Michael, they were everything to him.'

'We might never fathom why,' I say uneasily. 'He had a lot on his shoulders.'

'Yes . . .' Her gaze is absent as she rubs the palms of her hands on the paint-stained shirt front. 'I worry that I should have done more when I realised that he was upset. I never did get round to talking to Eileen about it. Maybe if I had, things wouldn't have turned out like this.'

'You've had a lot to deal with recently, I don't think you need to take any responsibility. Is Alan around?'

'He'll be back later, he's trying to finish the roof at Broadmeadow today.'

The wireless is on low, swing music playing. Tea towels are bubbling in a tall pot on the cooker, with sudsy water slopping over. Bev switches the gas off, pokes them down with a pair of wooden tongs and puts a lid on them.

'It's how my mum always used to clean the dishcloths. I try to do everything the way she did.'

'How are you doing now, Bev? Have you recovered?'

'Yes, thanks. I get terribly sad, but I'm fine physically.'

I sit at the table while she makes tea and finds a tin of biscuits. In her brother's old clothes, the trousers rolled up at the hems, she's like a ragamuffin. That's when there's a soft click in my head, and I believe that I can guess what happened and how, and the reason why. If I'm correct, Beverley's grief is mixed with a heavy dose of guilt.

We drink the tea and chat for a bit about Henry, the museum and what might happen now. Beverley's tears keep coming like a faulty tap, her blue eyes reddening. I'm growing impatient. If I'm on the right track, they're also tears of self-pity.

'I'll do whatever I can for Eileen and Michael too,' Beverley murmurs, picking at a nail. 'I can probably run the museum for—'

'I saw Tommie Carpenter again this week,' I interrupt.

'Oh? Why was that?'

'I was in London. She told me that her husband confessed about his relationship with you when they were at the hotel, before he went missing. He was terribly distressed and she was astonished.'

Bev blinks at me. 'He said he was going to tell her after that weekend.'

'Maybe that's what he intended, but sometimes secrets burden people and guilt gets the better of them, makes them act instinctively.'

'I suppose.' Bev has noticed my change of tone and looks unsure.

'The thing is, I've been going back over his words to her. He didn't say he was about to leave, just that he'd made a terrible mess of things and he couldn't work out what to do. That's not how you described your plans. According to you, it was all worked out and you were going to move into a flat together.'

'Maybe Ronnie couldn't bring himself to tell her everything there and then. I mean, if he just blurted it out and she got upset, he might have lost his nerve.'

'Or, maybe he'd already told you that he wasn't going to leave.'

'He did!' she cries. 'He did say he would!'

'Possibly, and I'm sure that he meant it at the time. When he was with you he longed for you to be together, but when he was back with Tommie, the weight of obligation caught up with him.' I'm working this out as I go along, but it makes sense and I can tell from the panic in her eyes that I've nailed the truth. 'I'd bet that Ronnie had changed his mind, and he'd told you that he couldn't desert his marriage before that weekend. He was devoted to Tommie.'

'He loved *me*!'

'No matter how mad he was about you, Ronnie was a traditional man. When the chips were down, would he really have upped and left Tommie? He'd given you the awful news that he couldn't abandon his wife, hadn't he? That must have been terrible for you, after his promises to you and the baby. You must have been in pieces. I can understand why you told me and Inspector Thaxted that you were going to be a couple. It would have been painful to admit the truth, that he'd discarded you after offering you a future, and left you to face the hardships of being an unmarried mother. In your position, I might well have done the same. We all need to hang on to some pride, and especially in a close-knit community like this.'

Bev responds to the sympathy, raising her bloodshot, brimming eyes to me. 'You're right. He told me he was going to stay with his wife a week before they visited Fernfield. I called him as we'd arranged, full of optimism, longing to hear his voice. I couldn't believe it, it was the last thing I was expecting. He said he'd been going over and over it, and he just couldn't do it. I begged him to keep his word, but he wouldn't budge. He became so cold, dismissive almost. He said he'd send money for the baby and me. Money! Then he put the phone down on me.'

She's off again, crying copiously. She and Tommie could fill a reservoir if they joined forces. I top up her tea from the earthenware pot.

'Here, Bev, drink up.'

She gulps the tea and I wait until she's more composed.

'Everything you said about Alan knowing nothing about Ronnie or the baby was untrue, wasn't it? He might have been unaware for quite a while, but after that awful phone call you came home and told him all about it, didn't you?'

She's shocked and frightened now. 'He was here when I came back from the phone box. I was in such a state, it alarmed him. I had to tell him what was wrong. How I'd met Ronnie, how we'd been seeing each other, the baby, and the plans we'd had. He was furious.'

'I can imagine. What brother wouldn't be? Was he angry with you?'

'Not really, although he had every right to be. He said that Ronnie disgusted him, messing me about and taking advantage of me. Alan reckoned that he was going to drop me completely, and that I'd be lucky to receive any upkeep towards the baby.'

Her defences are completely down. I might as well go for it. 'Did you realise that Alan was going to shoot Ronnie?'

'How do you . . . Oh, God!' She's frozen in the chair.

'You might as well tell me, Bev. It's all going to come out anyway. Tommie Carpenter saw you cycling that afternoon. You were helping Alan, weren't you?'

'Alan didn't mean to shoot him. It was a terrible accident.' She crosses her hands on her chest.

'Seems a bit odd to take a gun with you to meet someone if you weren't planning to use it.'

'He said it just . . . This is such a disaster and I'm the cause of it. I've made all this trouble for Alan. What's going to happen to us?'

I'm not sure that she's aware of all the crimes I suspect her brother of. I hope not. 'Bev, nobody but Alan is responsible for shooting a man in the head. After you told him everything, did he decide that he wanted to see Ronnie and have it out with him?'

'Yes. I was worried about them meeting, but I did hope that Ronnie might reconsider if Alan discussed it with him, man to man. Alan told me to phone Ronnie and ask him to meet me by Larch Bridge on that Friday. Ronnie refused at first, said that there was no point because I wasn't going to make him change his mind. I pleaded with him, and in the end, he agreed. I said he owed it to me.'

No wonder Ronnie was so conflicted in the hotel and ran from the room: his wife beside him, his pregnant lover half a mile up the road, waiting to cling to him and implore him to keep his promises. 'Once you'd arranged the meeting, Alan stole a car and he met Ronnie, not you.'

'Alan said he needed a car, so that he and Ronnie could drive somewhere and talk in private. That's all I thought was going to happen. I'd never have agreed to it if I'd realised that Alan had a gun.'

Does she really believe that Alan didn't set out with murder in mind? Maybe she'd had too much going on to work it out. Maybe she just didn't want to consider it.

'What was his explanation afterwards for taking the gun with him?'

'He said he expected that Ronnie might be stubborn or try to weasel his way out of his responsibilities — maybe even try to claim that the baby wasn't his. Alan wanted to make him understand that he meant business and wasn't going to let me be treated so badly.'

'Did you arrange to meet up with Alan that afternoon?'

'Yes, we agreed that I'd cycle over and meet him on a track near Larch Bridge, where he told me he'd drop Ronnie off again and then dump the car. He'd left his bike hidden near the farm he was working at, so I met him and then he cycled to the farm with me on the crossbar and I rode my bike back here. He said to wear some of his old clothes, so that if anyone saw me, they wouldn't recognise me.'

Sinatra is singing 'All This and Heaven Too'. Beverley leaps up and switches him off. 'I believed I was going to have my little heaven with Ronnie and the baby. Now every day's like hell.'

I want to comment that it can be a bit like that when you've played a part in someone's murder. 'Did Alan tell you that he'd shot Ronnie when you met him on your bike?'

'Not then, no. He just said that they'd argued and it hadn't done any good. He told me that he'd explain more later. He was on edge and keen to get back to work in case he'd been missed. When he came home that evening he told me. I was stunned. Alan said that Ronnie had got very angry when he turned up at the bridge instead of me, but he assumed that Alan was bringing him here. Alan drove to Broadmeadow and parked. They had a huge row and Ronnie refused to change his mind about leaving Tommie. He said awful things about me, that I'd pursued and trapped him and got pregnant on purpose. Alan saw red when he insulted me. They started fighting. Alan pulled the gun, they wrestled with it, and Alan accidentally shot him. Then he ran back across the fields to where we'd agreed to meet.'

Those insults don't sound at all like Ronnie Carpenter. I'd bet that Alan invented them to justify his actions to his sister. 'And you've protected your brother since. You've kept up a pretence about him. You had me ferrying you to hospital, worrying about you and making up excuses you could tell Alan about why you've been ill. There was me, believing that you were all alone with your guilty burden, no one to share it with.' I am upset, her deception gnawing at me. I'd sympathised with the plight Bev was in, understanding what it was like to feel alone in the world. 'I expect Alan was relieved when he came home and heard you'd had a miscarriage.'

'That's a horrible thing to say! I wanted that baby so much. And I didn't tell him that I'd been to the hospital with you. I kept you out of it. I said I'd dealt with it here, on my own.'

'Is that supposed to make me feel better? You've been pretty horrible, Bev, concealing the murderer of a man you loved. The father of your baby dumped in a car and his wife left to grieve.'

'Don't! Do you think I haven't been tormented? I haven't been able to sleep since Ronnie died. But Alan's my brother. He was standing up for me and he was worried about why you were asking questions, turning up at the museum and the farm. He told me it was important that I kept his contact with Ronnie to myself. He said that if I stuck to my story, no one could prove otherwise. Alan's all I have left. I had to lie. What else could I do?'

'That's right, Bev. You did the right thing.'

We both jump at Alan's voice. He's standing in the doorway, hands bunched in his khaki jacket pockets.

'What have you been telling her, sis? You been blabbing? I told you to keep your lip zipped.'

'Alan, I didn't mean . . . She guessed, she guessed it all. I've told her you didn't plan to shoot Ronnie! It was self-defence, like you said.'

Alan and I exchange glances and he can see I don't believe that for one minute. I'm too busy wondering where his gun is to worry about such details.

Bev gets up and runs to him. 'Have you heard about Henry? He killed himself!'

'I heard. Very sad. I suppose you're planning on going to the police now, Daisy Moore. You hang out with them enough.'

'You murdered a man. You should go yourself.'

'I would if I was the sort who likes punishment, but that's not me.'

I'm speculating about why he was so keen to get Ronnie Carpenter on his own, and what else he might need to be punished for, but I hold my tongue.

'Daisy, you're my friend, you've been so kind,' Bev pleads. 'Alan didn't mean to kill Ronnie. He was trying to make things right for me and the baby.'

'It's an interesting interpretation. You've done a lot of lying, Bev, to someone you regard as a friend, leading me up the garden path while I helped you out in good faith.'

'I've told you, I had to, because—'

'Bev, shut up and go upstairs. Every stupid remark you come out with makes things worse and gives her more to take to the police.' Her brother grabs her by the arms and pushes her through the door.

'But, Alan, maybe it's for the best and now we can—'

'Shut up, I said! Why do you always have to open your mouth and blab, you silly girl! Just go upstairs and keep out of the blasted way.' He gives her a hard shove.

I hear her stumbling up the stairs. I'm trying to see if there's a sharp knife or anything to defend myself with, and am gauging the steps to the back door, but Alan catches my movement.

'Stay where you are!' He crosses to me and looms over me, his fists clenched.

I look up into his unforgiving eyes, but I can see uncertainty there. He wasn't prepared for this, so he doesn't have a plan.

'If you harm me, you'll get caught. Bev won't keep quiet this time.' Although I'm not at all sure about that.

'Bev'll do what she's told.'

'And what about Pearl? She's made of stronger stuff and we're friends. She's nursing doubts about you, and she'll get suspicious if anything happens to me.'

'What do you mean, doubts? What have you been saying to her?'

'That's between me and Pearl, but you've miscalculated her.'

'Why have you involved yourself in our lives?' He's angry and flummoxed. 'I don't understand what's in it for you. You're just a jumped-up waitress.'

'For starters, you almost knocked me over in your stolen car, so that rubbed me up the wrong way.'

'What are you on about?' He's leaning so close, I can smell onions on his breath.

'I was cycling into town on that Friday morning and you nearly drove over me.'

'You're smart. Too smart for your own good.' Little flecks of spit bubble at the corners of his mouth.

'People often tell me that. It makes me even more determined. The smart thing for you to do now, Alan, would be to back off. But then, you're not that bright, are you? If you were, you wouldn't be in this quandary.'

He grabs my arms, trying to lift me from the chair. I hook my heels behind the chair legs and go limp. He curses and yanks at me. I manage to scratch his face, but he barely registers it. He's pulling me and the chair across the floor when there's a hammering at the front door and a loud voice.

'Open up! Police!'

'Alan!' Bev screams to him from the stairs.

He hesitates, looking towards the sitting room and I grab my chance, shaking free, shoving past him and running to the back door. I'm relieved to find it open. I fling myself through and over the side wall, grazing my hands on the jagged stones and landing badly on my ankle. I run, limping to the front of the house, where two policemen are breaking through the door while Inspector Thaxted shouts to another to go round the side path. He sees me as the door gives way and then he's in the house, where there are thuds and shouts.

'He has a gun!' I call and then turn to a constable who's standing by one of three police cars with his truncheon at the ready. 'He's got a gun!'

'Yes, miss, quite possibly. My goodness, you're bleeding!'

I stare down at the blood on my hands and hold them up as Alan Fanshawe is marched from the cottage in handcuffs by two constables, who shove him in the back of a car. A few minutes later, Thaxted leads Beverley out, guiding her to the second car. She's gripping his arm as if he's a lifebelt and keeps her head down. She's sobbing and shaking.

'Get this house secured,' Thaxted orders a constable, then turns to me. 'You can't cycle with your hands in that state.' He calls after the constable, 'Fetch a towel from the house for Miss Moore.' He shakes his head. 'We'll put your bike in the boot and drop you off at the cottage hospital.'

'Beverley told me that—'

'No!' He holds up a hand. 'Not now. Get in the car.'

I sit in the back, my hands wrapped in a towel while a constable sits up front with him.

Thaxted stares at me in the mirror. 'Mop yourself up and try not to get blood on my upholstery. My goodness, I've had my fill of problematic women today. First Mrs Carpenter and now Miss Fanshawe, both lamenting their fates. You're dry-eyed, Miss Moore? Correct?'

'Correct.'

'Small mercies.'

There's no other conversation on the way back, which is fine with me, although I'm dying to hear what led Thaxted to Alan and Beverley. My ankle is throbbing, my hands are stinging and there's a gash on the left one, where I launched myself over the wall. I press the towel against it, watching it bloom crimson and I can't help thinking of Beverley's miscarriage. What an awful mess her life has become.

At the door to the hospital, Thaxted turns around in his seat.

'You need to come to the station tomorrow morning, so that we can take a statement. We'll drop your bike off at the Dolphin. You should ring Jeffrey, get him to drive you home. I can't make a habit of providing police vehicles as taxis.'

The constable steps out and opens the door for me. I hobble into the hospital, weary and hoping for painkillers.

CHAPTER TWENTY-FOUR

The nurses clean me up with stinging antiseptic, bandage my ankle and stick a large plaster on my left hand. When I visit the loo and glance in a mirror, I see that my hair's askew and I have a dirty smudge on my chin. I splash water on my face, rubbing off the grime. I'm tired and sad, with Henry Claremont on my mind, but I can feel my heart pumping and the flow of energy in my limbs.

I'm too weary to go home, so I ring Felix, who gives me a lift to the hotel. I call JB from there, explain that Alan has been arrested, I've had an argument with a wall, and I'm staying in the hotel for the night.

Sharon is covering reception, listening in while pretending to read the bookings.

'What on earth have you been up to? Vera told that inspector you'd gone to visit a girlfriend. Is she a prize fighter?'

'Inspector Thaxted was here?'

'He phoned earlier, asking for you.'

Felix has gone to wait in the bar for me. Sharon adjusts her blouse over the swell of her bosom.

'Is he that Austrian chap, the refugee?'

'That's right, Felix Koller.'

'He's nice. I reckon someone needs to make a bit of a fuss of him. He lives at Lucinda Laidlaw's now, doesn't he?'

'Yep.'

'I've seen him around town. Romantic looking, with that curly hair and those huge eyes. Like a Georgette Heyer hero.'

'My mum liked her books.'

'I love her. I've just finished *Friday's Child*. So fascinating — the time just runs away when I'm reading her.'

Felix stays to have a nightcap with me. We both opt for brandy while I recount the evening for him.

'That man could have done you serious harm!' Felix stares at me.

'He didn't, though.'

'But Daisy, you shouldn't put yourself in such danger, take such risks. You could have had far worse injuries.'

'It's just the way it happened. I didn't set out to get bashed up.' *And at least I know I'm alive, that I've achieved something, been in the game.*

'Even so.' Felix shakes his head. 'If this Fanshawe took a gun with him to meet Mr Carpenter, that certainly reads like premeditation.'

'I suspect that his sister's quandary wasn't his only reason for meeting and killing Ronnie. Bev's situation was an added excuse to solve his own problems and enlist her help.' I take a warming drink. 'Bev tends to follow instruction and Alan's head of the household, so she did as she was told. He yelled at her to shut up and manhandled her in front of me. I'd say that has happened before.'

'What's his other motive?'

'My guess is that it's to do with the thefts from the museum, but I'll have to wait until tomorrow to hear the rest of the story.'

'Was the inspector cross when he found you at the scene this evening?'

'Cool, certainly.'

'You were only trying to help.'

'Try that on him. To be fair, he should probably still be in hospital, so he's allowed to be short-tempered.'

Felix points at my ankle. 'You and he have matching limps now.'

Sharon wafts in, pours a vodka and tonic and sits with us. Halfway down my brandy, my eyes start to close. I say goodnight. Climbing the stairs with leaden legs, I hear Sharon's rich laugh and Felix's low chuckle.

* * *

The red-cheeked Constable Emerson takes my statement the next morning. I wonder if Thaxted has given him the task as a penance. When we've finished, he asks me to wait as the inspector would like to see me, and, to my astonishment, he offers me a cup of tea.

After twenty minutes or so, he tells me that I can go through to the inspector, who's typing like a pro when I walk in.

'How are you, Miss Moore? Survived yesterday's excitements?'

'Torn skin and a slight sprain. Better than being shot.'

'We discovered Fanshawe's gun in the loft, so there was no immediate danger of that. I've read your statement. Miss Fanshawe has told me the same story. She's very cut up about you, by the way, and was relieved when I reassured her that you're still standing.'

'She doesn't comprehend the whole story about her brother, does she?'

His eyes look sunken, his lips pale. I get the impression that he's holding himself together. 'No,' he says, 'and when she finds out, it will be hard on her.'

'There'll be more weeping.'

'Yes, a great deal, I expect. What made you go to the house yesterday?'

'I was concerned about Beverley, but also, I'd been going over my conversation with Tommie and her comments about

213

the cyclist she saw. In recent weeks, I've mistaken a post-woman for a man, because of her uniform — trousers and jacket — and Sharon told me I can look like a boy, because I wear trousers. It struck me that Beverley is fairly slight, and dressed in trousers and a cap, she could have been Tommie's cyclist. Then when I got to the house, Bev was cleaning and dressed in her brother's old clothes. Things fell into place. Once I started probing, she told me everything. I expect it was a relief. Then Alan arrived home without us realising. He'd heard some of Beverley's confession.'

'I'm glad that you didn't suffer any injury from Fanshawe.'

'I was glad to hear you at the door. I don't think that Beverley would have intervened, she's too much under Alan's thumb. Has he talked?'

'He's admitted shooting Carpenter and claims that it was self-defence, because Carpenter attacked him in the car.'

'Did he carry out the thefts from the museum? I reckon he was responsible for at least one, if not both. He's not had steady work since leaving the army, yet he's able to buy gifts for Pearl Armitage.'

Thaxted swivels in his chair. 'He certainly executed the second robbery. His sister told him about the first one, and he learned the layout of the museum from working there, as well as how valuable the Charles I ring was. Goswick museum is sadly lacking in proper security and Fanshawe saw his opportunity, expecting that the second theft might well be linked to the first. We've questioned an Oxford man, Halse, who deals in stolen jewellery. He's admitted receiving the stolen ring from Fanshawe and selling it for four thousand pounds, but he insists he didn't deal with the tapestry. He says he heard that that was a job done to order from London, so I've put colleagues there on to him.'

'How did you get to Halse?'

'Bill Mackie gave me a tip-off. He'd heard rumours and decided he'd like to get himself off the hook and earn some brownie points with the police. Once we put this evidence to Fanshawe, he'll have nowhere to hide.'

I assimilate all this. 'Did Ronnie Carpenter have suspicions about the second robbery?

'He'd mentioned misgivings to a colleague, told him that he'd met Fanshawe around the museum and found him cocky and nosy, asking about the insurance claims and how the police inquiries were proceeding. That colleague told us that Carpenter phoned the museum a couple of times while he was considering the second insurance claim. He asked Fanshawe some questions about the stolen ring and his work visits to the building. That must have raised alarm bells with Fanshawe. Carpenter didn't take these doubts any further and he didn't pass them to the police. After all, this was Beverley's brother and he wouldn't have wanted to upset her or cause trouble. But once Beverley told her brother about her relationship with Carpenter, he must have seen an opportunity to shut him up.'

'Especially as Ronnie had ended the relationship with her, and might feel free to act on his suspicions about the theft of the ring. That was a big risk for Alan then.'

'I agree. Fanshawe had made good money from the ring sale and intended to keep it.'

'I bet that he left Ronnie's body at Broadmeadow to cast suspicion on Tony Armitage.'

'I'll find out in due course. Miss Moore, you failed to tell me that Beverley had had a miscarriage, when you acted, according to her, as "a guardian angel sent to help her".'

'I didn't see that I needed to. I did suggest to you that she might be pregnant. She'd lost the baby and she was distressed, so I got her to hospital. I'd no idea that she'd told her brother about Ronnie and the baby, and she kept up the pretence that he didn't know. I bet she won't consider me an angel when she has time to mull over all of this.'

'Miss Fanshawe is too confused to view anything clearly at present. I accept that she was unaware that her brother had a gun, or that he'd carried out the second museum theft. Also that she swallowed his claim that the shooting was self-defence. Once she absorbs the full picture, she'll realise that his actions undoubtedly contributed to the stress that led Mr Claremont to the river.'

'Poor Henry. He was so upset about those thefts. Will Beverley be charged?'

'That's under discussion at present. I can't see what good it would do, but the final decision won't be mine.' He reaches for a glass of water and drinks, his hand shaking slightly.

'How are you after your hospital stay? Are you in pain?'

His face shuts down. 'Thank you for asking. I'm taking my medication. I'll survive.'

'Inspector, why did you ring me at the hotel last night?'

'To warn you again to stay away from the Fanshawes. There was a familiar inevitability about hearing that you'd gone there. You got off lightly, given how cornered Alan Fanshawe must have felt. You do have a talent for getting into sticky situations.'

'And I have another one to deal with. I must get back to the hotel. I've a date with the ants, who are intent on stealing the sugar.'

I stand, giving an involuntary groan as I put weight on my injured ankle, and limp away.

'I'd lend you my stick, but I don't have a spare,' Thaxted says.

It's my turn to give him a frosty glare before I close the door.

* * *

The next Saturday, a small parcel is left for me at the hotel. Inside is a book, *A Life of Isaac Newton*, with a note attached from Inspector Thaxted. His handwriting is a beautiful italic script.

> *Here is a book that might interest you.*
> *Alan Fanshawe has been charged with the second robbery at the museum as well as the murder of Ronnie Carpenter.*

*No decision yet on Miss Fanshawe. She has been permitted to
go and stay with an aunt in Staffordshire.*

   *Thank you for your efforts. I hope that you have van-
quished the ants.*

   PT.

'Who's that from?' Vera asks, clutching her lower back.

'Inspector Thaxted. Is your back aching?'

'A bit. Baby's doing a jig. Is that policeman sweet on
you or something?'

'I wouldn't say so.'

'I should hope not. He's far too decrepit. A young
woman like you can do better for herself. There's a nice, fit
chap waiting out there and you'll trip over him one day.'

'I'll bear that in mind.'

'Make sure you do. Anyway, I don't know how the
inspector puts up with you interfering in his work and getting in hot water again. You never seem to learn. I thought
that Miss Fanshawe was supposed to be your friend. Odd
friends you've got, if they try to send you to the hospital.'

I'd have thought that Vera of all people would understand that things aren't always what they seem. I say nothing,
just fetch a cushion for her back. When I return she's turning
the book over gingerly.

'I presume you're not planning to read this at work,'
she says. 'I rely on you to keep sharp, Daisy.' She peers at
the cover. 'Crumbs, it looks like dry old stuff. Rather you
than me. You're a funny kettle of fish and no mistake.' She
leans down and brandishes a plunger. 'Is your right hand well
enough to use this?'

'I'd say so, it's much better.'

'Can you sort out the sink in the downstairs loo? It keeps
clogging and needs a good seeing to.'

I stand, plunger in one hand, Isaac Newton in the other.
This strange equation seems to sum up my life.

* * *

My hands and ankle are fully recovered, so I cycle to Broadmeadow Farm a couple of days later, deliberately timing my visit for after the drama that surrounds one o'clock dinner. It's a dreary, rainy day of low, granite-grey clouds and I have to concentrate on avoiding puddles. Pearl is subdued, but asks me in and offers tea. We sit on either side of the range.

She takes up her crochet, her fingers moving nimbly. 'You must be daft, riding your bike around on a day like this.'

'I'm used to it now, the weather doesn't bother me. I've come because you must be sad about what's happened with Alan. You were involved with him, weren't you?'

She carries on looping her hook. 'How did you guess?'

'You don't have much opportunity to meet men. He was here a fair bit, single and young. Then there were the scarf and brooch, an admirer's gifts. He spoke warmly of you when I met him here. Protectively.'

She makes a noise in her throat. 'We were sweet on each other. I wasn't sure that we'd last the course once my dad got wind of us. He had no time for Alan, just used him because he's handy. Alan wasn't scared of him though, which was reassuring. We'd managed to keep out of his view, but with Dad, it's always only a matter of time. Then Alan proposed a couple of days before he was arrested. He said he didn't care what Dad said. We were planning to go to Gretna Green next month and get married. I'm just twenty, and Dad would never have agreed if we'd wanted to marry around here.'

'Where were you going to live?'

'In the cottage first, with Bev. Alan said he'd square it with her and he'd get me a wool shop, in Oxford or maybe Fernfield. The lease is coming up on the fabrics shop that closed down in the High Street. Then he said he'd buy us a little place of our own.'

'I'm sorry.' No liberty for Pearl, no wool shop, no husband, just the ongoing tyranny of her father.

'Not as much as I am. I wasn't engaged for long, was I? But I wouldn't fancy being married to a murderer. I can't believe that Alan shot that man and left him on our land. I've never had any luck, so nothing's changed.'

'When you met me in the hotel and touched on someone doing something wrong, I imagined that you were referring to your dad, but it was Alan, wasn't it?'

'I wasn't sure what was up with him,' she replies morosely, 'but I could tell something was. He had more money than usual and he was spending freely, buying me stuff. I couldn't work out how he was going to afford shop leases and buying us a place to live on his jobbing wages. When I asked him about it, he said he'd had some luck. Then I remembered that there'd been thefts at the museum and I couldn't help worrying that he was involved. It played on my mind.'

'Does your dad know about Alan now?'

'No, and I'll keep it that way. No point in giving him something else to grumble about.'

'What will you do now?'

She laughs, a bitter sound. 'What can I do? Keep on milking the cows and bashing nails in fences. At least Alan had finished mending the roof. It's not raining in my bedroom now.'

'Don't give up on the wool shop. Things can change.'

'Not for me, they can't. No, there's no point in believing in over the rainbow. The only rainbows here are the ones stretching across the cowpats.'

Despite her dourness, I can't help liking her. There's a stalwart core to Pearl. 'Well, come into Fernfield sometimes and have a drink with me.'

'Maybe. Thanks for asking. I'd rather be on my own now, if you don't mind.'

On my way out, I meet Tony Armitage driving a mud-splashed jeep. He kills the engine and leans out. 'You again! You're not welcome here.'

'I came to see Pearl.'

'That's what I mean. You're no good for her.' He wags a filthy finger at me. 'She gets restless when she sees you.'

'Is that a bad thing?'

'In my book, yes.'

'Yours isn't the only book, though.'

He switches the engine back on and revs the jeep. 'Clear off out of here and stay away. This is my land and I don't want to see you on it again.'

He bucks the jeep through a pothole, spraying muddy water on me. I cycle back to town, aware that I look and smell as if I've been rolling in a ditch.

CHAPTER TWENTY-FIVE

London is crazy, beside itself, hysterical. I joined Father Hickey for a while in Walthamstow's celebrations and now I'm in a crammed Trafalgar Square for the victory parade, sandwiched between the priest and JB. Everywhere, people are singing, laughing, swaying, cheering and swinging rattles. The mounted policemen's horses are whinnying. Quite a few onlookers faint in the swarming throng and St John's Ambulance are busy with stretchers. Improvised hammocks swing from lamp posts, where the most eager slept out last night. I've seen a woman sitting on a kerb brewing tea on a primus stove. Half a dozen strangers have kissed me. One man in naval uniform asks me to marry him and doesn't seem rebuffed when I decline.

It's far too noisy to talk to one another. We've linked arms so that we don't get separated. The combined din of the crowds and the marching bands is astonishing. There are Scottish pipers, an Indian band wearing cream uniforms and blue turbans, another group of men wearing headscarves of pink chiffon, and many brass bands. They create a cacophony of sounds that swirl and linger. I cheer extra loudly when I see bus drivers marching, sure that I would recognise some of them if I was near enough. When the aerial parade swarms over, filling the sky with throbbing engines, men and women throw their hats in the air.

After a couple of hours, we agree that we've had enough and adjourn to a pub tucked down a quiet backstreet. Father Hickey's friend Abe is waiting for us, smoking a briarwood pipe. I met him last summer when he was helping the priest with his vegetable garden. He's tall and blonde, sporting a blue-and-gold-striped blazer with an open-necked shirt. His patterned tie is hanging loose around the collar.

'You made it!' Father Hickey grips him by the arm. 'Northampton released you from its clutches.'

'By the skin of my teeth.' Abe smiles up at him. 'Daisy, hello. I hear that you've been sleuthing again, and with success.'

'I have been busy.'

'Daisy likes to keep the Oxford Police on their toes,' JB says. 'Now, my round, lady and gentlemen. What's it to be?'

When we're settled with our drinks, JB raises his white wine.

'Cheers to us all for surviving, one way or another.'

We clink glasses. A woman is bashing out 'Down at the Old Bull and Bush' on an out-of-tune piano.

Abe and Father Hickey are drinking a vivid cocktail called a Green Dragon, which involves crème de menthe and gin. Abe holds his up to the light. 'This is the colour of jealousy.'

'I'm jealous of darlin' Daisy. She has far too much excitement beyont in Fernfield, following clues and mixing with villains,' Father Hickey says. 'Did Felix not want to come with ye today, Daisy? Ye said he might.'

'He's not keen on crowded places, so he decided not to. Sudden noises make him anxious.'

'Oh, I understand. Sure, I'm glad none of us fainted, they were running out of first aiders.'

JB chinks his glass against mine. 'Another cheers, this time to you, Daisy, for helping get to the bottom of the Carpenter case.'

'Do I only get a drink?' I ask. 'Last time you bought me supper at Rules.'

The three men exchange smiles.

'What?' I demand.

'Oh, nothing to bother yer head about,' the priest says. 'How does it feel to have solved another murder? Ye're certainly making a habit of it.'

'Mixed emotions, to be honest, just like last time. I'm glad a murderer's been arrested, but so many people — well, women — are caught in the fallout: Tommie Carpenter, Beverley Fanshawe, Pearl Armitage and Eileen Claremont. It leaves a sour taste.' And there's Henry. I can hardly bear to think about him.

'That must always be the case with murder,' Abe says.

'True, but it doesn't make it any easier,' I tell him.

'Is there anything you can do for them?' JB asks.

'Not much.'

'Exactly. Carpenter and Fanshawe created mayhem. You helped to clean it up. Right, Declan?'

'Absolutely. Them two made a hames of everything. Don't be carrying the world on yer shoulders, it'll wear ye out. And as I regard meself *in loco matris*, 'tis me duty to tell ye so.'

'I'll try not to.'

'Then down the hatch,' JB urges, 'because this place is filling up, rain's forecast and we have somewhere to go.'

'Where?' I knock back my drink.

'Where else but Rules?' The priest takes my hand and plants a kiss on it. 'Ye didn't think we'd only buy ye a lousy gin?'

Before we go, I visit the ladies. On my way back through the throng, I squeeze past Abe and Father Hickey and note their dangling hands, almost obscured by their chairs. Their little fingers are entwined. Some remarks and images fall suddenly into place. JB has seen me noticing. He catches my eye and winks.

We surge out into the night. There's rain in the air, that peculiar, melancholy London smell of damp cinders and ancient dust. Lights glitter, drunken men stumble off pavements, tired families wander home, arms entwined, children wave crumpled flags or are carried on shoulders, couples clinch in doorways, voices call the old London songs with 'Knees Up Mother Brown' fighting with 'Burlington Bertie'. Vera would purse her lips and say that there was no need for all this malarkey.

There are sad undertones to the outpouring of jubilation: too many people dead, too many others left destitute and homeless, but I recall Alice Weaver's comment that it's a poor heart that never rejoices. I join in with JB, Abe and Father Hickey as they stick their thumbs under their lapels and dance 'The Lambeth Walk' along the street.

THE END

THE JOFFE BOOKS STORY

We began in 2014 when Jasper agreed to publish his mum's much-rejected romance novel and it became a bestseller.

Since then we've grown into the largest independent publisher in the UK. We're extremely proud to publish some of the very best writers in the world, including Joy Ellis, Faith Martin, Caro Ramsay, Helen Forrester, Simon Brett and Robert Goddard. Everyone at Joffe Books loves reading and we never forget that it all begins with the magic of an author telling a story.

We are proud to publish talented first-time authors, as well as established writers whose books we love introducing to a new generation of readers.

We have been shortlisted for Independent Publisher of the Year at the British Book Awards three times, in 2020, 2021 and 2022, and for the Diversity and Inclusivity Award at the Independent Publishing Awards in 2022.

We built this company with your help, and we love to hear from you, so please email us about absolutely anything bookish at feedback@joffebooks.com

If you want to receive free books every Friday and hear about all our new releases, join our mailing list: www.joffebooks.com/contact

And when you tell your friends about us, just remember: it's pronounced Joffe as in coffee or toffee!

www.ingramcontent.com/pod-product-compliance
Lightning Source LLC
Chambersburg PA
CBHW020609180626
46810CB00007B/2700